LEGACY OF LIES

Jane A. Adams titles available from
Severn House Large Print

Killing a Stranger
Heatwave
Touching the Dark
Mourning the Little Dead

LEGACY OF LIES

Jane A. Adams

Severn House Large Print
London & New York

This first large print edition published 2008
in Great Britain and the USA by
SEVERN HOUSE PUBLISHERS of
9-15 High Street, Sutton, Surrey, SM1 1DF.
First world regular print edition published 2007 by
Severn House Publishers, London and New York.

Copyright © 2007 by Jane A. Adams.

British Library Cataloguing in Publication Data

Adams, Jane, 1960-
    Legacy of lies. - Large print ed.
    1. Blake, Naomi (Fictitious character) - Fiction
    2. Ex-police officers - Fiction 3. Blind women - Fiction
    4. Detective and mystery stories 5. Large type books
    I. Title
    823.9'14[F]

ISBN-13: 978-0-7278-7717-8

Printed and bound in Great Britain by
MPG Books Ltd, Bodmin, Cornwall.

One

Even a couple of years ago, Naomi thought, she would have been reluctant to step so far outside of her comfort zone, but she felt surprisingly relaxed this time. True, last year she had ventured further afield when she and Alec had spent ten days in Tenerife, but as she had been content to spend most of that either sleeping or lounging on the beach, it didn't really count in terms of adventure. She had been surprised, though, at how unbothered she had been when preparing for this trip. Perhaps that was because in her sighted days she had known this area well. Family holidays spent visiting relatives on the Fens, cycling and walking beneath the big skies that overarched the flat landscape, made this familiar territory.

She had never visited Alec's uncle Rupert, though. In fact, she had barely registered that he had an uncle Rupert – or Uncle Rupe as he called him – until Alec had announced that the old man had died.

'How old was he?' Naomi had asked.

'Rupe is ... was ... Dad's older brother. Dad is seventy this year and I think Rupe must have been seventy-six, or thereabouts.'

'How did he die?'

'Ah, well that's the odd thing. It seems Rupert had a heart condition I didn't know about. He went out walking one day, collapsed in the middle of nowhere, and was dead by the time a couple of hikers came across him.'

'That must have ruined their day. Sorry, that was flippant. Were you close? When's the funeral. Will there be problems getting the time off?' Naomi remembered from her own time as a police officer, just how hard it could be to take holidays without a lot of prior warning. 'Are we going?'

'You want to go with me?'

'Don't see why not. I know you hate funerals. We can give your parents a lift over. Doncaster way, isn't it?'

'Lord, you have a memory like an elephant. I can't have mentioned him more than a couple of times, and no, we weren't close, though I liked him a lot. But Mum and Dad won't be going. They and Rupe had a major falling out, years ago. I doubt Rupe dying will change the way Dad feels about him. I mean, I'll ask, but I think the answer will be no.'

And the answer had been no. Naomi had

been there when Alec broached the subject. His mother had added her voice to his pleading that Rupe was dead now and Arthur, Alec's father, should let the past go, but he was adamant and in the end Alec had given in. Surprisingly though, Arthur had stolen a moment to speak to Naomi just before they'd left.

'I'm glad the two of you are going, actually,' he said awkwardly. 'What happened between myself and Rupert, well, it was a personal thing and perhaps the two of us should have made peace somewhere along the line. But my quarrels shouldn't be my son's and I'm well aware that Alec kept in touch with his uncle.'

'You didn't mind?'

'What was there to mind?'

'But you still feel you can't go to his funeral?'

'No, I can't go. Naomi, funerals are an opportunity to say goodbye to those you love and respect. Honour, I suppose. I don't think I quite stopped loving Rupe, which is why I'm glad Alec kept in touch. I believe everyone deserves to have some family, some connection, if you see what I mean. But respect? No. I didn't honour or respect my brother, so my going to *pay* my respects would be somewhat hollow, don't you think?'

And so, Naomi thought, it was just the two of them. Three, if you counted Napoleon, Naomi's guide dog, snuffling on the back seat, snoring and twitching as he dreamed.

'Must be chasing rabbits,' Alec said.

'Napoleon's an urban dog. I doubt he's even seen a rabbit. Wouldn't recognize one if he saw one.'

'Trace memory,' Alec said wisely. 'All dogs have a trace memory of rabbit chasing.'

'Well, out here, he might just get the chance.'

'If Uncle Rupe's garden is the way I remember, he might get the chance in there.'

'Big garden, is it?'

'Fallowfields was once a farmhouse. Rupe bought it with an acre of land, started to create a garden and then, typically, got bored. The section around the house, maybe a third of the land, is landscaped and lawned and all that. The rest ... well, I seem to remember he called it his meadow. In the spring it's all wild flowers and scrubby, self-seeded birches.'

'Sounds nice. It's going to seem strange staying in his house, though.'

'Not superstitious, are we?'

Naomi could hear the smile in his voice. No, she could not be described as superstitious.

'It just seemed easier,' Alec went on. 'We

could have stayed in the local pub, but the closest one is all steep stairs and awkward rooms and I don't think either you or Dog would like it very much. At Fallowfields he can run around the garden and you can get used to the layout without crowds of drinkers and family lunchers getting in your way. Rupe wouldn't mind. He'd be happy about it.'

Naomi stretched, shifting position in the passenger seat.

'Uncomfortable?'

'Tired of sitting. Much further?'

'Fifteen minutes. Ten maybe.'

'What's it like round here?'

'Well, actually, it's very un-fenlike. The big open spaces don't really start until we're out past Fallowfields. Here, it's all very green. The road is enclosed either side with trees and high hedges. In fact, Rupert's house is surrounded by what I'm told is a very ancient hedge. But you get about a mile from the house and it all opens out. Massive fields and those deep drainage ditches banked on either side. I never did like it very much.'

'Oh, I don't know. On our family holidays it was good for cycling and I used to love watching the storms roll in.'

'There is that, I suppose. Rupe always liked a good storm. I remember, when I was just a little kid, going out into the garden with him and getting drenched because he wanted to be out in it. There's a terrace runs the length of the house at the back with steps down on to the lawn...'

'Very Lady Chatterley.'

'Oh, very. There are these plinth things either side of the steps. I suppose they were meant for planters or something. Anyway, Rupe stood on one, and me on the other, and we perched up there, cheering every time the thunder crashed, watching the lightening strike and trying to count how far away it was.'

'Wonder you didn't get struck!' Naomi laughed.

'I was frozen through and soaked to the skin by the time we got back inside. Rupe ran me this hot deep bath. The baths are Victorian and so deep you cause a drought just filling the damn things.'

'Baths? More than one?'

'Oh, there's an en suite in Rupe's room and a second bathroom on the floor below. Rupe took over the attic. Dad always said he hoped Rupe had the ceilings reinforced before he installed the second bathroom.'

'Your parents visited the house?'

'Oh yes. When I was small we visited often. The storm incident; that was on a family visit. Mum and Dad had gone out somewhere and left Rupe in charge of me.' He laughed. 'I often thought I should be in charge of Rupe. That day, Rupe got me in the bath then made this massive jug of hot chocolate. We sat in that great big kitchen of his, Rupe in this elaborate burgundy dressing gown, all velvet and quilted silk – very Noel Coward – and we drank chocolate and Rupe told stories. He knew the scariest ghost stories. I don't think I slept for weeks after that.'

Naomi laughed. 'I can't see your mother being pleased about that.'

'Oh, she wasn't. Not about any of it. Of course, Rupe hadn't bothered to hide the evidence. There were my soaking wet clothes strewn all over the bathroom floor and, of course, I blurted the whole thing out as soon as Mum and Dad got in, just in case the sopping trousers hadn't given it away.'

'So, when did this quarrel happen?'

'I'm not sure. I know after I was about eight years old we stopped coming, but I was away at school by then and everything was changing. I don't think I really thought about it too much. I still heard from Rupe at birthdays and Christmas, still got cards with cash tucked inside and long rambling letters about nothing in particular. Rupe was good at that kind of thing. I missed the summer trips, but I don't think I gave it too much

11

thought at all. You don't at that age.'

'I wonder what it was all about.'

'So do I, but Mother won't say if Dad won't and he was adamant. None of my concern, he said, and you know Dad. Once he takes up a position, his feet are set in concrete...' Alec paused and Naomi could almost feel the thoughts ticking by. 'Oh,' he said finally, 'we're here. I forgot how fast the house came up after that bend.'

He slowed and Naomi heard him shift down the gears, the rattle as they hit something in the road.

'Cattle grid?'

'Yes. Rupe installed a hedgehog ramp.'

'A what?'

'A ramp for hedgehogs to climb up if they fell in.'

'Seriously?'

'Oh yes. He liked hedgehogs.'

The sound beneath the wheels had changed and Naomi heard gravel. The car lurched slightly as Alec hit ruts and uneven ground. 'You'll need to watch yourself on here,' he said. 'It's paved closer to the house, but the drive is quite a length and very uneven. I think the gravel just hides the pot holes.'

He turned and then pulled up, cut the engine. 'OK. This is it. Fallowfields.'

He sounded excited, Naomi thought.

Excited and just a little nervous. She wondered at that.

Alec opened the door and let Napoleon out. As Alec helped her from the car Naomi could hear the dog sniffing and snorting at all the new smells.

'Watch your footing. Two steps and you'll be off the gravel and on to the paving.'

Naomi extended her cane as he led her forward. She felt the small stones shift beneath her feet and then the smooth, if still slightly uneven, feel of the flagstones. 'Has it rained?'

'Looks like it.'

'I thought so.' The air smelt fresh and the heat of the sun brought out the scents of rose and honeysuckle and damp grass. It also made the flagstones slightly slippery and she could feel the algal slime of stones not scrubbed in a very long time.

'OK.' Alec stood behind her and moved her slightly to the right. 'You are now in line with the front door. The house is symmetrical, Georgian style, you know, balanced. Three storeys including the attic floor and with sash windows Rupe had to prop up on sticks. Of course, he might have got them fixed by now...'

'But you don't think so.'

'Um ... Uncle Rupert was into quirky. Apparently early sash windows *were* held up with props. The weights that are supposed to keep them open came later. Or so he used to tell me.'

'And you believed him?'

'Like I said, Uncle Rupert told good stories. OK, walk forward about five paces ... good. Now there's a small step up.'

'I've got it.' She could feel the step as her cane nudged up against it.

'There are pillars each side of the door making a sort of porch. If you reach out your hand...'

Cool stone beneath her fingers. Smoothly carved. 'Nice.' She hopped up on to the doorstep.

'Just watch yourself. On your right there's a foot scraper. Big cast iron thing.

Naomi swung her cane. Found it.

'You'd know about it if you stubbed your toe. Another step and you'll be at the door. Big, black, shiny and ... what do you know? Rupert must have had it repainted.'

'Well, I should hope so. It has been three decades, near enough, since you were here.'

'I suppose it has.' Alec sounded surprised.

Naomi explored the door with her outstretched hand. Smooth, solid, with the beaded panels she had half expected to find. Letterbox, large door knocker. The casting felt like swags of leaves. To her right she found a doorbell. Large, metal surround, cold to the touch. 'Oh! It's a bell pull. Does it work?'

'It used to. Try it and see.'

Naomi tugged at the knob. Somewhere inside the house a bell jangled cheerfully.

'It rings in the hall and down in the kitchen. The kitchen is slightly sunk ... sort of half below ground level. Rupert had bigger windows put in. There's all the servants' bells still up on the kitchen wall, though they aren't attached any longer. Or, at least...' He seemed suddenly struck by how long it had been since he was last here. 'They used to be there. You're right. Who knows *what* he did to the place in the past however many years.'

'Does it feel very strange to be back?'

'Oh yes,' Alec said softly. 'Very, very strange.'

Naomi waited outside while Alec went through into the hall to check for any obstacles. She leaned against the smooth stone pillars and listened to the near silence. Only Napoleon's padding and snuffling and the song of a blackbird broke the stillness and quiet. The sun had come out after what had been a cloudy start to the day. It seemed to be making up for lost time and Naomi thought she could almost hear the garden drying. Green scents rose all about her and she closed her eyes – a habit from her sighted days – to intensify the sensations and focus on the warm, moist fragrance of earth and flowers. This would be a fabulous place to laze and doze and let the world slip by, she mused.

It occurred to her that Alec was taking quite a time and she figured that he must be taking a chance to explore the house alone. That, she thought, was what she would have done. The experience of returning here had caught him off guard. He had been unprepared for the reawakening of forgotten memories and impressions and she knew that he would be regretting having not returned in Rupert's lifetime. She wondered what Rupert's house was like inside and how much it would have changed from Alec's memories. And just what sort of quarrel could have kept the family apart for all this time.

Two

Waking in a strange place was always something of a trial, especially when the bed was so comfortable. Reluctantly, Naomi dragged herself back to something like consciousness

16

and turned over.

No Alec.

She sat up and called his name, suddenly anxious that she would not be able to remember the layout of the house. Then she heard his footsteps on the stairs and the sound of the bedroom door being pushed across thick carpet.

'I thought I'd make us both tea. Start the day in a civilized manner,' Alec said, depositing a tray on the chest of drawers that, Naomi remembered, stood beside the window.

'I wondered where you'd gone.'

'Sorry. I thought you'd sleep until I got back. You looked very peaceful.'

Naomi stretched, listening to the domestic, comforting sounds of tea being poured and sugar being added and then stirred. She liked hers without but Alec was a lover of strong and sweet. 'I slept well,' she admitted, slightly surprised. 'It's so quiet here.'

'Apart from the birds making a racket at five in the morning.'

She laughed. 'I didn't hear that. Anyway, that's supposed to be enjoyable, isn't it?'

'Five in the morning is never enjoyable. Here you go.'

He placed the mug in her hands and tugged her pillows into a more supportive shape against her back.

'What time will we have to leave?'

Alec fetched his own mug and climbed back into bed. 'It shouldn't be more than a fifteen-minute drive, so about eleven, I suppose. I've fed Dog and let him out. The kitchen door's open ready for when he's finished exploring and before you ask, don't worry, I checked the garden is secure.'

'Good. You sure it's safe to leave the door open?'

'Naomi, this is the middle of nowhere. To get into the garden someone would have to struggle through a thorn hedge and cross a ditch and then climb a wall. I don't see the average burglar bothering, really I don't.'

'Maybe they breed hardier souls round here. Thieves that don't mind the thorns.' Naomi objected, but she wasn't really worried. Alec had explained to her the night before that a wall running either side of the house separated the rear garden from the front drive. A small, wrought iron gate gave access through the wall, but it was locked and presented no gaps big enough for Napoleon to squeeze through. The rear garden was also walled close to the house and the remaining land could be approached through a second small gate set into the back wall. Safe for Napoleon and with enough room for him to run. It didn't entirely prevent her from worrying, but nearly.

'What time is it now?'

'Eight thirty or just gone. We can have a leisurely breakfast and explore a little more of Rupe's domain before we leave for the funeral. No rush.'

'I wonder how many will be there.'

'I don't know. Uncle Rupert mentioned a lot of people in his letters, but I only met his business partner once. They'd been running that antique shop together for years.'

'It's good of him to have arranged everything,' Naomi mused.

'It is, yes. Not sure what the wake will be like. From what I recall of Marcus Prescott, he liked his booze. Come to that, so did Rupert.'

'Well, unless you want me to drive, which might prove interesting, you'll have to leave him to drown his sorrows alone.'

'True, though I'll have one drink just to bless the old boy, and I thought when we got back we'd see if Rupert still kept his cellar as well stocked as he used to.' He paused and then said, 'You know, love, part of me feels as guilty as hell for not keeping in better touch and the rest just keeps wanting to laugh when I remember what Rupert was like. Then I feel guilty again because I really did like him and...'

'People lose touch,' Naomi said gently. 'I'm sure Rupert didn't hold it against you. He must have known you were in an awkward position after he fought with your dad.'

She felt Alec shake his head. 'That's just it. It wasn't difficult. Dad never made it hard for me to do anything and I always read bits of Rupert's letters out to him and Mum. I must have been well into my teens before I even realized there was a problem between them. No. No excuse, Nomi, I could have come to see him. I was just too busy living my own life.'

'But you wrote back?'

She could hear the smile in his voice as he replied. 'Yes, I wrote back. Equally rambling and insignificant letters. I know Uncle Rupe liked them even if I didn't make sense half the time. I never was what you'd call an expert letter writer.'

'Then stop beating yourself up and remember the good stuff,' Naomi told him. 'From what little I know about your uncle, I don't think he'd have borne any kind of grudge.'

As it happened, Marcus Prescott had company in plenty, all eager to toast their dead friend without Alec having to worry about it. The church in Epworth was full to bursting. Naomi listened to the buzz and hum of conversation and tried to guess just how many were present.

Marcus Prescott had met them at the door and led them portentously to the front of the church, insisting they take their places beside him as chief mourners, and made such a fuss of Napoleon that Naomi wondered if he knew anything at all about dogs.

The big black dog now lay quietly at her feet, his harness cool against her leg. Alec clasped her hand and held it tight and she was surprised to feel that his grip was trembling very slightly.

She tried to gain some sense of space and size of the church from the way the voices echoed, but was still taken by surprise at the sudden volume as the choir broke into song in front of her. A choir at a funeral? And on a weekday too. That was a first in Naomi's experience. She associated choirs with weekends and weddings.

The congregation joined the anthem at the second verse. It was not a hymn Naomi knew and she was surprised to hear Alec's voice join with the others. He sounded as though the words and music were familiar to him. Alec, to her knowledge was not a churchgoer. Was this another of Uncle Rupert's legacies?

Another surprise: the eulogy was given by a minister who claimed to have known Rupert very well and, from the anecdotes delivered, Naomi had no reason to doubt

21

that claim. He spoke of a humorous, generous man. A man for whom friendship and loyalty were all and whose sense of fun and fair play was known to all of those who called him friend.

And then, Marcus Prescott was called upon to say his piece.

Naomi was not initially surprised at this; he was Rupert's business partner after all and long-term friend, but she was taken aback at the tone of his address.

'It is always sad,' Marcus said, 'to bid farewell to a loved friend and, as one grows older, it seems a more frequent occurrence. Sad enough when the loss is through illness or due to the simple ravages of time alone, but to lose a loved one through violence; that is a greater tragedy.'

'Violence?' Naomi whispered. 'What's he on about?'

'I have no idea.'

Naomi could hear that Marcus's statement had caused consternation elsewhere too from the restless movement and murmured questions that rippled through the congregation. She heard the vicar speaking softly to Marcus and the uncertainty in the man's voice even though she could not make out the words.

Marcus, however, would not be constrained.

'Violence I say, and I will stand by that. To suggest that our friend died of natural causes is, I am sure, to ignore the truth of the matter. Rupert Friedman was found in a spot so remote and so removed from his usual haunts that I cannot believe he found his own way there. He had no reason to be there. No reason to have died, alone, uncomforted.'

'Alec,' Naomi breathed. Marcus's voice cracked with the emotion of what he was saying and Naomi's heart went out to him even though she could see no sense in what he was saying.

She felt Alec get to his feet and heard, in the hushed silence, his clear firm steps as he went up to Marcus Prescott.

'It's all right,' Marcus Prescott said with some acerbity. 'You don't need to come and fetch me off my soapbox. I've said my piece, but if you loved your uncle half as much as he loved you then you'll look into his death and you'll find out that I'm right. Rupert was killed, sure as if some villain plunged a knife into his heart.'

I love the rain. Love to hear it falling when I'm snug inside and love to walk in it, provided I have a decent coat and a sturdy umbrella. I love to watch the clouds gather ready for a decent storm and the charcoal skies that prevail in the

Fenland winters. If I could move Fallowfields a little closer to the sea then it would be a perfect place to live. To sit in my bedroom and watch the clouds roll in off a mean ocean would be the ultimate bliss, but to be truthful I can have no complaints. Life, with a few slips, has been a good ride and I like to think that even those slips have been put right.

The day I die it will be raining. I know this with the kind of certainty that strikes one at certain times. Rain washing my life away, washing me back into the rich brown earth.

Three

The wake was an odd affair. Marcus had hired a room in the local hotel and they retired there en mass. Alec lodged Naomi and Napoleon in a corner of the large room, close beside the window and with a table, behind which Napoleon could lie out of the way of careless feet and Naomi could keep people at a distance should she feel the need. He described the space to her: the double doors, the tables along the back wall set out with food, and the small bar in the corner.

'How many people?'

'Oh, must be close to fifty. Some from the church seem to have gone and others turned up for the free food.'

'Alec, don't be so cynical.'

'Who's cynical? I just know people. So do you. Marcus is holding court. I suppose I should mingle.'

'Get me some of that free food first,' Naomi teased. 'Breakfast seems a long time ago.'

'Will do. Sure you'll be all right if I go and look like the bereaved nephew? I'd like to find out who's here and what they were to Rupe.'

'I'll be fine,' Naomi told him. 'And you do need to make yourself visible, you know.'

Alec kissed her. He fetched food from the buffet table, picking items she could identify easily and gave her a brief rundown of what he'd put on her plate and where, then he kissed her again and left. Naomi ate, breaking her own rules and slipping the odd treat to Napoleon. Alec had brought wine and a glass of water and she sipped the wine slowly alternating with deep gulps of water. The room was stuffy and the sun through the window too hot on the side of her face. She wondered if she could manage to move.

The sound of people moving and chatting shifted around her. She caught snatches of conversation and was unsurprised to find that Marcus's outburst in the church was a major topic of debate.

'What was he thinking of?' A woman's voice.

'Was he drunk?' This time a man. He sounded quite young, Naomi thought.

'You never can tell with Marcus. Puts it away all right, but I've never seen him actually sozzled.' An older man, this time. He had a broad accent with a warm burr to it that Naomi knew was local.

'Not like dear old Rupert...' The woman again.

'Rupert was never ... oh, I know he liked his pleasures, but...' The older man. He sounded, Naomi thought, as though he too liked his pleasures and had already indulged.

'Think there's anything in what he said? Marcus, I mean.' The younger man sounded excited at the prospect.

'Marcus has a lively imagination and too much time on his hands,' the woman said firmly and Naomi got the distinct feeling that this would mark the end of the discussion. Mother and son, she decided, reflecting upon their relationship, though she didn't place the older man as the father. For some reason she couldn't quite explain, the tone of the older speakers did not chime with their being man and wife.

She was right about the conversation

26

change, though, and proved obliquely right about the relationship.

'How are the plans for the wedding?' the older man asked.

'Oh, going very well, aren't they, Phillip? You know, she is a lovely girl, but I'm not so sure I like the parents.'

They drifted away and Naomi focussed on identifying another conversation. She bit into one of the little cherry tomatoes Alec had put on her plate, savouring the burst of flavour, and then sampled something long and crispy that turned out to be a cheese straw. From across the room she heard Alec's voice, but not the words. Directly in front of her she heard a woman laugh. Off to the left a couple bickered. Naomi listened with momentary interest, but as the object of disagreement seemed to be a mother-in-law – whose, she wasn't sure – she decided it would soon become a boring exchange and not worth the attention.

The sandwich was odd. Goats cheese? And something fruity, like a plum chutney. She was in two minds as to whether the ingredients went together, but finished it anyway and then took another sip of wine. Two men were discussing the price and profitability of sugar beet and Naomi was about to dismiss them when she heard one man say, 'Bit of a rum deal him being out your way, Frank. I knew the old bugger liked to walk, but he usually kept to the Peatlands trail. I never knew him to *off-road*, like.'

'Off-road.' Naomi was amused. It made it sound as though Uncle Rupert moved on wheels.

'Never knew him to come out that far, that's true. And the couple what found him noticed he weren't dressed for walking. Got his town shoes on and you know how particular the old bugger were when it came to his clothes and such. No coat, neither.'

'It *was* a hot day.'

'True, but he were an old fashioned sort of bloke, weren't he? Never saw him in shirt-sleeves, not any time. I reckoned he never felt dressed without his jacket.'

The second man laughed. 'Careful, Frank. You'll be agreeing with old Marcus next and we all know he's barmy!'

'Not a bit of it. I'm just saying that it were strange, that's all. The couple what found him, they came straight up to the farm and I called the police and then went out with the man while the missus looked after the girl, like. We went back to where they found him and there he is, lying on his back. Face up to the sky, he was. Looked as shocked as any man I've ever seen and I seen a few dead 'uns, as well you know.'

Naomi wondered why he had seen dead

people often enough to make a comparison but didn't really feel that she could ask. Instead, she took another sip of wine and listened hard, hoping for more. Inconsiderately, it seemed the men had now spotted an acquaintance and were calling him across. To Naomi's disgust the conversation turned once more to crop prices and kids and other domestic issues and it was obvious that she would learn no more.

'Are you all right over here all alone?'

She recognized Marcus's voice and smiled in his direction. 'I'm fine, thank you. We thought Alec should get on and do the mingling bit. I'm still a bit wary in company and places I don't know.'

Marcus dragged out a chair and flopped down beside her. He set something that sounded heavy down on the table and then a second lighter object. 'I've purloined a bottle,' he said. 'Want a refill? You look to be drinking red.'

'Thanks. There seem to be a lot of people here.'

'Free food and booze,' Marcus said dolefully, echoing Alec's sentiments, then he laughed, embarrassed. 'Oh, don't take any notice of me, my dear. Truth to tell most of them were friends to varying degrees and it's good of people to want to pay their respects. Truth to tell, too, I really miss him. Miss him

29

terribly.'

'I'm sorry,' Naomi said. 'I wish I'd met him. From the stories Alec tells he was quite a character.'

Marcus laughed softly. 'Oh, he was that all right. But he was a good man and ... I cared for him. Cared deeply.'

Were they more than friends? Naomi wondered. 'What you said in the church...?' she asked tentatively.

'What I said in the church, my dear, I meant. Meant every word and I'm hoping and praying I can persuade young Alec to take me seriously. God knows the local constabulary can't or won't. Rupert had a heart attack, they say. That's what killed him. Lord knows, Rupe wasn't in the best of health, but the doctor reckoned he could last a good ten more years if he took care of himself.'

'And did he? Take care of himself?'

Marcus was silent. Naomi sensed him shake his head. 'No,' he said at last. 'Rupert was his own man, did his own thing as we used to say. He loved life and, I suppose, he did indulge himself a little too much but ... My dear, if I'd come to the house and found him dead in his chair, I would have accepted that. Lord knows, I expected it. Every time I came to Fallowfields I wondered if that would be the time I found my old friend dead. I made him give me a list of people I should call, just in case. But this way? It's all wrong.'

Wrong shoes and no jacket, Naomi thought.

'Was there an investigation?'

'No, dear. Nothing. He'd seen the doctor a few days before and when they ... cut him open, they found that his heart had just given out. Nothing suspicious. Just an old man out walking who had a heart attack and couldn't call for help. That's what they decided and nothing I can say makes them believe any different.'

'Maybe that's all there is to know?'

Marcus poured more wine into his own glass. Naomi had not been aware of him drinking it and she had not touched her own during their conversation. 'I've tried to believe that,' he said. 'I don't want to think of my friend in trouble, frightened, even in pain, I know he must have had the pain and that is bad enough. To suspect it could have been worse than that...'

'But what exactly makes you think...?'

'That he was murdered? Naomi, do you believe a man can be frightened to death?'

'I don't know. I think it's possible.'

'Well, I know that Rupert was afraid. He'd begun to lock his doors. Rupert, in all the years I knew him, *never* locked his doors.

Then he monitored his telephone calls, used the answer phone; he hated the darn things. And there were people who came looking for him. Two men, he said, asking questions. One, I know, went to Fallowfields and Rupert was afraid.'

'Didn't he tell the police? Did he give you any idea who they were or what they wanted?'

'No. No, nothing. He wouldn't listen to me when I said he should report the incidents. He didn't tell me who the man was or what was said or why he was suddenly scared of his own shadow. Naomi, in the days before he died, he didn't even come to the shop. Rupert loved our little shop. He thrived on it; meeting people. To cut himself off from that. From his friends...'

'From you,' Naomi said softly.

'From me. Yes. Rupert was my friend. My dear, dear, friend.' His voice broke with the pain of it and Naomi reached out, hoping to find his hand without knocking over the wine. She touched his arm and laid her hand on the rough tweed of his jacket.

'Alec has to do something,' Marcus said fiercely. 'He must do something. Rupert is dead and he cannot, in all conscience, just accept that and walk away.'

Four

Naomi was very quiet on the drive back to Fallowfields. She was not sure how seriously she should take Marcus Prescott; she sensed that Rupert's death would have been almost more than he could bear no matter how it had come about. Worse almost than the death was the sense that his old friend had been unable or unwilling to confide his worries.

Naomi had no idea what it was that Rupert might have been worried about but she did wonder if, perhaps, something personal had been bothering him. Something *too* personal to have talked to Marcus about. That Marcus had been so used to being in the know would have made any secrecy on Rupert's part seem out of character and it would have been easy – natural even – for Marcus to see his death as suspicious following so soon after this change in behaviour.

'Penny for them,' Alec said. 'I saw Marcus had you cornered but you seemed to be holding your own, so I called off the rescue attempt.'

'Not sure if they're worth a penny,' Naomi told him. She took a deep breath. 'I've agreed we'll have lunch with him tomorrow.'

'You've what? Naomi, I really don't think ... I mean, I'm sympathetic and everything, but don't you think the old boy's losing his marbles?'

Naomi was thoughtful. 'No,' she said finally, 'I don't think he is. At least, not the whole bag full. Anyway, we'll be seeing him in the morning at the solicitors. It made it a bit difficult to say no. I thought, well, lunch in a public place, get it over and done with. He wanted to come out to Fallowfields and that would have been far more awkward. You could hardly throw him out if he got to be too annoying.'

She smiled in Alec's direction and heard him laugh. 'All right. I know when I've been organized. Won't hurt, I suppose.'

'No, and I think you owe him anyway.'

'You reckon? How so?'

'Oh, for Rupert's sake, I suppose and also because Marcus was his closest friend...' She hesitated, not sure if she really believed the next thing she planned to say or if she had been infected by Marcus's zeal. 'And because I think there might be something to what he said,' Naomi admitted.

★ ★ ★

34

Tired, they had gone to bed early that evening but Naomi woke in the early hours. She felt her way to the en suite bathroom, proud that it was getting so much easier to orientate herself in strange places.

She found, to her annoyance, that she was now fully awake. Back in the bedroom Alec's soft, steady breathing just added to her sense of irritation. He obviously hadn't even noticed she had got out of bed. She sighed, stifling the irrational desire to get back into bed and wake him up and then pretend to have been asleep all the time.

Don't be such a baby, she told herself.

She stood in the doorway recalling what Alec had said about the room. He said there was a window seat overlooking the garden. She would sit there a while. One window was open and she made her way towards it, guided as much by the slight breeze squeezing through the gap as she was from memory. The window seat was deep, comfortable and padded; an alcove really, with the window on one side. She pulled up her feet, wrapping her arms about her knees and leaned back against the wall. She laid her head against the closed pane and breathed deep of the night scents rising from the garden.

Back home, in her flat, she could smell the sea at night. By day the traffic smells blocked the tang of salt, but by late evening, when the tide came in and the cars made their way home, the wind carried the smell of seaweed and damp tide.

They were further from the sea here, she thought. Thirty, maybe even forty miles. The dominant scent was of jasmine and rose and it was so quiet. *So* quiet. Too early even for the birds to be chattering.

A car passed in the lane, the engine noise breaking the silence and she found herself wondering who they might be and where they were going at this time of the night. She listened hard, straining to hear as the sound receded into the distance. She liked the house, loved the location and the peace, but wasn't so sure she could get used to this degree of isolation. And, she reminded herself, Rupert had lived alone. She was sure she could not have done that. Not here. Her little flat was her very own, personal space and she had chosen it after she had lost her sight because of the welcoming feel to it the first time she had visited and the easy layout. Yes, she lived alone there, but she was always aware of others around her. Her upstairs neighbours were quiet, but the occasional thump or heavy step or closing door reminded her that there were people close by and even at night there were street sounds and occasional cars and cats prowling and yowling, barking dogs in the next street...

This was isolated, Naomi thought. At least, to her mind it was and yet several times she had heard those who were used to such seclusion speak of the place where Rupert had died as being in the middle of nowhere.

If Fallowfields was generally counted as being *somewhere* then just how desperately alone must Rupert have felt on the day he died.

Five

Morning brought a series of shocks.

'I'll run through the finer points in a moment, but, to be brief, apart from his share of the shop, he's left everything to you.' Donald Grieves, Rupert's solicitor peered at Alec over the top of his bifocals.

'To me?' Alec turned to Marcus Prescott. 'You knew about this?'

'Of course. Rupert and I made out our wills at the same time. Whoever passed on first took over the shop. Rupert wanted the rest to go to you. I believe, apart from the house, there's some seven hundred and fifty thousand pounds in a savings account.' He

37

looked at Donald Grieves for confirmation.

'Something of that order,' Grieves nodded.

Alec was too stunned to say a word.

'Why Alec?' Naomi asked and Alec glanced first at her and then back at the solicitor.

'Yes, exactly. Why me?'

It was Marcus Prescott that replied. 'Rupert liked you. Loved you. He wanted those things he loved to go to someone he felt the same about, and, as he and your father were no longer on speaking terms, that direction was never an option. Rupert said you always kept in touch and he had adored your visits to Fallowfields when you were younger. He used to talk about one day when there was a storm rolling in from the sea. Do you remember that?'

Alec nodded. 'Oh yes,' he said softly. 'Yes, I do.'

'He rated you highly, my boy. Said you were honest and kind and just that little bit driven. All qualities *I* loved in Rupert. You know,' Marcus continued thoughtfully, 'I always thought he'd have made a good father.'

The solicitor laughed uncertainly. 'Pity he never found the right woman.'

Marcus deliberated thoughtfully, and Alec could see that he had revived Naomi's ruminations of the day before. She no longer thought that Rupert and Marcus had been lovers, but she still questioned whether Rupert would have been interested in 'the right woman'.

'So, what happens now?' Naomi asked.

'I'm stunned,' Alec added unnecessarily.

'Well, everything has been set up to make the transfer of deed and so forth as easy as possible. Um, Rupert was concerned that, even with keeping the house, there will be tax to pay, so he made some provision for that. There's the bank account, though, with inflation etc, it may not cover everything. I do know that he was keen you should keep Fallowfields. Said so on a number of occasions, said it would stand you in good stead for the long term, but I'm sure he would have understood should you decide to sell. No rush, of course.'

'No,' Alec said. 'I mean. I have to think about this. I've still not taken it in.'

'No, no, of course. I've put a little pack together for you. Copy of the will and other paperwork relating to the legacy. You can go through it at your leisure and, of course, don't hesitate to contact me with any questions.'

Alec allowed himself to be guided to the local hotel where Marcus had arranged for them to have lunch. He felt numbed, shocked. He had hoped for some small legacy from his uncle, just something to remember him by. To have been allowed to take a couple of books from the extensive library or perhaps a few of the family photographs Rupert had framed and dotted about Fallowfields would have been more than enough. To have been left so much ... that shifted the balance of Alec's world.

He had never been badly off. His father, as a doctor, and his mother, as a teacher, they had valued education and experience and Alec had acquired the best of both. He had been loved and cherished and grown up perhaps a little too much aware of his own imagined importance. University and then policing had changed his perspective and brought him into contact with a wider variety of people and backgrounds, but on the whole his transition from high achiever in school to high achiever in the workplace had been smooth and seamless and the salary had followed, supplemented by the investments his father had made on his behalf when Alec was a child.

He owned a house and a car. Both above averagely nice. He did pretty much what he wanted as regards holidays and consumer luxury, but this legacy was something else. A brief look at the paperwork he had been given told him that his assets, even after taxes had been paid, would leave him with something like half a million.

Pounds.

Sterling.

Plus the house.

Not enough to retire on, maybe, but certainly enough to change his life one way or another.

But it wasn't just this that shocked him, Alec realized. Wasn't just that he now had a rather large house with a very large garden and an extremely comfortable bank account. It was that it had never occurred to him that Rupert might have had money. Not at all. Rupert had bought Fallowfields at a time when such property was cheap. He had furnished it comfortably but never to a particularly luxurious standard. He had always driven ageing and somewhat quirky cars and...

A thought struck.

'Marcus, did Rupert still drive?'

'Yes. He had that old Austin Healey. Why?'

'Did he keep it at Fallowfields? It isn't in the garage.'

Marcus looked curiously at him. 'What are you thinking?'

'Did he drive to where they found him?'

Marcus shook his head. 'I thought that, but there was no sign of the car.'

'So...'

Marcus sighed. 'Alec, that's just one of the

things I want to talk to you about. Look, here's the hotel, let's get our table and order and then I'll fill you in. Naomi dear, there are three steps, quite narrow but shallow and I've checked ahead, our lovely Napoleon will be more than welcome. There's a bit of an alcove in the main dining room. Napoleon can lie down out of the way and not be trodden on.'

'Thank you, Marcus.'

Alec made to take her arm to find that Marcus had beaten him to it and was guiding her up the steps. Completely unnecessary, Alec knew. She and Napoleon could manage just fine, but it was a natural reaction on his behalf and, he supposed, on that of Marcus as well.

It struck him, not for the first time, that he should have brought her to visit Rupert. His uncle would have loved her and adored the dog.

He found that he felt a terrible guilt. That this man had evidently thought so much of Alec and Alec done so little in return, though he had cared deeply for Rupert and genuinely grieved at his death.

He followed Marcus and Naomi into the dining room of the hotel. Noting the plush and rather overblown decor, all dark wood panels and deep red carpet, but the staff seemed friendly and the menu, when he remembered to look at it, was varied if not deeply imaginative.

Solid, country fare as Rupert might have said.

Marcus was reading the options to Naomi and discussing the merits of the various dishes he had sampled there. Alec could hear him promoting the merits of the steak and kidney pudding.

It all felt faintly surreal.

'Alec, you'll feel better if you eat,' Naomi said gently and he nodded, knowing she was right. He had skipped breakfast, never a good move and now she had drawn his attention to it he realized that his gut churned emptily just adding to the hollow feeling at the centre of him.

'The salmon,' he said, falling back on the familiar. 'And the soup for starters. Thank you.' He waited until the waitress had departed. 'Marcus?'

'Yes, Alec.'

'Time to talk, I think.'

Marcus nodded. He took his napkin from the table and unfolded it then spread it carefully on his lap. The wine arrived and, once Marcus had approved it, Alec accepted a glass.

'Alec?' Naomi was surprised. Alec rarely drank at lunchtime.

'If I have more than one we'll get a taxi

back to Fallowfields,' he said.

'OK,' she sounded dubious, anxious even.

'Nomi, it's been a strange couple of days and an even stranger morning. Frankly, I think I could do with a drink.'

'OK,' she said again then reached for her glass and sipped. 'Mmm, nice.' She smiled suddenly in Alec's direction. 'I think in that case we should order another bottle.'

Marcus laughed softly and then sobered. 'Rupert,' he said. 'Of course, you will want to know everything I can tell. Truth is, Alec, it's mostly suspicion and conjecture but, believe me, I know something is wrong about it all.'

'Go on.'

'It's knowing where to start.'

'Well,' Naomi prompted. 'How about you start with when you noticed something was wrong with Rupert. When his behaviour changed?'

Marcus nodded. He played with the stem of his wineglass, frowning at the deep red liquid. 'It's hard to know,' he said, 'but I think, the first time I really noticed something odd was about three weeks before Rupe died.

'I live in the flat over our shop. I'm not like Rupert; never felt the need for a garden, and the isolation of a place like Fallowfields would drive me mad, I think. Anyway, this one particular morning I heard someone banging on the shop door long before we were open, so I looked out of the window to see who it was and there stood this teenager – a boy, really – banging on my door and shouting for Rupert.'

'You didn't recognize him?'

'No. Not at all. And he wasn't the kind of customer I'd expect in our shop even during opening time. He wore those baggy trousers young people seem to like these days and a hoodie, I think they call them, don't they?'

Alec nodded.

'Anyway, I called down and asked what he wanted and he said he had to talk to Rupert. So, I told him Rupert wouldn't be in until ten and to come back then, to which he said he couldn't, he must see him now. I gained the impression that he thought Rupert lived at the shop and he seemed very put out when I told him otherwise.'

'Did you tell him where Rupert lived?'

'No.' Marcus shook his head emphatically. 'That I'd never do without Rupert's permission and, besides...'

'You didn't like the look of him?' Naomi asked.

Marcus hesitated. 'It wasn't that, dear. I'd be the last to hold the way someone looks against them. My dear, I recall some of the so-called fashions I indulged in my youth and besides, he was polite enough in his own way. No, it was more that he seemed afraid. Kept looking over his shoulder all the time I was talking to him. It was as if he didn't want to be discovered asking for Rupert. That he was afraid of the consequences should he be found out.'

'And when you told him Rupert wasn't there?'

'Oh, he took off down the road as if the devil himself was chasing him. He didn't come back again either.'

'And what was Rupert's reaction? Did he recognize the boy?'

'He said not, at first. Then, as though it had just occurred to him, he said it might be one of the people he'd been interviewing that had sent the boy. I didn't believe him, but I didn't press the matter. I really, truly wish I had.'

'Interviewing?' Alec questioned.

The first course arrived and they all fell silent until once more they were left alone.

Marcus played with his soup. 'He collected local tales, you knew that, I suppose?'

Alec nodded. 'He sent me copies of the little books he wrote. He was a member of the Folklore Society or something, wasn't he?'

'Oh yes. For years and he must have published a dozen of his pamphlets. We sold them in the shop and the local galleries and tourist places took them as well. He even had an account of the Fen Tigers published by a major publisher some years ago. I believe it was well received.'

'Fen Tigers?' Naomi asked. 'Surely there were never big cats around here. Or was it something like the Beast of Bodmin?'

Marcus laughed. 'No, my dear. Not big cats as such. They were protesters. Guerrilla fighters you could say almost, back in the eighteenth century when the drainage of the fens took place. They attacked the workers, destroyed the workings, tried to stop the whole process.'

'Why?' Naomi wondered. 'Surely the creation of new farmland was a good thing.'

'For the landowners, perhaps,' Marcus agreed, 'but the drainage destroyed an entire way of life for many, to say nothing of an ecosystem we are only just beginning to value. And worse, so far as the locals were concerned, the engineers were foreigners from the Netherlands. But I think what interested Rupert the most was the way the drainage destroyed the ... what you might call the supernatural ecology.'

'The what?' Alec was confused.

'Don't let your soup go cold. It's very good.'

Alec glanced down and belatedly began to

47

eat. Marcus, he noted, had all but cleared his plate, and that despite the fact that he had barely ceased his talk. How, Alec wondered, did he do that?

'Anyway, as I was saying. Boggarts, bogles, tiddymen, black dogs, they had them all in plenty to say nothing of the various water sprites and Lord knows what else. Rupert loved all that stuff, went about collecting the residual tales and adding them to the established ones. He said it was amazing just what oral history could preserve.' Marcus chuckled fondly. 'I think it actually *troubled* him that these mythical beings had been displaced. In fact I think it troubled him almost more than the displacement of the actual people.'

Derek Reid had wandered out into the barn to check the car. He'd brought a gallon container of petrol to top up the tank, or at least provide enough for an emergency. His little red car was economical, but Sam's bloody great Ford Granada was thirsty. Derek reckoned it was an odd choice of car. Not even one of the newer models – newer, he laughed, hadn't they stopped making them ten years or so ago? It was a big black thing with electric everything, the sort Sam would have owned back in the eighties.

Sam wasn't good at moving on, not even in

the small ways, Derek thought.

He unlocked the cap and poured the petrol into the tank. He reckoned it would be about half full by now. He'd been bringing in a gallon a day from one petrol station or another for the past ten days and Sam had only made a couple of short trips out so, added to what he already had in the tank, there should be ample there for anything he might need to do.

The sun shining through the double doors didn't quite reach to the back of the building. Derek wandered back into the shadows and regarded the second car parked there. Boy, that had taken some getting back here. The Austin Healey was a quirky little number, that was for sure.

He shook his head, recalling the events of that day. Heavy rain, despite it being the middle of June. Glowering clouds. He'd been half frozen waiting. Sam wouldn't let him stay in the car, said he had to stand and wait where Rupert could see him. Then they'd forced the old man into Sam's car and brought him back here.

Derek went over, stroked the ageing vehicle. He kind of liked the look of it, quirks and all. It had character.

Sighing, Derek picked up his petrol can and made his way back upstairs to where Sam waited in the partially completed conversion. The owners had once had big ideas, Derek thought. The house wasn't up to much but it was all mod cons up here. Or would have been had they got around to finishing.

'Here,' Sam Kinnear handed him a slip of paper. 'Stuff I want and things to do, and keep away from that bitch. She's not part of the plan, Derek, remember that.'

Derek nodded, taking the list from Kinnear's hand.

'Fuel in the car,' he said. 'Plenty for tomorrow. You still want me along?'

Kinnear scowled. 'And what sort of a question is that.'

Derek shrugged. 'Better be off,' he said. 'It was the funeral this morning, I went to check the place out like you said. There's just the two of them there, I reckon. We could have...'

'Could have what?'

'I don't know, gone there while they were at the funeral.'

Kinnear stared hard and Derek shifted uncomfortably beneath his gaze. 'Bit too late for that,' he said. 'I want him to know. I want the bastard to be afraid. Just like the old man.'

Derek nodded and left as swiftly as he could without actually running. He started his little car and drove away, relief at being away from Kinnear growing as he put the miles between them. He thought about Sharon and he smiled.

'And she's not a bitch,' he told the absent Sam Kinnear.

Six

They took a taxi back to Fallowfields, leaving the car parked where Alec had left it round the back of Marcus's shop. Wholly Marcus's shop now, Alec thought.

Alec had not spoken on the return trip, he sat lost in thought with Napoleon beside him on the back seat. Naomi chatted with the driver; her sleek black companion the predictable focus of their conversation.

Back at Fallowfields, Alec helped her from the car and then stood outside the front door as though something was bothering him.

'Don't say you've forgotten the keys,' Naomi teased.

'No, I have them here.'

'What then?'

'I think someone's been here.'

'Why?'

'Tyre tracks,' Alec said. He left her side and

51

she heard him crunch across the gravel.

'How can you tell in the gravel?' she asked. 'They're probably ours anyway.'

'No.' Alec's voice came from low down so she guessed he was crouched or kneeling.

'What do you see?'

'Well, there's a grass verge, then flower beds each side of the gravel drive. It looks to me like someone turned their car around and the back wheels ran on to the verge and then into the bed. There are deep ruts.'

'Not there yesterday?'

'No. I'm sure of that. There's been no rain here for a while, then we had that torrential downpour early this morning. Not enough to soak the verge; that's still hard, though you can see where the grass has been crushed because it's not been mown in, I'd say, several weeks. The flower bed though, that did allow the wet to penetrate and there are tyre tracks and the plants have been crushed. The leaves are still green so...'

'So someone came here while we were out.' Naomi thought about it. 'Someone lost? Needing to turn around?'

'If they only needed turning space there's plenty down at the road end of the drive. If someone came here asking for directions, which I think is unlikely, then they were unusually careless turning round. There's plenty of space for manoeuvre, Nomi. Whoever swung around here did it in a hurry and either didn't pay attention or didn't care what they drove over. Plus, I'd say they spun their wheels. There are deep indents in the gravel and it's been sprayed out on to the verge. That's what I noticed first.'

'Odd.' She reached out and pushed the door. 'Still locked. What about the side gate?'

She heard Alec crunch across the drive again and shake the wooden gate. 'Locked,' he said.

'I hear a but in your voice.'

'Not a but, just a maybe. I'm wondering how hard it would be to climb.'

'Best check inside and round the back.'

Naomi heard him slide the key into the lock. She followed him inside, Napoleon trotting behind her, nuzzling at her hand and clearly puzzled as to what was going on. 'Anything wrong in here?'

'Not that I can see.'

She waited in the hall while he checked from room to room. The French doors in the dining room were old fashioned and fastened with a large key that hung from a hook hidden behind the curtain. The back door in the kitchen had a bolt and a deadbolt, she recalled. Window locks on the front windows had been fastened before they went out. Windows at the rear were old and not as secure. Alec had taken her on a tour on their first night, making sure she knew how each door fastened and that she could manage everything for herself.

'Anything?' she asked again as he came back into the hall.

'No, it all looks fine. I don't know, maybe I'm being a bit paranoid. It could easily have been someone took a wrong turn or something.'

'You don't believe that,' Naomi said.

'No, I don't believe that.' He sighed. 'I don't know about you but I could use a coffee. I really shouldn't drink at lunchtime.'

Naomi giggled. 'Poor old thing. Look, I'll see if I can manage coffee and you get up to Rupe's study. I know you're itching to get in there after what Marcus said.'

'That obvious am I?'

'Oh yes.'

'Sure you can manage?'

'I think so. You put everything next to the kettle on the right-hand counter?'

'I did. Give me a shout and I'll carry the tray.'

'Will do.' She waited until he had run up the stairs and then she reached out to rest her hand on the wall. Layers of thick paint covered what felt like mouldings but which Alec told her was some kind of embossed paper. She let her hand slide down to find the dado rail. 'First door, living room. Right.

Corner, then kitchen door. Counter. OK. Now, Napoleon, two steps down and then, I think, about two steps to the table? Yes, right.' She found the nearest chair and hung her bag on the back. 'Counter to the right. Ah, kettle. Bit of a challenge this, Dog.'

She heard his tail thump against the cupboard door as he wagged. 'Sink.' She followed the counter round and felt the cold metal of the draining board beneath her fingers, found the taps and placed her finger close to the spout so she could check that the water was directed into the right place. 'Hope that's not too full. Should have thought to bring my coffee maker, Dog. If we're going to be here long I think we'll have to buy one. I'm not a big fan of instant.'

Napoleon grunted agreement.

'Mugs. Bet he didn't think to leave them out. Second cupboard I think he said. Yes, right. You know, Napoleon, I'd love to be able to see this place. Or maybe I wouldn't, might be scared off by the decor. I mean, who gloss paints wallpaper, hey?'

She busied herself with the rest of the coffee making, pleased at how well she managed. True, it took her a bit of time to navigate around a strange kitchen, but Alec had taken time and trouble to make sure she was familiar with most of it. It felt good to be able to take control. Another big step.

'And what do you make of it all?' she asked the dog. 'Did Uncle Rupert meet with foul play?' She chuckled at her own sententious tone. 'Or is old Marcus allowing his imagination to run away with him?'

Napoleon grunted again. 'You think so, do you? Yes, I'm inclined to agree. There's something not quite right here and I've a nagging feeling that you and I are going to be stuck here in the back of beyond whilst Alec tries to find out what.'

Alec guided her to an old leather chair that stood beside the wall and she sipped her coffee and listened to him riffling through the desk drawers, the captain's chair in which he sat squeaking in mild protest as he finally leaned back and lifted his own cup from the blotter.

'Did you find the laptop?'

'No, definitely not in here. His notes seem to be where Marcus said they would be and there's also a stick drive in here. I'll try it in my computer later, see what's on it. Funny, I half expected to find a stack of manky floppy disks, not a stick drive, but then I wouldn't really have credited Uncle Rupe with entering the computer age.'

'Marcus reckoned he was a bit of a wiz.'

'So he did.'

'What are the notes like?'

'Well, they're just readable, I suppose. I don't imagine Rupe expected to have to show them to anyone else.' He sat forward and set the mug down with a bump.

'Thought of something?'

'Hmm, yes. When I stayed here I seem to remember Rupert having a safe or strongbox or something. I wonder...'

'You remember where?'

'A floorboard, I think. Somewhere over near the fireplace. Let's see.'

The wooden boards creaked as he knelt down and pulled back the rug and Naomi heard him tapping at the floor.

'Won't it all sound hollow?' she asked. 'It's a floor. The only bit that won't will be where the joists cross.'

'Well, yes, but ... I'm trying to remember. Something loose, I think, that could be lifted. God, it was so long ago, I just can't...'

He fell silent and Naomi fancied she could almost hear the cogs turning as he thought about it. 'I'm on the wrong side,' he decided. She heard him shuffling and tapping in a different place.

'Yes!'

'Found it?'

'I just need something to...' Keys jangled as he searched his trouser pockets, found the little multi-blade penknife that their young friend Patrick had given him for Christmas.

'Just need to slide the blade down. There!'

She heard him lift something from the hole, metal scraping on wood as he caught the boards on either side. He came over to where she sat and dropped down on to the floor at her feet. 'I don't have the key but I think Patrick's knife might get me in.' He poked and scraped and levered and Naomi heard the lid break free of its catch and drop back against the floor.

'Well? Talk to me. What do you see?'

Alec sat back on his heels and riffled through the contents. 'It's all a bit ordinary really,' he said. He didn't really know what he'd expected but felt oddly disappointed. 'Just his passport and some insurance documents, for the house, it looks like and ... well, there's a couple of floppy disks and this.'

'This? Can't see, remember.'

'A locket,' Alec said. 'Heavy, gold, engraved. Looks Victorian to me.' He fumbled with the tiny catch. 'There's a lock of blonde hair inside.' He closed it up and passed it to Naomi, watching as she fondled the oval shape and the heavy belcher chain.

'Pretty,' she said. 'There's some weight to it, too.'

'Hmm.'

'Something wrong?'

'I don't know. I suppose not. I just have the feeling that I've seen it before.'

'Quite likely when you were here,' Naomi commented. 'You knew about the box, you probably saw what was inside. You'd have just forgotten, I expect.'

'Oh, I'm sure you're right. It just seems a little out of place.'

'Could it have been a family piece? Rupert's mother's, something like that? It would probably be the right age to be a family piece.'

'Likely so.' He laughed. 'I knew there'd be some floppy disks somewhere. The stick drive was just too much.'

'Pity you can't look at them. Your laptop doesn't have a floppy drive, does it?'

'No, a lot of the newer ones don't. Still, I can have a read of what's on the stick drive and I'll bet the shop computer will have a floppy drive. I expect Marcus will be happy enough to let me use that.'

He took Naomi's hand and pulled her to her feet. 'More coffee,' he said. 'You get the kettle on again and I'll dig out the laptop and I've got a phone call to make.'

'Oh?'

'Marcus gave me the name of the officer who dealt with finding Uncle Rupe. I'm hoping, as a professional courtesy, he'll agree to meet us where Rupert was found.'

It's disturbing, the way one drifts through life

and never really thinks about what will happen when one is no longer there. All of the flotsam and jetsam collected through life will belong to someone else and all of the responsibilities passed on.

I hope I won't leave too many of those but there are a few. I will, of course, do my best to sort the problems before I pass on, but as another birthday approaches far too fast, I realize that I really ought to set things in order.

Marcus has talked about making a will and I think I will make mine too. It will all go to Alec, of course. There is no one else, really. Elaine will be settled as I've always promised myself, but the rest can go to Alec. I loved the boy and I respect the man. I don't know of many who have fulfilled all their youthful promise, but it seems to me that he has and it is good to know that even as we have both grown older there has been room for the occasional letter and that he is still capable of enjoying our humorous swipes at life.

So, I will make my will and leave it all to Alec and hope he has the sense to trust his old uncle and not to dig too deep into things not his, or by that time, my concern.

Seven

It had rained during the night but the temperature remained high and Naomi had not slept well. She and Alec had their breakfast on the terrace, the air heavy with the scent of roses and damp grass and filled with birdsong and the sounds of one very happy dog rolling in the damp grass.

'Sure you'll be all right?' Alec asked.

'I'll be fine. I just want to laze for a while. Your taxi should be here in a few minutes. I'm going to sit here for a bit and then explore the house, on my own, no one to see when I forget where I am.'

Alec laughed. 'I know when I'm not wanted but, Naomi, make sure you have your mobile with you all the time, just in case.'

His taxi arrived and Alec set off to retrieve his car from the pub where they'd had lunch the day before. Naomi continued to sit, enjoying the sun and the warm, fragrant air and debating whether or not she could be bothered to go and make herself more tea.

When the doorbell rang it took her by surprise.

'Who on earth is that?'

Napoleon scampered back on to the terrace and Naomi stood irresolute. She wasn't properly dressed yet, hadn't bothered to do more than pull on sweatpants and a T-shirt, and it occurred to her that this might be some friend or acquaintance of Rupert's who had not heard the news of his death.

The bell rang again, this time followed by loud knocking. Whoever it was didn't seem about to go away.

Slowly, Napoleon at her side, she made her way back through the house. The banging had not ceased. Naomi decided she wasn't keen on opening the door.

'Hello, who is it?'

The banging stopped.

'Hi, who's there?' Naomi asked again.

There was a pause, then: 'I want to talk to the new owner.'

'About what?'

'Look, just open the door and let me in. I told you, I want to talk to the bloke Rupert left this place to.'

Naomi had decided she was definitely not going to let this man in but she felt stupid and childish talking through the door. She fumbled for the chain and fastened it in place before cracking it open just a little.

'I'm afraid he isn't available at the moment. If you'd like to leave a message...'

'What are you? His bloody answering service?'

Naomi didn't reply. She had, as Alec had instructed, slipped her mobile phone into the pocket of her sweatpants and she debated now if she should use it. Alec's number was on speed dial, but how soon could he get back?

'If you take that tone,' Naomi said, 'then you can damned well stay outside. If you have a message to give tell me now then clear off.'

He pushed the door. Naomi, taken by surprise was shoved off balance. Angry now she pushed back only to find something was blocking the door's return. Damn the man, he'd put his foot in the way. She swung her full weight against it and pushed harder. 'What the hell do you want?'

The man leaned in close. He seemed unconcerned about the pain she must be causing to his trapped toes. She could feel his breath on her face and smell his aftershave. It smelt expensive, she noted almost absently, and didn't gel with the rest of her experience of him. She tried to keep her voice steady. 'I asked you what you wanted.'

'Rupert Friedman owed me money,' the man snarled. 'As I see it that means the bloke he left it all to owes me on his behalf. Now let me inside.'

'No way,' Naomi told him. She released her pressure on the door just for an instant and then rammed it back against the intruding foot. The man pushed back. Her hand pressed hard against the edge of the door, but Naomi was startled to feel his fingers curl around hers. He tugged her grip free and started to pull on her hand.

Naomi felt panicked, then angry. Just before he dragged her hand through the gap in the door, she leaned in and bit him. His skin felt rough against her tongue. She bit harder. He swore and let go. She slammed again against his foot. This time that too moved away.

'Little bitch. I'll have you!'

She slammed and locked the door. Pressing her ear against the heavy wood she could still hear him swearing and cursing as he stamped upon the gravel. Then a sound that chilled her to the bone. He's coming over the gate.

She knew the way easily now. With her hand against the wall as a guide she almost ran back through the house and slammed the French doors closed, locking them with the old key. Footsteps on the terrace told her that he was round the back and a moment later he was banging his hands against the

French doors. Naomi knew they wouldn't hold for long. Not if he was determined to get inside.

She heard a crash as he smashed the breakfast tray from the table on the terrace. Naomi turned and headed back through the house. She had not expected this, not this level of violence. Most people took time to ramp up. This man obviously had a very short and very dangerous fuse.

The safest place to be? Where would be the safest place?

Calling Napoleon she began to climb the stairs. Rupert's study was next to the guest bedroom she and Alec occupied. It had a heavy, solid door and a decent lock. Below in the dining room, wood splintered. What the hell was wrong with this man? It had dawned on her that he might have been watching the house and seen Alec leave. It had also occurred that there might be two of them. The footsteps on the terrace had sounded different, now she thought about it. Lighter, faster. She had gained the impression from the man at the front door that he was heavily built.

Stumbling on the top step, Naomi reached out to find the wall, searching for the wood panel and the dado rail that separated the panelling from the paper above. She hauled herself up and then moved towards the study

door, relieved to feel the solidity and reassuring weight as she swung it open and
then slammed it closed. Alec had left the key
in the door as, he'd told her, Rupert had
always done. She turned it now, then stepped back from the door and stood, listening
to the sounds coming from below – crashing
and splintering and breaking glass.

She fumbled in her pocket for the mobile
phone and dialled the three nines.

'I need the police,' she told the controller,
horrified to hear the shake and sound of
barely controlled terror in her own voice.
'Someone's broken into my house and I'm
alone. Yes, they're still here. I've locked
myself into a room upstairs and it sounds
like they're wrecking the place.'

She listened to the calm voice of the controller on the other end and a surge of impatience, driven by pure fear sharpened her
tone as the panic rose. 'Look, I need someone now. Please.' And then she broke her
own unwritten rule. 'Look,' she said. 'I'm
blind. I can't see.'

The controller stayed on the line, her calm
voice meant to reassure. She was playing a
role that Naomi had played many times in
her days as a police officer, before the blind-
ness had taken her career and transformed
her life beyond recognition. She spoke gently
and firmly, telling Naomi that help was on

its way, keeping her on the line and asking for reports of any sounds she could hear, any movement through the house.

'He's coming up the stairs,' Naomi whispered. 'I can hear him on the stairs.'

'You've locked the door?' the woman on the line confirmed.

'Yes, I've locked it and it's a heavy door but...' She could hear him now, standing at the top of the stairs, then two steps to the study door, rattling the knob.

'I've called the police,' Naomi yelled at him. 'I've called the police and they're on their way.'

She backed away from the door and bumped into the desk. The controller was still talking to her but Naomi could no longer hear. Napoleon whimpered, sensing her anxiety. He nuzzled at her hand and Naomi slid down beside the desk and gathered the big black dog close to her.

'Naomi, are you listening to me?'

Naomi lifted the phone to her ear. 'He's outside the door.' She tried to stay calm. She took long controlling breaths. Damn it, she told herself, she'd been in tight spots before and not panicked like this. She'd been trapped in a burning building, taken hostage in a bank siege, almost been thrown off the roof of a building, but she had never felt like this.

The difference, she decided, was that at

those other times there had been other people to think about. Other concerns. In the fire, Patrick had been with her and she had been more worried about getting him out than she had been scared for herself. In the siege too, she had taken control then, fallen back on her training and pushed her own fears aside in order to calm other people.

This time, apart from Napoleon, she was truly alone.

'I've called the police,' she shouted once more, then strained to listen. The door knob creaked again and weight thudded against the wood, then a muffled shout from down below.

So, he wasn't alone.

She heard the footsteps again, but this time they turned back to the landing, becoming muffled on the carpeted stairs.

'I think they're going away,' she whispered into the phone. 'I think they're going away.'

'Officers will be with you in just a few more minutes,' the controller informed her. 'Stay where you are.'

Naomi had no intention of leaving the illusory safety of this room.

She strained her ears, praying that the men had really left but angry that they might now get away. 'Tell them to hurry. Please.'

'Just hang on and stay put. They'll be with

68

you in no time at all.'

Still straining her ears, Naomi caught the sound of an engine and car tyres on gravel. 'They're getting away. I can hear the car.'

A moment later and the sound of distant sirens had her gasping in relief. She heard the cars in the drive, arriving at speed and tyres spinning in the gravel.

'They're here,' she told the controller, trying hard to keep the tears from thickening her voice. 'Thank you, they're here.'

She stumbled from the room and down the stairs, falling over the debris that the intruders had left in the hall. The front door banged open as she reached the hall and she cried out more in shock than fear.

'Police,' a voice announced. 'It's all right, love, you're all right now.'

Hands rested lightly on her arms and someone led her towards the door. 'Let's get you sitting in the car, shall we?' His accent was local, thick with burr and drawn out vowels.

Naomi allowed herself to be led outside and seated in the car. 'In you get, big fella,' the voice continued and Napoleon scrambled up inside, resting his big head on her leg.

Naomi leaned her head back against the seat and allowed the tears to flow.

Eight

Alec arrived about a half hour after the police. Naomi had, in the end, refrained from calling him and the policewoman now sitting beside her in the car had concurred. No point in risking an accident because he had driven back too fast.

She heard his car come into the drive and skid to a halt. He ran across the gravel, calling her name and she heard the officer who had been first through the door asking who he was.

'It's Alec,' Naomi told the woman sitting beside her, and a moment later Alec had replaced the WPC and was inside the car with his arms tightly around her.

'What the hell happened? Are you OK? Why didn't you call me?'

'I'm all right,' she reassured him. 'Just a bit shaken up. A man came, just after you left. He banged on the door and—'

'You let him in?'

'No, I didn't let him in. I'm not that stupid.'

70

Alec was contrite. 'I'm sorry. I'm just—'

'He or another man broke in round the back. Dog and I locked ourselves in Rupert's study and I called the police.'

Quickly, she filled him in on other details. Alec, reassured that she was all right, had switched, she noted, into policeman mode. He asked her questions, looked for more detail then, hugging her again, he got out of the car. 'Stay there, love. I'll be right back.'

Naomi sighed and leaned back into the seat once again. Her head hurt and, unaccountably considering the circumstances, she was now ravenous. She wanted to get away from this place, check into a nice safe hotel and find some breakfast or brunch, or whatever it was time for.

Panic and fear, Naomi noted, not for the first time in her life, promoted hunger. Vaguely, she wondered if this was a common reaction and decided that it probably was not.

It seemed that she had almost been forgotten now. She eased herself from the police car and stood listening to the conversations. SOCO had been called, but no one knew when they'd arrive. Alec had explained who he was and was now in deep discussion with the first officer on scene. Hand resting on Napoleon's head, Naomi now made her way over to where Alec stood.

'You feeling better, love?' the other officer asked her. 'I still think you should get checked out by the doc.'

'Thanks. I'm OK,' Naomi told him. 'Have they done much damage inside?'

'Right mess, I'm afraid,' he told her. 'I'm DS Fine, by the way. We didn't get a chance for proper introductions earlier.'

Naomi held out her hand. 'Pleased to meet you,' she said as he shook it, aware that this was all just a little bit surreal. His handshake was firm and the hands slightly calloused. She remembered the man who had put his hand around the door frame and grabbed her own.

'I bit him,' Naomi said. 'I bit hard, I think I might have drawn blood. There might be trace on the door frame.'

'Trace?' Fine was clearly surprised by her technical use of the term.

'Naomi was a DI,' Alec explained. 'Until...'

'I had an accident,' she said.

'I'm sorry.'

She smiled. 'Life happens. Look, I'm ready to make a statement now.'

'Sure you're up to it?'

'Best now, while it's still fresh.'

'I'll get someone to drive you both to Epworth.'

'I'll drive us,' Alec told him. 'I think we'd

72

better find ourselves a hotel, too. Can I get some clothes and such together?'

'He ... they ... didn't go into the bedroom,' Naomi said. 'The man that came upstairs stood outside the study door and turned the knob, then he was called back downstairs. I shouted at him that I'd called the police. I think they knew they'd better leave.'

'Right. OK. Alec, DC Roland over there has laid out our path, so you'd best let him show you where you can go. We'll secure the place before we leave and someone will hang on here until SOCO arrives.'

'Thanks,' Alec said. 'Could you help Naomi and Napoleon to my car and I'll be as quick as I can.'

Sitting in the front seat of a familiar vehicle, selecting her favourite channel on the radio and allowing Rachmaninov to soothe her nerves, Naomi closed her eyes as she still always did when trying to shut out extraneous thoughts.

She replayed the time from when she had first heard banging on the door right through to when the police arrived. It hadn't, she realized, been that long. Ten, fifteen minutes, perhaps from start to end, but it had seemed like an eternity.

Napoleon woofed a greeting as Alec dumped their luggage in the boot and then got into the car. He took Naomi's hand and

73

squeezed.

'It's a right mess,' he said. 'But you're all right. That's what matters.'

'You know,' she said, 'they must have been looking for something. Rupert owing money might be true, but I don't think that was the important thing. They wanted to get inside the house and I'm sure they saw you leave. I think they might have assumed I'd gone with you and were just checking things out by banging on the door.'

'Speculation,' Alec said. 'You can't know that.'

'No, I can't and I'll just stick to the facts in the statement. I know the drill. There was a strange thing though, Alec. The man who came to the front door. He got so angry so quickly that it was almost unnatural. It was as if he'd already worked himself up and what I did just tipped him over.'

'Whatever the truth of the matter,' Alec said, 'we won't be going back to Fallowfields for a little while, I don't think.'

'But we won't be going back home either, will we? Just as well you booked more time than you thought you'd need.' Just as well there was nothing dramatic happening back at work either, she thought.

Alec sighed. 'I think if we had doubts before about Rupe being in trouble they've now been well and truly swept away. I've got to get to the bottom of this, Nomi.'

'I know.'

'But if you want to go.'

'Right. I'm really going to clear out now, aren't I. You know me better than that.'

He reached out and squeezed her hand again. 'Thanks,' he said. 'But I don't want you in any more danger.'

'I'll be fine,' she said. 'I'm not keen on being on my own in strange places just now, but apart from that...'

'You think I'm going to leave you alone ever again?' Alec half joked. 'You can't be trusted. Trouble magnet, that's what you are. Always have been.'

Naomi smiled but she could hear the anxiety in his voice and her own mind replayed the violence the men at Fallowfields had exhibited. What would have happened, she wondered, had they been given time to break down the study door?

Nine

Naomi's head was aching but she was beginning to feel better. A shower, a change of clothes and the promise of a late lunch helped in that regard.

They had checked into the hotel that Marcus had taken them to and considered themselves lucky to get a room this time of year. Alec had gone downstairs while she finished dressing, to order lunch and try and remember what the wine had been called. He hadn't wanted to leave her, even in the safety of the hotel room, but Naomi had insisted. She knew she had to be alone, just for a few minutes, to get back her nerve. The longer she put it off the harder it was going to be. Alec would come back up and escort her downstairs but she needed that few minutes alone just to prove to herself she still could.

Behind her she heard Napoleon shift and snuffle. He was lying contentedly in a patch of sunlight that flooded in through the bedroom window. 'Don't get too comfortable,' she told him. 'You're not staying up here on your own. I'd come back and find a hole eaten in the bedspread.'

Napoleon beat his heavy tail on the floor and grumbled to himself. 'Well, no, I've never actually known you to eat bedspreads, but there's always a first time.'

She fumbled for her eye shadow and applied it carefully, blending the two shades, and smudging the lighter one away into nothing. A tiny piece of masking tape stuck to the compact reminding her which was the darker of the two green-grey shades. She had given up wearing make-up for quite some time after the accident, but her sister had insisted she learn how, sitting with her in front of the mirror because that was the way she had always done it before the accident, and coaxing and coercing her into trying out new shades and methods. Naomi was truly grateful for all the fond bullying her sister and her friends had done, though at the time it had seemed so terribly hard and so unfair. Now she applied her 'face', as her sister called it, with almost as much confidence as she had in her sighted days and, with a bit of practise, she had even mastered lipstick, and recently had begun to trust herself to apply the richer, deeper shades that went so well with her dark hair.

Alec opened the door and announced

himself. 'It's me. You ready, love?'

She nodded and stood up, turning to face him. 'I look OK?'

'You look great.' He inspected her as he always did. She was still slightly paranoid about going out in badly matched clothes. 'I like the new eye stuff.'

'Thanks. Thought I'd try something new. I'm starving.' She called Napoleon and allowed herself to be escorted downstairs. 'We should tell Marcus what happened,' she said.

'I tried to phone him, but just got some woman who said she was looking after the shop today and he'd be back this evening.'

'Right, he's going to be upset by all of this.'

'Hmm, and Reg Fine, the DS you met at the house,' Alec continued, 'he's going to arrange for us to be taken to where they found Rupert.'

'When?'

'Hopefully tomorrow. All we are going to do today is eat and rest. Doctor's orders.'

'What doctor?'

'Doctor Friedman.'

Naomi laughed. Alec seated her at their table and settled Napoleon. 'Seriously love, you had a really bad fright. I want you to be all right.'

'I'm fine. What I'd really like is to have lunch then go for a walk and just have some unwinding time. We've not had a proper chance to look around yet. Let's make like tourists for a while?'

'Whatever you want to do. We can do the John Wesley trail, if you like. That would be a good way of finding out about the town.'

She nodded. 'I'd forgotten about the whole Methodist thing. Nonconformist territory, isn't it, around here? I vaguely remember Mum insisting we did all that one holiday. Looking at Wesley's tomb and an old rectory, I think.' She shook her head. 'It was a long time ago.'

'Funny how we both spent our holidays round here,' Alec commented. 'OK, we'll do all of that and see what the shops have to offer. The girl on reception told me there's a ghost walk tonight, if you feel up to it.'

'Um, maybe.' She was aware that she was not responding with the enthusiasm Alec would have liked and aware that would worry him even more than he was already, but she couldn't seem to do anything about it. Though she was trying to seem outwardly calm and her heart rate had long ago returned to normal, there was a little piece of her brain still switched into panic mode and when someone close by dropped a glass it was all she could do not to leap to her feet and run away.

Her response made her angry, irritated

with herself. She'd been in worse situations, she reminded herself. Under greater threat, or equal threat at least. Hadn't she?

To be truthful, she was no longer certain that was the case. Something about the way the man had responded to her. The rage she had sensed, and which had been barely contained, unsettled her. No, more than unsettled; it shook her to the very core. It wasn't normal, Naomi decided. It wasn't right. It wasn't sane.

Naomi attended to the starter which had just arrived and tried to divert her thoughts. The statement had taken a while to make. First off she had presented what had happened in bald facts, trying to keep events in the right order and tell her story as clearly as possible. Gently, Alec had coaxed the finer details from her. Naomi was surprised at how much she could in fact remember. The scent of aftershave. The taste of tobacco on the man's skin when she had bitten him. The rough skin at the side of his fingers. The lighter footsteps of the other man.

'What are you thinking?' Alec asked her.

'Nothing much.'

'Nomi?' Alec chided gently.

She took a deep and slightly quavering breath. 'I was going over the statement in my head,' she said. 'In case I'd forgotten anything.' It was, she thought, only a small lie.

Just a little omission.

He reached across the table and took her hand. 'Forget it now,' he said gently. 'Let's enjoy ourselves for the rest of the day. Tomorrow when we see DS Fine again, we may have more information to add to the puzzle. Nothing you can do about it now.'

She knew he was right and she wanted so much to be able to put this from her mind and allow herself to be distracted. She wasn't fooled for one moment that Alec was any less preoccupied and in part she wanted to tell him to stop pretending and just give in and talk this thing to death. The more sensible, thinking part said there was no point and that Alec was right. Let Reg Fine do his job and tomorrow may well bring further revelation.

Most of all she wanted to tell Alec what she felt about the man who had come to the door at Fallowfields and she shuddered inwardly at the knowledge, pure and simple, that he would be back.

Ten

'How far away are we from Fallowfields?' Naomi asked as DS Fine stopped the car.

'It'll be ... let me see. Fallowfields is on the other side of Epworth, actually a bit closer to Owston Ferry, and we're now about a mile outside of Crowle, not far from the river Don and up at the top end of the Isle of Axholme, proper. All in all, it'll be about eleven, twelve miles. We're now in part of the Peatlands nature reserve. Much of a nature lover was he, your uncle?' he asked Alec.

'Only in a general sort of way. I don't recall that he went bird watching or anything like that.'

'Pity,' Fine said. 'This is the place for it. I saw a hen harrier here a week or so ago, brought my lad up with me.'

'You have children?' Naomi asked.

'Oh aye. Two of them. Boy's ten and the little lass is nearly eight.'

The burr, Naomi noticed, seem to have thickened as they drove further out into the country.

Alec got out, then opened the rear passenger door for Naomi and Napoleon.

'So, what's it like?' she asked, turning her head and catching the sound of birds and the rustle of wind blowing through grass. There was another sound too, one she had previously associated with the Somerset Levels, an almost subliminal hiss of saturated ground. 'Marshland,' she said. 'Of course. Was this area not drained then?'

'Not completely. No, the Dutch engineer Vermuyden and his men managed to suck the water from the sponge most everywhere back there in the sixteen hundreds but there's the odd spot wouldn't give in.'

Naomi heard the satisfaction in his voice and smiled in sympathy.

'There are old peat diggings all over here and on the Thorn and Hatfield moors. Anyone coming here should stick to the paths until they know their way around. They can literally end up in deep water, and that before they know it.'

'And Rupert, did he keep to the path?'

'It doesn't look that way. The hikers that found him said he were lying face up about thirty yards off the track. Pure fluke that they spotted him at all. He was part hidden behind some thorn bushes and when they first spotted him they thought he might be twitching, bird watching, you know.'

Naomi nodded.

'But then it occurs to the woman it's a bit strange, lying on your back looking up at the sky when the sky had nothing in it worth looking at. Not even a cloud, she reckoned. Anyway, they left him to it, and walked on aways, but as they'd joined the track at Belton, and that's a good six miles back and Thorn is another seven, eight mile further on, they decided not to go so far, so half hour or so later, they come back, intending to grab a bite at Crowle and then walk back to Belton. And there he is, still lying on his back.'

'How long had he been dead?' Naomi asked.

'They wanted to know same thing,' Fine told her. 'They were worried that they might have saved the poor chap had they called for help sooner, but no hope of that. The doctor reckoned he'd been gone hours before. Time of death was estimated something between four and eight the previous evening, going on liver temperature and considering the night had been warm, and that's as precise as the pathologist wanted to go.'

'That's not the most accurate way,' Alec began. Then: 'Oh, I see.'

'What?' Naomi asked. The best way of ascertaining the time of death was decay of potassium in the eyeball. That was very precise. Why hadn't that been done? 'I don't think I understand.'

'Crows,' Alec said. 'He was lying on his back. They go for the eyes.'

'Oh my God. I never thought.' She shuddered. She had, in her career, encountered bodies in many states and conditions but that particular variation had escaped her thus far.

'It must have been a shock for the hikers,' Alec said.

'I imagine so. Look, I brought you a copy of the post-mortem report seeing as you asked for it, but I have to warn you, it don't make pleasant reading. This is the middle of nowhere and there are foxes and badgers and the like. They don't fuss too much over what they eat.'

'No, I understand.' Alec paused, taking this in. Naomi guessed that Fine would not have been as blunt had Alec not been a fellow officer.

'So,' Alec said, 'is it far from here?'

'About a fifteen minute walk, I'd say.' Fine turned to Naomi. 'Now, do you want to take my arm, or Alec's or something?'

'Thanks, but no. You and Alec walk on, Napoleon and I will follow. So long as he's got someone leading he'll keep me on the path.'

'If you're sure. It's this way then.'

She heard them set off, feet crunching on stones and then quieter as they reached earth and grass. She urged Napoleon to follow Alec, feeling a little nervous because the place was strange to her and to the dog and, being a route he'd not been trained on, he was effectively as lost as she would have been. She knew from experience, though, that he would be fine if Alec took the lead and she sensed that Alec needed that space, that opportunity to switch into inspector mode and try to separate from the raw emotions that must come with hearing the intricate details of Rupert's death.

It was so much harder when it was personal.

Naomi listened to the landscape: flowing water, bubbling through what sounded like a narrow channel; shrieks of a bird she could not identify; and the cawing of those damned crows. She liked the Corvidae as a group, had a particular affection for jackdaws, but found herself suddenly repulsed by the thought of scavenger crows.

It was so hot. Wide, open skies and a landscape almost empty of trees made for baking heat and she wished she'd thought to bring a hat. The sound of water, bubbling and trickling on either side of her jarred oddly with the dry heat of the windless day.

'Was it as hot as this when Rupert died?'

she asked.

She heard Fine turn. 'No, we'd had a wet spell. In fact the day he died was a misery. The ground beneath him was still soaking when they lifted him, but the day he was found was nearly as warm as this and he'd have dried where the sun caught him.'

'Any reason?' Alec asked.

'Not really. I was wondering about tyre tracks. But why would he want to come out here on a wet day? Surely there'd be better places to meet someone even if he didn't want them coming to his home.'

'Rupert was always eccentric,' Alec reminded her, 'and I never knew him mind the rain, even the sort of rain you get round here.'

Fine laughed at that. 'You're on to something there,' he said. 'If the Inuit reckon they get fifty kinds of snow, I reckon we get twice that in species of rain. But no, we didn't find any significant tyre tracks. Tourists and hikers, and locals too, are in and out of that bit of car park all the time. It'd be very hard to tell if Rupert had driven here in his own car, especially as we can't find it.'

'Marcus said it was the Austin Healey...'

'And you'd think that would be easy to find, wouldn't you, but we've had no sightings. Not one. My guess is it's either parked up in a barn somewhere or it's under water.

Frankly, we don't have the resources to do more than put out an all points bulletin and hope someone spots it.'

'So,' Alec mused, 'the best guess is that he drove here, with someone else who then left him either before or after the heart attack and drove off in Rupert's car.'

'Makes the most sense. Of course, he could just as easily have driven out here to meet two somebodys and one drove his car off afterwards. Right, we're there. Mind yourself, Naomi, the ground is very uneven and there's tussocks and humps all over.'

She released Napoleon's harness and accepted the offer of Alec's arm for the walk across the rough terrain. Naomi tried to imagine what it would have been like in the pouring rain. She could feel the dampness of the soil that slipped beneath her feet, the scent of thyme and bog rosemary rising up on the heated air. Alec had not been wrong about the rain, she thought. She recalled wet holidays imprisoned in the caravan, or the chalet her parents rented when their finances improved. Playing cards and board games while horizontal storms raged at the windows and beat a tattoo on the roof so loud it drowned out the radio. She would not have chosen to come out here in that kind of rain.

'He was lying here,' Fine said.

Alec left Naomi's side and she heard him

moving slowly, casting about the scene.

'I don't suppose the area was searched?' he asked.

'Only in a general way. There wasn't a mark on him and a phone call to his doctor suggested what the PM might show up. We cordoned the area for a couple of days, but didn't have the manpower to keep anyone here. I'm sorry, Alec, but there seemed no need. To tell the truth I'm still not fully convinced any different.'

'Not even after those men came to Fallowfields?' Naomi realized she sounded indignant.

'Why wait this long?' Fine asked. 'The funeral notice in the local paper had contact details for both the undertaker and the solicitor. Marcus Prescott was very careful to make sure of that.'

'Oh, why particularly?'

'Because Mr Prescott was anxious that anyone who had dealings with Rupert could get hold of someone. Apparently he'd mentioned some purchases he wanted to make, but Mr Prescott didn't seem sure about the details. You'd have to ask him.'

'So, if Rupe owed someone money – legitimate money, that is – they could have spoken directly to the solicitor.'

'Or even gone to the shop,' Naomi pointed out.

'True.'

'Of course,' Fine went on, 'I'm personally not ruling out foul play in one sense, especially considering those two that came to Fallowfields.'

'In one sense?'

'I always did find it a bit strange that he had no pills with him. My father's got a dicky ticker and he won't go from one room to the next without his medication. Seems to me some bugger might have frightened the old man so much his heart gave out and then took his pills away.'

Eleven

Marcus had a tiny office at the rear of the shop. With Alec, Naomi and Napoleon all present, it was something of a crush. The young woman Alec had spoken to on the phone was minding the shop while they talked. Her name was Emma, Marcus told them, and she cleaned his flat for him and sometimes helped out in the shop.

'Sugar in your tea, my dear?'

'No, thank you. I'm not like Alec.'

'Sweet enough, I think.' Naomi could hear

the smile in his voice.

They had been discussing the research Rupert had carried out for his new book.

Marcus picked up the conversation where he had left it before preparing the tea. 'Rupert usually advertised in the *Axholme Herald*. Occasionally he would use other local papers, but the *Herald* has a good circulation and usually served his purpose. They were always helpful, I believe, and once or twice even ran a little piece. Did an interview, that sort of thing.'

'Did that happen this time?'

'Oh yes. Rupe's latest obsession was treasure, you know, and everyone likes stories of buried treasure. Rupe saw it all as a bit of fun. I don't think he took the stories seriously, but they did all tie in with his writing on other stuff: the supernatural ecology I told you about. Boggarts and bogles and fen lanterns are often associated with treasure.'

Naomi recalled Marcus telling them this. 'Did they print a picture of him?' Naomi asked.

'Why yes. Very flattering it was too. He looked very dapper.' He opened his desk drawer and rummaged around. 'There,' he said, 'I've kept the clipping.'

He slid it across the desk to Alec. 'You're right,' Alec said. 'Very dapper. He did love his clothes. His waistcoat collection must run to fifty or more.'

'What does it say?'

'Not a lot really,' Alec told her. '"Esteemed local author" – he would have loved that – "Rupert Friedman sets off on another journey into our shared past. This time the focus of Rupert's investigation will be buried treasure, and he would like to invite us all on his hunt." Essentially it then goes on to appeal for local stories and oral traditions. Then a PO Box address through which they can contact him.'

'Was that his usual way?' Naomi asked.

'One of them,' Marcus confirmed. 'When he first started out he was a bit worried about the cranks, but as time went on he worried less, I think.'

'There's also an email and what looks like a mobile phone number,' Alec said. 'Marcus, I didn't think Rupe had a mobile. If he had a mobile, why didn't he call for help?'

'Because...' Marcus opened the desk drawer again. 'It was here, plugged into the charger. He rarely carried it with him, Alec. What he did was programme it to divert to voicemail and any messages he had he'd respond to later.'

'But he never carried it with him?' Naomi would, she thought, have been lost without hers these days.

'He considered them rather vulgar objects,'

Marcus said. 'He absolutely hated it if he was having lunch with someone and their mobile went off. He always said that if he'd arranged to see someone then that time was theirs and theirs alone and the rest of the world could shove off for an hour. So, no, he could only see the use in having one because it meant he didn't have to use either his home number or that of the shop. He always said he could never understand why people wanted to be tethered to an electronic dog lead.'

'I can see his point,' Alec said. 'This is probably the longest time I've had uninterrupted by work in what ... since our holiday last year. Marcus, can I take the phone? I might be able to find out who called him.'

'You can do that? Well, my boy, take it and welcome. I can barely make a call on the damn things. Rupert took me to buy mine and we asked the lad in the shop for the most basic he had in stock. It still sings and dances and does things I don't even understand the names of. Did you find his laptop?'

'No, not yet.'

'And no idea what they might have been looking for at Fallowfields? That was a terrible business. You must have been terrified, my dear.'

'Nothing yet. We're going back later to see if we can work out what they were looking for or if anything was taken,' Naomi told him.

'But to be honest,' Alec continued, 'we aren't familiar enough with what was there to know for certain. We wondered if...'

'If I'd come and take a look? I'd be glad to. I'm just so relieved that someone is finally taking this seriously.'

'Marcus, did the police give you Rupert's effects? The clothes he was wearing on the day, that sort of thing?'

'Yes, yes, they did. Though, I'm sorry, Alec, I've not had the heart to look at anything. They're in the storeroom. I'll get them in a moment, but I managed also to find this. Some notes Rupert made on his interviewees. Look, you see the one's he's crossed out, they were dead ends, but he colour-coded the rest with highlighter pens. Red for a really good lead. Green for someone whose story he was definitely going to use and blue for something he thought worth following up but wasn't yet convinced was useful.'

'That's very precise,' Naomi commented.

'That's the way he was. I hadn't realized the list was still here. He sat at this desk just a day or two before he ... before he died and added his colours. That's why I recall so vividly. I assumed he'd taken it with him, but here it is, together with some of his notes. I found them in the back of the day book. Or rather, Emma did when she was writing up a sale yesterday.'

'Day book?'

'Oh, it's what we call the little ledger we use to record daily sales.'

'Can you show me?'

'Of course.' Marcus sounded surprised. He left the room and came back a few minutes later. He placed the book on the desk in front of Alec and something else on the floor near Naomi. She could hear the crinkle of heavy paper and knew that inside would be Rupert's effects from the day he died. Paper allowed the contents to breath, which was important if the fabric was damp or bloody.

'Look,' he said. 'We record what is sold and the details of the buyer so we can send out mailshots, that sort of thing. Most people are happy for us to do that but, of course, some don't want more junk mail. There's the sale price and any comments we might deem useful such as here, look, this buyer wanted us to keep an eye out for similar items. Later, Rupert would enter whatever was relevant on a spreadsheet. He could cross-reference with original cost and source and all manner of things.'

Marcus sighed. 'I don't frankly know how I will manage.' He laughed uncertainly. 'I don't suppose you've ever thought of a career change?'

'I don't think so,' Alec told him. 'But I know someone who could probably help out with this side of things. He's very young, but he's a real ... wiz ... with computers.'

'You're thinking Patrick,' Naomi said.

'I'm thinking Patrick. I'm also thinking we don't have the evidence to call in a forensic computer expert. Not unless we can really prove foul play.'

'You think we need it?'

'I think Rupert was more attached to the twenty-first century and its technology than I ever thought. We can't find his laptop, but it's entirely possible he might have recorded something on the shop computer.' He stood up. 'Marcus, I won't take up any more of your time now. We'll arrange to go out to Fallowfields tomorrow, if that's all right.'

'Tomorrow? Why not today? I could be free right now if you like.'

'No, I want to talk to DS Fine again and call Patrick and take a look at Rupert's mobile. Marcus, where would the day book normally be kept?'

'Oh, in the shop, beside the till.'

'And the notes Rupert left? They were where?'

'Inside ... I'm not sure where. Emma didn't say.'

'Don't worry, I'll ask her on the way out. Look, Marcus, I'm sorry for doubting you,'

Alec said. 'It's beginning to look as though Rupe's death is more complicated than we first thought. And I'm sorry Marcus, but there's also the possibility that Rupe was involved in something ... well something...'

'Something not quite kosher,' Marcus finished. 'Look, Alec, I'd rather know. Rupert was a good friend and I think we all need to know the truth, don't you?'

Twelve

'Are you serious about asking Patrick to help?' Naomi asked.

'I am, why?'

'Harry might not like it. Alec, we don't know what's going on here. I don't want Patrick involved in any more drama because of us.'

'If necessary I'll take the hard drive to him. I don't think Harry could object to that.'

Harry, Patrick's father, probably wouldn't, Naomi mused, but in the last couple of years Patrick had been forced to cope with a great many things, the latest being the suicide of a close friend. It was a lot for a seventeen year old to cope with, but then again Patrick had helped out before with computer-related stuff.

'I suppose his exams are over and his school has broken up now for the summer,' she conceded.

It had rained while they'd been chatting to Marcus and the air smelt fresh and clean. Napoleon snuffed and snorted at the freshly revealed smells and hoovered at the pavement as they wandered slowly back to the hotel.

'What do you make of the notes Rupe left in the book? It sounds odd.'

'It sounds as though he hid them in a hurry,' Alec said. 'Or is that allowing my imagination to run away with me?'

'Maybe.' Naomi frowned. 'Marcus was rather eager to get out to Fallowfields. Or is that just *me* being over imaginative too?'

She felt him shrug. 'I think we're both a little guilty of that,' he said. 'Blame Marcus, he got us seeing foul play where no one else did.'

'Marcus didn't imagine the men that came to the house.'

'No,' Alec agreed. 'I wish he had. I wish Rupert's death had been just due to a stupid mistake on his part but...'

'Looks less likely now.'

'Much less,' Alec agreed.

★ ★ ★

98

The phone rang and Marcus hesitated before picking up.

'They've left then,' the voice on the other end said.

'Clever of you to state the obvious.'

'Don't try to be smart Marcus, or pretend you're not shit-scared. What did they say?'

Marcus sat down heavily. 'Not a great deal,' he admitted. 'They've been out to where Rupert died and they still can't find his laptop.' He heard the man swear and then turn away from the phone to mutter something he could not quite catch.

'So, what are you going to do about it?' the man said.

Marcus sighed. 'I'm going out to Fallowfields with them tomorrow. They want me to help out, see what you and your friend might have taken, I mean,' he continued, a sudden surge of anger momentarily overcoming his fear. 'What were you thinking of, threatening Naomi like that? I could have gone there at any time, quite legitimately.'

'My friend is impatient,' he was told. 'Anyway, you had your chance and you didn't deliver. My friend also gets impatient with people who let him down.'

The phone went dead and Marcus replaced the receiver with a hand that shook so much the plastic rattled against the cradle. He sat very still, staring at it, afraid it might ring again. He should have told them he had given Alec the mobile phone and the notes, he thought, though he had no idea if either would be relevant anyway. 'Not good to hold things back though,' he said softly. 'Oh Rupert, what a mess you've got us into.'

Back in the hotel room Alec began to lay out the contents of the bags he had taken from the shop. The only area big enough was the floor and Napoleon wanted to help, sniffing loudly at each object as Alec extracted them.

'Sorry, old man, but you're going to have to shift,' Alec said, shoving the large black dog away. 'This is evidence, don't you know, not a feast for canine senses.' Napoleon snorted and flopped down in the patch of sun beneath the window.

'Maybe we should give him something to sniff and take him back to the crime scene,' Naomi suggested half seriously. She sipped at the tea Alec had ordered and felt for the plate of biscuits he had placed on the dressing table.

'If I thought it would do any good I'd do that,' Alec told her.

'So, what do we have?'

'Well, nothing unexpected. A pair of grey flannel trousers, shirt, shoes and socks. Contents of pockets are: keys, pocket change, a wallet...' He opened it. 'Money and cards still there,' he said in surprise.

''Course they are. Whoever he was with wanted an accidental death not a robbery.'

'True. I wasn't thinking. Small pocket diary.'

'Anything for the day he died?'

'No, nothing. Odd appointments for the week before. I'll have to cross-check with his notes and ask Marcus about them later. Flicking through there's nothing that seems to turn up regularly and most of the entries are just times and initials.'

'Maybe he kept more details elsewhere. Or maybe they were such regular meetings he didn't need more detail.'

'Um, well, we shall have to just slog through, see what we can find out.' He continued with his inventory. 'Folded pocket handkerchief, comb. That would seem to be it.'

'That's odd,' Naomi said.

'What is?'

'Well, the amount of stuff he had with him. There's too much there for trouser pockets and he wasn't wearing a jacket.'

'You may have a point,' Alec said. 'I'll talk to Fine, see where these things were actually found. Not that it tells us much, just adds a level of mystery.'

'What are the keys?'

'There are three, on a ring that has a fob

101

for a local garage. Probably where he had his car serviced.'

'Car keys?'

'No, but it makes me wonder if someone took his ignition key from the ring. There's one here that looks as though it might be to a desk drawer. It's like the one back at Fallowfields. No door keys, at least...' He got up and Naomi heard a metallic jangle as he took his own set of keys from his jacket pocket so that he could compare the two sets. 'I'm making a guess that one is the garage key, it looks as if it would fit a padlock, and I never did find that back at the house. Then there's an old fashioned looking thing that might open the side gate. Nothing for the house.'

'Why not just take the lot?'

'Well, as you pointed out, it wasn't meant to look like anything but a tragic death.'

'Then why take the car key?'

'Presumably so they could get away. They needed the car.'

'But wouldn't that kind of give the game away. I mean, wouldn't people then start to ask how he got out there?'

'Well, no one but Marcus *did*, did they? DS Fine was saying they all assumed he'd parked up at some other point and walked on to the Peatlands trail from there. They were surprised, he said, but everyone they interviewed attested that Rupert was his own man, did his own thing, and still loved to walk. Everyone knew about his research and the assumption was he was out there soaking up the atmosphere.'

'Soaking up the rain, more like.'

'He never minded the rain,' Alec said. 'But...' He fell silent and Naomi could sense the sudden tension even across the room.

'But what?'

'Fine said it rained all day, didn't he? All the more reason for wearing a coat.'

'Yes. He said the ground beneath Rupert's body was still wet. Alec, what is it?'

'They weren't looking so they didn't see,' Alec said. 'They didn't see.'

'See what?' Naomi demanded.

'His shoes, Naomi. There's no mud on his shoes. Just a smear on the heels where he'd been lying on the ground, but there's no splashed mud on his trousers. Nothing. Just a pattern consistent with him lying on his back on wet ground. I'll lay odds Rupert didn't walk there or even drive himself. He died elsewhere and his body was dumped up there on the moor.'

Derek sat in his car about a mile from the barn and called Sharon on his mobile. He needed to hear a friendly voice and Sam Kinnear certainly didn't qualify. Sam had been furious at Marcus's failure to turn up the goods and at the way the woman had behaved that morning. But then, Sam Kinnear was always furious.

But he had really disgusted Derek that morning, although it had been a little thing, he supposed. It was the jacket Kinnear had worn, the Harris tweed, lightweight for the summer, but still too hot in Derek's opinion. But it wasn't that, it was the fact that it had belonged to the old man.

Derek thought with a shudder of how the rapidly cooling body had felt as he'd crammed Rupert's possessions back into the pockets of his trousers. Some had fallen on the ground as he'd laid the body down, but he didn't have the nerve to pick them up for a second time and shove them back into the old man's pockets.

'I like his coat,' Kinnear had said and stripped it from his body, emptying his pockets out and dropping everything on to the floor.

The little plastic pot with his tablets inside had rolled under the car and Derek had only found them a few days later. Not knowing what else to do, he'd dropped them into the door pocket in his car and thrown them from an open window later in the day. Then he'd worried about kids picking them up.

Kinnear had worn the jacket that morning. Worn it like it was his own.

Sharon answered after what seemed like an age. 'Sorry, love, in the shower.'

Derek relaxed a little visualizing her, damp and soapy clean. 'Tell me more,' he said.

Thirteen

Alec was studying the post-mortem. 'No indication that his position was changed after death,' he said. 'Haemostasis is consistent with him having been laid on his back after death and not moved again.'

'Which means,' Naomi mused, 'that he was moved very soon after. Within an hour or so, before the blood settled to the lowest point. If he was then laid out in more or less the same way, there'd be no obvious inconsistency.'

'And the PM just showed massive heart failure,' Alec added. 'Nothing surprising or out of place.' He sighed and Naomi could hear the frustration in his voice as he continued. 'I don't blame the local police for *not* looking further than the obvious but...'

'Would you have handled it any differently?'

'I don't know. I really don't. No sign of foul

play and you can just bet that when someone first called Marcus and told him Rupe was dead he'd have assumed it was his heart and probably said so. I'd probably have handled it the same way, and that's supposing I'd been involved. Likely this didn't get further up the chain than uniform and the local beat bobby.'

'Did Fine give you a copy of the police report?'

'Yes, he did. The first officer on scene was DC Steven Hythe. He got the call and went straight to the place the body was found. The male hiker, John Armstrong, had stayed there. Said he was worried about kids coming by and maybe seeing something they shouldn't. Anyway, it seems Hythe is a local, born and bred, and his report comments that in his opinion all marks on the body were consistent with the work of the indigenous wildlife. PM confirms that: crows, badgers and probably a fox. Not pleasant but certainly not suspicious.'

'And the constable was able to come to that decision straight away; that the damage was all done by animals?'

'I guess you get used to knowing what to look for. Down our way you find a body that's been in the sea, you can make a fair guess which injuries were caused by rocks and breakwaters and which look suspicious.'

'I guess so.' She could hear how hard Alec was finding it to remain detached. After all this body had been a man he'd loved, admired. 'You want to talk to this Detective Hythe?'

'Gone on leave, apparently. I already asked Fine. He's somewhere in the Canaries.'

'There's always the phone.'

'And I would ask him what?'

'You don't have to snap.'

'Sorry.'

'It's OK. Look, let's have a recap. Rupert was found in a place where he most likely didn't die. He appears to have died of natural causes, which begs the question why move the body. And why there. It sounds like someone who knows the area.'

'True and Rupe could not have died far from that spot either. No sign of earlier haemostasis so the body must have been moved very soon after death and moved no great distance. Pity he was cremated. A second PM would very likely reveal any inconsistency.'

'Right. We can probably plot some kind of search parameters. The chances are too that he wasn't transported in his car. There'd be some fairly obvious indication if he'd been propped up in a car seat, no matter how quickly they'd moved him. No, he was laid out, maybe in a van or something similar, then carried and placed on his back.'

'Which suggests whoever did it had either thought through the process or they'd just got lucky.'

'My bet is on lucky. But why move the body?'

'Because they didn't want Rupert linked to the place he died.'

'Right. What else. The car. Still no sign. But the key is missing which suggests they either moved it or are anticipating the need.'

'OK, so, as Fine said, it's either under cover somewhere or it's under water. Both equally possible round here.'

'What else do we have?'

'Rupe's treasure hunt,' Alec said. 'No, I can't see this being about buried treasure, satisfying as that would be somehow.'

'Satisfying?'

'You'd have to have known Rupert, I think.'

'OK, but it's still worth following up on the list. He may have said something, hinted at something, even behaved oddly. And there's the boy that came to the antique shop. We've still not figured out if he belongs to "buried treasure" or "men at house".'

'True,' Alec agreed. 'And there's the mobile phone and the shop computer to examine and the laptop still to search for.'

'I don't think that's at Fallowfields. My

guess is it's wherever the car is. But you've not looked at the disks yet or the USB drive.'

'Damn, I forgot to ask Marcus about using his computer. Though there might be a shop in town where I can get an external disk drive for my laptop.'

'You'd rather not ask Marcus?'

Alec hesitated. 'I'd rather do what we can on our own,' he said.

'Any reason?'

'Just a feeling.'

'I'm not sure I like your feelings. They usually mean trouble.'

Alec pulled up a chair and sat down beside her at the dressing table. She heard him help himself to a biscuit. 'Tea's cold,' he complained. 'I have a feeling,' he continued, 'that this time it's big trouble.'

Following directions given at the hotel reception they found a tiny computer shop crammed in-between a bookstore and a small café. For such a miniscule emporium, it was surprisingly well stocked and Alec was able to purchase the drive and cable he required. The book shop proved irresistible and Naomi chatted to the owner while Alec browsed, eventually returning to the counter with a stack that fell over as he set them down.

'What on earth? Sounds like you've bought

109

half the shop.'

'No, just some local history guides, including two of Rupert's and a few old paperbacks.'

'Like?'

'Oh, the usual, you know.'

Naomi laughed. Alec loved forties and fifties pulp detective stories from both sides of the Atlantic. They were getting harder to find, though, and he had taken to haunting car boot sales and rummaging in the furthest corners of second-hand book shops to fulfil his desires.

'These sell very well,' the shop owner said. 'The local history guides, I mean. So sad that he isn't with us any longer.'

'It is,' Alec confirmed.

'We were so looking forward to his new one. Guy, in the computer shop next door, he reckoned we should stock up with metal detectors. Free book with your treasure detector, that kind of thing.'

Naomi laughed. 'So everyone knew about the new book then?'

'Oh yes. Rupert, Mr Friedman, was a regular in here. And then there was that piece in the local rag, with a picture and so on. I'd already got my order in. Like I said, he always sold well.'

She totalled Alec's purchases on a calculator. 'These old things don't scan, of course.

Rupert was a real character. Did you know him?'

'Yes,' Alec told her. 'He was my uncle.'

'Oh, I'm so sorry. He was a lovely man. I'm surprised you don't already have copies of his books, then?'

'I do,' Alec assured her. 'But at home, not here. I didn't think we'd be staying long enough for sightseeing.'

'It's nice round here,' the woman said. 'Plenty to see. You take care now.'

'Of course,' Naomi said as they stepped out on to the pavement and the shop door rattled shut behind them. 'Everyone knew Rupert and what he was up to.'

'Or thought they did.'

Slowly, they wandered back towards the hotel. It was market day and the square had been crowded and humming with noise when they'd walked through earlier. Traders were now packing up; Naomi listened to the crack of a trestle being broken down, voices shouting instructions, a van with a reversing alert beeping across to her right. The pungent smell of bruised cabbage and overripe fruit wrinkled her nose and suddenly...

'Alec!'

'What?'

She let go of his arm and spun around. 'I just heard him. The man from Fallowfields. I just heard him.'

'You certain?'

'Of course I am.' She turned her head trying to get her bearings, trying to catch the voice again.

She heard it shout, 'You bloody well watch where you're going!'

'Over there. He just shouted.'

'I heard. Stay here.'

'Alec!'

Damn. He was gone. Clutching Napoleon's harness Naomi cast about, trying to pinpoint the direction Alec had taken, straining to hear the man again. Someone pushed past her and then apologized.

'Mind your back love.' Someone else eased by, brushing Naomi with the boxes he was carrying.

Reaching behind her she groped for the wall, then fumbled in her bag for her folded cane. Not there. Furious with herself, she realized she had left it in the hotel room, assuming that, with both Napoleon and Alec present, it would be superfluous.

'Alec, where the hell are you?'

Naomi was both angry and afraid. She wanted him to get the man, but she didn't want to risk him being hurt and, though she was flattered – or knew she would be later – that he'd made no concession to her needs and just taken off after the man as he would have done had she been a sighted colleague, she was also furious with him for having left her.

Sounds surged and broke around her; noises seemed suddenly too loud as though the space in which she stood condensed and concentrated them. Naomi took a deep breath and pulled Napoleon closer to her side. He nuzzled at her hand.

She could do this, she told herself. Just stand still until Alec came back. She could do that. But what if he didn't come back? The insistent thought nagged at her. What if he got hurt? What if he actually caught the man? He'd have to hold on to him while he called for back-up and ... Impatient both with herself and with Alec, she reminded herself unnecessarily that they were not on their home turf and that back-up would neither be automatically on tap nor swift to arrive.

Where the hell had he got to? Naomi concentrated on the sounds flowing and flooding all around her, listening hard for signs that he would return. Voices shouted instructions as the remaining stallholders packed up for the day. A man laughed loudly; a burst of sound quite close by, which jolted her even though it was a pleasant sound. A woman spoke to a child and another chatted to a friend; the sort of 'I said she said' conversation to be heard the world over.

She did not hear the man again and she caught nothing that sounded remotely like Alec coming back.

Alec had lost sight of the man as he struggled to cross the market square. Crowds still jostled the remaining stalls, looking for late bargains, and the cries of the traders drowned out anything further that the man he pursued may have shouted.

Alec dodged around a half dismantled trestle. His feet skidded on something that smelt like rotten fruit. Cursing, he regained his footing and ran on, searching over the heads of the crowd for the individual he had glimpsed only for a second or two. A big man, heavy set and balding. Not young, but from what Alec had seen and Naomi's description of his actions at Fallowfields, very capable of taking care of himself.

Alec was not a fighter. He had boxed in his teens and kept himself fit, but he resorted to using his fists only in the direst emergency and it occurred to him, even as he skated and dashed across the crowded space, that he didn't have a clue what he'd do should he actually catch up with the man who'd tried to break down the front door at Fallowfields. Driven by anger at what might have happened to Naomi, he had thought no further than catching up with him.

And right now he could not even see him.

Alec had reached the opposite pavement. Able now to see ahead he scanned for a sight of his quarry. There! The dark jacket and bald head. The man was tall and Alec could see him now through a gap in the crowd. He pushed his way forward, making better speed now that he was moving largely with the flow and not across it.

He reached the corner of the market square in time to see the object of his pursuit disappear down a tiny side road. Glancing across he could see Naomi and the dog pressed nervously against the wall.

Bugger, Alec thought. He *really* hadn't thought this through but it was too late now. Briefly he thought about breaking off his search and returning to Naomi but he'd almost caught up with the man now. Instead, Alec groped in his pocket for his mobile and called DS Fine, grateful for the foresight and habit that had impelled him to place the officer's number on speed dial. His relief, when Fine picked up, was profound.

'Reg, it's Alec Friedman ... Out of breath? Yes I'm running. Naomi heard the man who came to Fallowfields ... Yes, she's sure.'

Fine listened as Alec filled him in and gave his location. Fine was several miles away but he promised to get someone to him.

'Alec, this man is dangerous. Stay back.

Observe but keep out of the bugger's way.'

'Do my best,' Alec said and rang off, hoping that Fine would be as good as his word. He could see the man he pursued very clearly now. The side street was relatively empty of people and the man walked at a deliberate but unhurried pace.

Alec slowed and caught his breath. Fine was right, he should stay back. Observe. There was little cover here and should his quarry choose to turn around he would see Alec. Would he know who I am? Alec asked himself. He had come to Fallowfields demanding to speak to the new owner, but did he actually know who Alec was or what he looked like? The suspicion Naomi had voiced that day, that the two who had broken in had waited until Alec was out of the way, resurfaced. Oh yes, Alec thought. You know who I am. He slowed down again, aware that he was getting too close now and there were far fewer people around.

Halfway down the street was the back entrance into a pub yard, and to Alec's surprise and discomfort, he saw the man open the gate and slip through.

What did that mean? Was he staying at the pub? Was this where Rupert had died? Impatiently, he reminded himself that he still had no direct connection between Rupert's death and the men who had threatened

Naomi, however strong his intuition was that they were involved.

Cautiously, he slowed even more and stood uncertainly a few yards from the gate.

He should wait. He should call Fine again. He glanced back towards the market place, hoping to see the cavalry racing to his assistance, but he saw only a middle-aged couple wandering hand in hand towards the square, and a woman with a pushchair, loaded down with shopping, walking slowly towards him.

He tried Fine's mobile again. Engaged. He was on his own.

Alec sighed and knew he was now committed. He took the final steps and, cautiously, standing well back, pushed the gate. It swung open easily on well-oiled hinges and Alec stepped inside.

Fourteen

Alec scuffled, trying to find some purchase for his feet but they seemed to be too far off the ground. The man had him by the throat and he was struggling just to breathe. Alec grasped the hand with both of his own but the fingers gripped like steel bands.

He felt his assailant's weight subtly shift and wondered what was coming next, but then the rabbit punch delivered to Alec's kidneys drove all coherent thought from his head. He was dropped, unceremoniously, to the floor, sprawling on the concrete as the waves of pain surged through his body. A kick to his exposed abdomen, followed by another to the ribs, and all the air in his body followed through in its abandonment of him.

Alec lay curled in an instinctive, protective ball, just trying to draw breath back into his lungs. A shadow fell across his face and the man knelt down beside him. Alec did not have the breath to move even if he could have thought of some way of escape.

He waited, his body too pained to tense for the anticipated attack, although some corner of his mind still screamed in panic.

His attacker did not touch him again.

'I know you, Friedman.' The voice was surprisingly soft. 'Take this as payment on account. Your uncle owed me, big time.'

'Who ... who the hell are you?' Alec gasped-ed.

The face split in a wide and mirthless grin. 'Someone you really don't want to know,' he said. 'Pity you don't get a say in the matter, isn't it?'

Then he was gone. Alec heard the gate swing closed behind him and struggled to move but his body had other ideas. Nothing seemed to work. His legs, his arms, even his head, were attached like dead, lead weights to a torso that throbbed and shrieked with pain. For a terrifying moment Alec was convinced that he was paralysed, that he would never be able to move again. Grimly, he forced his hands to close, his feet to push against the concrete, his head to lift. No one knew he was here. He tried to get his hand into a pocket to find his phone, not even sure which pocket it might be in, suspecting anyway that he might be lying on it. He managed to roll from his side on to his hands and knees though they shook and trembled as if he'd run a dozen marathons. He knew he couldn't even attempt to stand. His head swam and his breath burned as he drew air hungrily into lungs that felt blocked as though the man's hand still gripped his throat.

Somehow, he reached the gate, dragged it half open and began to crawl through. That was how they found him, barely conscious and half in, half out of the gate, one hand in his pocket clutching the now broken mobile phone.

Fifteen

There are times when you just *know* and Naomi knew when she first heard the sirens that they were coming for Alec. Desperately, Naomi tried to head towards the sound but she had no idea what obstacles were in her way. She stepped awkwardly off the pavement, urging Napoleon on when he tried to pull her back. A car horn sounded and a voice shouted. She jumped, stumbled on a raised paving stone, felt the dog press against her side and guide her towards the wall.

'Are you all right?' A woman's voice, local from the sound of the accent. 'Are you lost, dear?' The voice was earnest, even slightly patronising, but at that moment Naomi was prepared to forgive that.

'My friend...' she began, then realized how mad it would sound if she tried to explain. She didn't even know for sure what had been going on since Alec set off in pursuit of the man.

'I got separated from my friend,' she managed at last. 'My dog doesn't know the area.'

She shrugged helplessly. 'So yes, we are lost,' she admitted.

'Oh, my poor girl! Where did you lose your friend? Oh, I'm sorry dear, of course, you wouldn't know, would you. Now let me see. What best to do?'

Naomi, thankful of the help, but a little impatient with the procrastination, wondered how she could make use of her new-found friend. She didn't have DS Fine's number in her mobile otherwise calling him would have been her next move.

'Look, I feel really stupid getting lost like this. I really don't want to put you to any trouble. Is there a policeman about, or even a traffic warden? Someone like that?'

'Well...' Naomi could feel the woman turn and look around, then abruptly, she left her side.

'Seems to be the day for it,' Naomi muttered wondering if she was about to be deserted again. Then she heard her would-be rescuer calling out to someone from a few feet away.

'I say. Yes, I say. Yes, officer. I've found one,' she told Naomi triumphantly. 'He's coming over here now.'

Naomi sagged with relief as the officer arrived and took charge.

'The ambulance,' she demanded almost before he'd had the chance to ask her name.

'The ambulance, were you on scene when it arrived?'

'On scene? Miss, I was there but—'

'The man they picked up. It was a man, wasn't it? Was his name Alec? Alec Friedman.'

He was clearly taken aback. 'We're not certain yet,' he said slowly. 'Miss, what is going on here?'

'Alec was with me,' Naomi said. 'He went off, chasing after a man I...' It dawned on her that he had not been certain of the identification. 'How badly is he hurt? Tell me, please.'

She reached out and grasped the officer's sleeve. 'Can you take me to him, please? Or put me in a taxi and send me to the hospital. I don't care either way, but I've got to get to Alec.'

How many hours, Naomi wondered, had she spent hanging around in hospitals? In her days as a serving policewoman she had waited to interview suspects or victims. Since then, she'd waited with a friend for news of their son who had been stabbed. Now, she waited to hear about the man she loved and felt as guilty as sin because she had sent him out after his attacker.

It did no good to remind herself that Alec was his own person; that he had chosen to go racing off in pursuit of a very dangerous man; that Naomi hadn't really had a say in the matter. All she could think was that *she* had alerted him to the presence of the thug who'd beaten him, half strangled him, left him unconscious.

'Naomi?' DS Fine sat down beside her on another of the uncomfortable plastic chairs. 'Alec knows you're here. He was worried sick.'

'Any news?'

'The doctor will be with you shortly. He was on his way then got called to another patient. Alec will be fine. He's got a couple of cracked ribs and he's bruised to hell, but nothing permanent; nothing life-threatening. Doc reckons the bastard kicked him in the ribs and belly and they want to keep an eye on him overnight, watch for any internal bleeding, but, apart from being bloody uncomfortable, he's all right.'

'Can I see him?'

'That's what I've come to fetch you for. Dog will have to wait out here, I'm afraid.'

She nodded, allowed Fine to lead her out of the waiting room and down what felt like a very long corridor. The sounds and smells of the ward reached her as Fine opened swing doors and held them while she passed through. Dinner time evidently, from the aroma of food and clatter of plates. Voices, sounds of machinery, footsteps on a hard smooth surface.

'He's in a side ward,' Fine told her. He took her hands. 'We have to clean our paws with this gel stuff. Just rub it in and it evaporates.' He pumped the alcohol gel into her cupped hands and she rubbed it over her hands and between her fingers.

'But he'll be all right?'

'He'll be all right.' Fine opened the heavy door and then led her over to the bed.

'Alec?' She reached out. The relief when he took her hand was utter and profound. She couldn't help herself, she began to cry. Harsh, dry sobs that shook her entire body and brought relief only when the tears began to fall.

Fine had her driven back to the hotel. Alec had been ordered to sleep and Fine, having taken a statement and a description from him, had arranged to come back in the morning. Later there'd be time with a police artist or computer ID, but for tonight there was nothing more to do or that could be done.

Fine had alerted the reception desk to what had happened and Naomi was finally left alone in a very quiet, very empty feeling hotel room. She sat on the edge of the bed, listening to Napoleon snuffling his way into sleep, and the need to hear a friendly voice became an overwhelming urge. She fished her mobile out of her bag, set it on speaker and listened as she scrolled through the list until she reached 'Harry'.

He picked up on the fourth ring and she realized she had been holding her breath. She could not have borne it if the call had gone unanswered.

'Naomi? You sound upset? What's wrong?'

The story spilled out. The men who'd come to Fallowfields, Alec being attacked. The mystery surrounding Rupert's death.

Harry broke in before she was really through. 'Naomi, where are you staying?'

Momentarily confused, she told him.

'Then just hang on for a couple of hours and we'll be there.'

'No, Harry, I can't ask you to...' Though she realized as he said it that this was exactly what she'd hoped he'd do.

'Don't be silly. What else would we do? Now, have you had anything to eat?'

'No, I don't suppose I have.'

'Then get on to room service and order yourself a decent meal. Patrick and I will be with you as soon as we can.'

Naomi rang off. Relief flooded through her and her hands shook. She felt suddenly drained and also very hungry. She fumbled with the room phone, trying to remember what Alec had told her about getting through to reception and, more by luck than anything else, managed to order sandwiches and tea.

'A man just called,' the girl told her. 'Someone called Harry Jones? He said he was a friend and booked a room for himself and his son.'

Naomi replied to the question the girl had made of this statement. 'Thank you,' she said. 'He said he was coming. Yes, he's a good friend.'

A very good friend, she thought as she put the receiver back on to its cradle, feeling carefully to make sure it was properly seated.

She thought of all the four of them, Alec and Harry and Patrick and her and all they had been through in the past few years, and she was relieved beyond words that soon she would not be alone.

Sixteen

The side ward was rather crowded. Naomi hoped that the nursing staff would continue with their tolerant attitude; the number of visitors allowed technically being only two per bed and with Harry, Patrick and herself they were already one over.

DS Fine's arrival added to the visitor infringement.

Naomi introduced Patrick and Harry, and Fine greeted them with an air of formality that jarred Naomi's senses, setting them on edge.

'What's wrong?' she demanded.

'That obvious, am I?'

She shrugged. She heard Fine pull up a chair and deposit something papery on Alec's bed. 'Recognize anyone, Alec?'

She listened, straining for audible clues as Alec picked up the folder and flicked through the pages.

'Him,' he said at last.

'You're certain?'

'I'm certain. I got a decent look at him, both when I was following him across the square and when he had me by the throat.'

'Right,' Fine said.

'So? Tell,' Naomi prompted.

'We found a partial print on the doorframe at the house.'

'He put his hand on the door,' Naomi remembered.

'Most of the print was smudged, but there was a partial of the index finger. There aren't enough points of similarity for it to stand up in court but enough for us to run the print. We got a match. This man. Alec just picked him out from a sample of twenty mugshots,' Fine explained for Naomi's benefit.

She nodded. She knew how it was done. There had to be a selection available for the witness to choose from or the accusation could be levelled that the officer was leading the witness. Or, in this case, the victim. 'So, who is he?'

'His name,' Fine said slowly, 'is Samuel Kinnear and if ever a man needed to go on an anger management course, it's him.'

'Kinnear,' Alec mused. 'There's something familiar...'

'Armed robbery seems to have been his speciality, but he's implicated in everything from murder to extortion. Been inside for the last fifteen; released eighteen months ago. His parole officer lost track ten days in and no one's seen hide nor hair since.'

'So, what's he doing here?'

'That's what we'd all like to know,' Fine said, 'and by all I include our friends in the Met. Kinnear's a long way from his home patch.'

'London?' Alec was surprised.

'With a career that stretches back to the Kray twins,' Fine confirmed. 'Rumour, only on that score, but rumour says he worked as an enforcer and he wasn't too particular on whose behalf he enforced, provided they paid up.'

'He's not a young man,' Alec said thoughtfully. 'I'd say he had a good ten, fifteen years on me.'

'Date of birth 1952,' Fine said. 'So that makes him, what, fifty-four?'

'So...' Naomi calculated what she could recall about the gangland situation in Kray's London. 'He must have caught that particular wave at the tail end and only been young. Eighteen, twenty maybe.'

'That fits with the rumours,' Fine told her. 'He was an army brat, grew up following his old man across Europe and the Middle East. The family settled in the East End when his father left the forces. Samuel didn't seem to get along with his old man and left the family home soon after, but he was trouble even before that. Got himself thrown out of two different schools by the time he was fifteen, charged with assault when he was seventeen. Charges were dropped...' He paused. 'Alec, I don't have many details, I'm afraid, and I can't begin to guess what his connection with your uncle might have been, but—'

'But it sounds as though I got off lightly,' Alec finished. 'Reg, you're not going to like what I'm planning.'

Naomi could hear the frown in Fine's voice. 'Which is what?'

'I'm moving back to Fallowfields.'

'You're right. I don't like it. Alec, my advice would be for you and Naomi and your friends to get off home. End it here, let us sort this one out.'

'I can't do that,' Alec told him. 'Whatever this Kinnear is after might well be at Fallowfields or, at any rate, there might be something to explain what's going on. I agree, Naomi and the others should go—'

'Well, Naomi doesn't agree,' she told him tartly.

'Naomi, I don't have the resources to—'

'Um, I don't think you'll need them,' Harry informed him. 'Patrick and I will stay. We're with Alec on this.'

'Harry?'

'Alec, if the roles were reversed, you and Naomi would be there. You've both proved that time and again. I'll make arrangements for new doors, locks, maybe a panic button?'

'I can arrange a direct line, yes,' Fine conceded.

'That's good,' Harry said. 'And maybe you know a decent locksmith?'

Fine sighed. 'I can manage that as well. But Alec, Harry ... I don't think—'

'What you mean,' Patrick butted in, 'is that you don't see how my dad and Alec can protect a blind woman and a boy.'

'I wasn't going to put it quite like that.'

''S'all right,' Patrick told him. 'We've been in worse scrapes. And Dad's right. You don't walk out on a friend.'

Fine left soon after and so did Harry, Patrick staying on to help with the practicalities of Naomi getting back to the hotel. 'I've brought your laptop,' Naomi told Alec, 'and the disks and your other stuff. Keep you out of mischief.'

'Thanks, love. But I'll be out sometime today.'

'You won't,' she told him. 'I talked to the ward sister this morning. They want you here for another day.'

'Then I'll discharge myself.'

'No. No, you won't. I'm fine now. I have Harry and Patrick and you need more time to heal and rest. Alec, I'm not going to argue about this. Play with your files and get some

131

rest and I'll be back for proper visiting this afternoon.'

'I'm fine,' Alec protested.

'So fine you got out of bed this morning and fell flat on your face. That fine? The sister told on you.'

'Vertigo. That's all.'

'I'm not listening.'

She got up from her seat by his bed and kissed him. 'Nothing is ever simple, is it?'

'No,' Alec agreed regretfully. 'It never is.'

They left the ward and collected Napoleon from his place in the waiting room. Patrick took her arm and Naomi reflected that he seemed to have grown again. She thought of the shy fourteen year old he had been when she had first met him three years before, small for his age and terribly unsure of himself. Patrick had grown up.

She paused to switch her phone back on and found she had a missed call: Marcus.

Of course, she hadn't told him what had happened to Alec.

Once in the taxi she called him back. 'Are we still on for Fallowfields today?' he wanted to know.

She had, she realized, forgotten all about the promised search. To be reminded now was irrationally and absurdly irritating. 'No,' she told him. 'It won't be possible.' Quickly and perhaps more acerbically than his enquiry had warranted, she told him why.

Marcus was shocked; she could hear it in his voice, but to her astonishment, once he had expressed his horror and his sympathy he asked again, 'So we won't be going to Fallowfields today?'

'No, Marcus. Frankly, that's the last thing on my mind just now.'

'Naomi dear, if you gave me the key, I could make a start. One less job for you.'

Naomi frowned. 'For one thing, Marcus, it isn't just a question of the key. The police secured the doors and windows. It will take more than a key to get in. For another, I'd much rather wait until Alec is up and about before we do anything more.'

Silence on the other end of the phone. She could feel Marcus working out what to say next. Why so impatient? she wondered. What was so important?

'Marcus? Are you still there?'

'Of course. I'm sorry, of course. You must be too concerned about Alec to want the bother of such secondary things.'

'I'll call you, let you know.'

'Problems?' Patrick asked as she rang off.

'I don't know,' Naomi told him, wondering at the tension in Marcus's voice. It came to her again that there was something Marcus wasn't telling.

Seventeen

Two days later they returned en masse to Fallowfields. Harry had been as good as his word. New locks secured the front door and the French windows had been reinforced and re-glazed with a deadbolt added.

'Best we could do with that.' Harry was apologetic. 'Anything more would have meant replacing the entire lot and that's a major undertaking. Be a shame, anyway, to take the French windows away and replace them with one of those patio things.'

Naomi stepped out on to the terrace. She listened to the garden noises as she had on the day the men had broken in. Somehow, she had expected them to have changed, to have registered the aggression and violence that had interrupted the peace of this garden, but the birds sang and the trees whispered and the scent of roses continued to fragrance the air. She breathed deep and tried to relax.

She hadn't wanted to come back here and her palms felt clammy, sweat trickled down into the waistband of her linen trousers. Her head felt as though a band had been tightened around it; a band with extendable rods that reached down to press upon her shoulders.

'We started to clear up the mess,' Patrick said, 'but we only did enough to make the floor safe for Napoleon. There was broken glass and stuff.'

Napoleon, Naomi smiled, not her. Patrick had his priorities right.

'We thought we should leave it in case the stuff they chucked about might give us a clue to what they were looking for.'

'Did they go upstairs?' Marcus asked.

'Um, yes,' Harry said. 'Into the study.'

'The study?' Naomi was puzzled. 'No, the police arrived. They didn't have time to get into the study.'

'Which means they came back later.' Alec's tone was flat, emotionless. He had been discharged the evening before and spent a restless night at the hotel. He was still in pain from his ribs, Naomi knew, but more than that, he'd had time for the implications of the attack to sink in and to consider what might have happened to Naomi had the police not arrived.

He was not a happy man.

'Fine didn't know about the second breakin?'

'Fine secured the place as best he could but he didn't have the resources to keep anyone on watch. Harry, did you notice anything when you got here? Was the place secure?'

'The front was and the side gate. To be truthful I didn't take a good look round the back. DS Fine sorted out the locksmith and the carpenter and I just waited for them to arrive and left them to it. I mean, I did stay, but I sat in the car and listened to the radio, I'm afraid. I didn't like to, you know, go inside until I had you with me.'

Harry and his old fashioned sensibilities, Naomi thought.

'Well, we should let Reg Fine know,' Alec said. 'And meantime, everyone keep out of the study. I doubt there'll be prints but you never know.'

'But the study...' Marcus began. 'Surely that is likely to be ... Anyway, don't you already have prints from that terrible man?'

'We've identified one,' Alec said. 'We know there were two. Until the crime scene investigator's had another chance to look around we keep out.'

'What state's the kitchen in?' Naomi asked. 'If Patrick gives me a hand I'll make us all some coffee.'

Setting Napoleon free to wander in the garden, she and Patrick made their way back through the dining room and into the kitchen. She could hear Alec taking charge and allocating tasks. 'Watch the steps,' she told Patrick. 'The kitchen is on a slightly lower level.' She reflected that to an outsider it might sound odd to be giving that advice to a sighted person but she knew Patrick. He'd grown fast lately and seemed not to have worked out yet where his newly extended limbs ended. She closed the door behind them.

'Open the back door, will you, Patrick. Let some fresh air in. Then you can tell me what you don't like about our friend Marcus.'

Patrick laughed. She heard him release the bolts on the heavy door. 'They didn't come through here anyway,' he said.

'Good to know.' She found the kettle, filled it. 'We'll need extra mugs. Second cupboard on the right. No, your other right. So, Marcus?'

She heard him open the cupboard and remove china, placing it on the counter with extra care. 'I don't really know,' he said. 'It's just a feeling. I don't think he's actually lying and I really do think he's cut up about Rupert dying and he's genuinely afraid that it was foul play...'

'But?'

'But. Big but...' Patrick paused as though thinking it through.

He was good at reading people, Naomi thought. He wasn't so good at taking notice of what he read, but there was nothing wrong with his actual perception.

'I don't think he's saying everything. I think he knows ... knew about those men before Rupert died and that's really what made him suspicious, what scared him. And I think he's very scared, Naomi. I think he's trying very hard to hide it but I think if he thought he could get away with it he'd have skipped the country well before now.'

'Skipped the country?' She was amused by his choice of phrase. Then more seriously she asked, 'So, what's stopping him, I wonder?'

'You agree with me?' He sounded surprised.

'I think I do. Question is, why he is hiding what he knows.'

'He's more scared of them than he is of you.'

'Fair enough. Except he's never encountered Alec, not when he's got the bit between his teeth. Next question is, did he get Rupert involved with them or was Rupert the link?'

'Rupert,' Patrick said with confidence. 'Bet you a fiver.'

She nodded. Much as she disliked the thought of damaging Alec's rosy memories of his uncle, she felt pretty sure that Patrick was right.

The day passed slowly and inconclusively. It would have helped, Patrick observed, if they had any idea what they were looking for.

By the time Marcus had left it was after four. SOCO had aleady been and gone, their promptness leading Alec to comment that either Reg Fine had pulled a lot of strings or that this must be an amazingly crime-free county. Patrick and Naomi had joined the search, Patrick describing what he found, Naomi telling him whether to return it to where he'd found it, or to keep it to add to the growing stack of documents and note-books Alec had gathered on the kitchen table.

Harry and Naomi cooked while Alec and Patrick sorted through what they had re-covered.

'Diaries,' Patrick said. 'Going back to 1983. I don't think he threw anything away. A couple of old address books from the study and the one from by the telephone in the hall.'

'More notes for his book,' Alec went on. 'More names to add to the list of inter-viewees. Plans for volume two of his Fen Tigers thing. Bank statements, credit card statements, usual stuff. It's going to take weeks to check up on all this.'

'Then we prioritize,' Naomi said. 'Look for unusual transactions on the statements or anything regular that isn't a utility or named. Cash withdrawals, that sort of thing.'

'I'll do that,' Patrick volunteered.

'Feel free,' Alec told him. 'I'll go through the phone bills and cross-reference with the address books. Harry, could you give Patrick a hand after dinner? There's miles of the financial stuff and an accountant's eye...'

'Be glad to. You didn't say, was there anything of interest on the computer disks?'

'Of interest, yes. Relevance, not that I could see. The stick drive had a back-up of his book. It looked to be about ninety percent complete.'

'How can you tell?' Naomi wondered. 'Harry, how do you want your steak?' She prodded it with a finger. 'It feels medium rare.'

'How do you work that out without seeing it?' Harry wanted to know.

'Oh, there was this chef on television. He said if you pressed the base of your thumb then what that felt like, when you prodded steak, was medium. The ball of your thumb felt like well done.'

'Presumably if it felt like the knuckle it meant you'd burned it,' Alec mocked. 'You must have asbestos fingers. I'd like to find that laptop. And, as to how I know the book was ninety percent done, he's already got a table of contents. Twenty-five chapters and most already written.'

'Um. Right. There might not be anything more on the laptop, you know,' Naomi pointed out. 'He might just have used it for his writing.'

'Perhaps so, but it would be nice to be certain. So far there's nothing that remotely links Uncle Rupert to Samuel Kinnear, or anyone else of his ilk.'

He paused. 'I have a very vague memory that Rupe lived in London for a short time but...'

'Your dad would remember?'

'Probably. Naomi, I'm going to have to leave for a couple of days. Will you be all right?'

'Leave? For where?'

'London. Follow up on some of the information Fine gave me.'

'You're not fit enough for that. Can't you call?'

'No, I can't do this over the phone. I'll be OK. Harry and Patrick are here or I'd insist you went home.'

'Like to see you try.'

'Who are you looking for?' Patrick wanted to know.

'I have a few contacts there but I also want

to go to Colindale.'

'Colindale?'

'Newspaper archive. Sometimes it helps to look beyond the official records. Fine's given me some directions to look and a couple of names.'

'It all sounds a bit vague,' Naomi objected, not happy about Alec going anywhere, especially while he was still so obviously in pain. She couldn't see him wince when he stretched or pulled the damaged ribs, but she had slept in the same bed last night. Or rather, lain awake while he tried to find a position in which he could comfortably sleep.

'It's all vague,' Alec confirmed irritably, but nothing they could say could dissuade him from leaving the next morning.

Later, Patrick and Naomi wandered into the garden and through the gate in the back wall that led to what Alec had called the meadow.

'What's it like?' she asked.

'Um, I don't know. Rough grass, little trees and a hedge with bigger trees growing in it.' He turned, scanning the boundary. 'It's big,' he said. 'Big for a garden, looks more like a field.'

'Any way anyone could get through the hedge?'

He left her side, Napoleon bounding after

him. Naomi stood, listening to his commentary. Patrick was very good at remembering to tell her what was going on.

'The hedge is taller than me,' he said. 'It's mixed, which means it's old. There's thorn and elderberry and what I think might be wild roses. There's rose hips. Nettles like you wouldn't believe and a couple of ash trees.'

'So, quite a barrier.'

'Yes, that is. Ah, maybe not.'

'Oh, what do you see?'

'Hang on a minute, I'm trying to find a way past the blasted nettles.'

'Be careful.'

'OK. There's ... well, it's not exactly a gap. There's a fence just here. A bit rotten looking but low and climbable.'

'Look as if anyone's climbed it lately?'

'Hard to say. No obvious scuff marks or mud on the rails, but, Naomi, it's pretty low. Easy.'

'What can you see over the fence?'

'I'm getting to that. It's a field with cows. No, bullocks, not cows. After that there's a farm. House, barn, couple of other buildings. Hedge all round the field, but I can see a gate across the other side and a car's just gone by so that must be the road. It sort of loops round. But if someone did come across here they'd have to come all the way across the field and then over the wall.'

'No, the gate wasn't locked, remember. Just latched. I'll get Harry to put a bolt on it, I think.'

She sighed, glad she'd not known before about the unlocked gate. Relieved in the same breath that the men who'd come to the house probably didn't know about it either or they'd probably have come through that way. Patrick had been certain that there was no sign of anyone entering the garden that way, he'd had to clear long grass from the foot of the gate before they had been able to pass through.

Patrick was back with her now. 'It's getting dark, isn't it?' Naomi asked.

'You can tell that?'

'Not exactly. I've just noticed that the air round here feels damp in the early evening once it starts to get dark. I remember it used to get that way when I stayed on the coast. Where's Napoleon?'

Patrick called to him. 'He's over there. Your left. He seems to be rolling in something.'

'Oh great. That'll mean a bath.'

They wandered over to where the black dog wriggled happily. The damp grass released the heat of the day, fragrant beneath their feet and Naomi caught the warm scent of wild thyme and chamomile beneath her feet. It reminded her of the day they had gone to the Peatlands.

'Looks like he's been digging,' Patrick commented.

'Digging? Sure it's not moles?' Napoleon, in her experience, was not a digger. He caught frisbees and rolled in unspeakable things and occasionally poked his nose into something that made him sneeze, but he didn't normally dig.

'Not moles,' Patrick said. 'There *are* mole-hills, but not just here and they don't look like this. No, someone's been digging. With a spade, that kind of digging. Shift over, Dog.' Unceremoniously, he moved Napoleon out of the way. 'The earth's soft and still loose, so not long ago, I'd say. I can get my fingers right down. Call Napoleon will you, Naomi, he's trying to help.'

She called the now disappointed black dog back to her side. 'Any idea how deep it might be?'

'Hard to say. Deeper than I can easily scoop out anyway. We should get some lights out here and a spade. You OK here for a minute while I run back to the house?'

Naomi thought about it. Was she fine about that? 'Sure,' she told him, still not totally convinced. She heard his feet on grass then on brick as he went back through the gate and on to the garden path. Then she listened to the silence. There was a soft wind breathing through the trees but little in the way of birdsong, only a lone blackbird defining his territory before he retired for the night, and then the faint lowing of cows in the neighbouring field. Funny, she'd only ever thought of cows mooing, not the male animal. Cars. Two or three of them passing on the narrow road. Two or three together almost amounted to gridlock round here, Naomi thought.

Then the less defined sounds, rustles in the hedgerow, and the faint whirring and clicking as something insect-like but mysterious to her ears buzzed close by.

As always when she focussed on what she could hear, her sense of smell seemed to increase. Overlaying the scent of thyme and chamomile, crushed now beneath her feet and releasing its almost apple fragrance, was the damp air that she had mentioned to Patrick. It carried its own earthy smells, faint must and moist soil, newly turned now by Patrick's digging. Drawn by the scent, she moved cautiously forward, Napoleon at her side. She knelt down where she guessed Patrick might have done, reached out, felt grass and a stray, sneaking bramble runner; drew her hand back from the pain of grasped thorns. She reached out again a little more towards her left. Her fingers sank this time into soft earth that had been churned by the boy's fingers, granular and friable beneath her fingers. A tremor of excitement ran though her belly, though she could not have explained exactly why. Maybe it was all that talk of buried treasure that chimed so readily with her childhood fantasies when she and her sister had dug up half the beach searching for pirate hoards.

She wormed her fingers deeper into the hole, then drew back, almost in alarm.

There was something there. There really was.

'Naomi?' she heard Alec calling to her. 'Where the devil are you?'

He couldn't see her? Of course, it must be fully dark by now and the overgrown garden was shadowed by the thick hedge. It was funny to think of him at such a disadvantage.

'Over here. Don't you have a torch?'

'Torch but no batteries. Patrick's gone upstairs to find his. Reckons he's got a little Maglite packed away somewhere.'

She heard him swear as he stumbled over something in the dark. 'Watch yourself, there are nettles that think they're Triffids and brambles sneaking about in the grass.'

'Thanks. I know that. Now.'

She stood up and a moment later he had his hand on her arm. 'I can see you now,' Alec said. 'Eyes getting used to the dark. Not often I'm in a place with so little light pollution. You can't even see the house from here.

You said you found something?'

'Yes.' She squatted down again, taking Alec's hand and drawing him down beside her. 'Here, dig your fingers down into the mud.'

'Do I have to?'

'Don't be a baby. Here, let me show you.' She found the place again, feeling for the scooped earth and then guided Alec's fingers into the hole she had made.

'You're right. Something hard, like the edge of a box. Hey, Patrick, bring that light over here.'

Naomi could hear Patrick running across the grass, Harry following behind.

'Shine it there. You've got something to dig with?'

'Didn't know where to find a spade or anything, but I've got a paint scraper from the kitchen drawer and a couple of large spoons.'

'That will do, it isn't very deep, whatever it is.'

'There's really something there? Here, Naomi, can you shine the torch while we dig?'

Before she could voice any objection she might have had, he had placed the torch in her hand and positioned her arm so that the light shone down upon their little excavation. Harry joined them, accepting his spoon. Alec had taken possession of the scraper.

'Er, you realize this is a silver spoon,' Harry stated.

'Well, I guess it'll wash. You take that side and Patrick, you start there. I'll go down where Naomi found whatever it was.'

She listened as they set about their task; the occasional scrape of metal on stone or a shuffle of feet and knees as someone changed position the only sounds that told her anything about their progress. Even Patrick had forgotten to commentate.

'Do you see anything?' she asked at last.

'I've got an edge,' Alec told her. 'Something plastic, wrapped in a supermarket bag and...'

'You know what it is, don't you?' Naomi could hear the excitement in Patrick's voice. 'It's Rupert's laptop. That's why no one could find it. He's buried it out here.'

Eighteen

It seemed such a bizarre thing to do; bury a laptop and, it turned out, it wasn't just a laptop Rupert had sunk into the ground.

They carried the bags back to the house and laid the contents out on black bin bags spread across the kitchen table.

'This has to be what they were looking for.' Patrick's excitement was obvious.

'We don't know that...' Harry, cautious as always.

'No, we don't but it's a definite possibility,' Naomi agreed with Patrick. 'But why bury it? That's the sort of action that indicates a real and immediate threat.'

'Marcus said Rupert was frightened.'

'Then ... I don't know ... why not remove the hard drive and mail it to a friend?' Naomi wondered

'Um, two possible reasons I can think of.' Harry was the surprise respondent this time. 'He'd have had to explain to the friend and that might have led to all sorts of questions Rupert didn't want to answer. And it's a laptop. It isn't like an ordinary PC. I've got a little caddy thing for mine so I can take the hard drive out any time I need to.'

He sounded quite proud of his grip on technology, Naomi thought.

'Which you've never used,' Patrick pointed out.

'Well, no, but I could, but my point is that to take the hard drive out of a laptop you have to dismantle the thing. I certainly wouldn't like to try.'

'Why not just wipe the drive?' Alec said.

'Because wiping it doesn't get rid of the

information. You can recover it with the right software,' Patrick pointed out.

'Specialist stuff,' Alec argued.

'Possible to get hold of though,' Patrick told him. 'There are sites that specialize in hacking software and there's usually re-covery stuff on them.'

'Patrick, I'm not sure I want to know and I definitely don't want to know how you know. Anyway, from what I've seen of Kinnear, that's way too subtle,' Alec argued again.

'I think we may be missing the point here,' Harry said. 'We don't actually know if there's anything *on* the laptop.'

'If there's nothing, why bury it?'

'Um, good point, I suppose. What about the other stuff?' They had not yet examined the other contents of the protective plastic bags.

'Time to take a look,' Alec agreed. 'Patrick, would you run upstairs and grab my laptop. I think the leads will fit this one. Harry, would you mind popping the kettle on. Now, what do we have here?'

Naomi heard the crinkle of plastic as Alec explored the contents of the bags.

'They're a bit damp,' he said. 'Rupe didn't wrap the books quite as well as the laptop, but I think they'll dry out OK.'

'Books?' Naomi asked.

'Yes. Three small hardback ... journals

from the look of it and ... Harry, this is more in your line, I think. It looks like a ledger of some kind.'

Patrick returned with Alec's laptop and Alec gave him the job of firing up the one they had found in the hole.

'Make sure everything is dry,' Harry warned. 'I don't want you starting a fire or anything.'

Naomi, impatient now, realized that she was the only one not doing anything. 'So? What do they say? Why did he hide all this stuff?'

'I think it's going to take more than a two-minute peek to answer that one,' Alec told her. 'OK, journals was probably too grand a name. He didn't keep a daily diary or anything. The first entry is from 2001, March 2nd. The next isn't until the following week. You know, I think I remember seeing a book like this in the study.'

'But these?'

'Naomi, hold on there. I don't know yet. The first entry is something about a trip to the theatre in Doncaster and in the second entry he's rather pleased with himself for picking up an arts and crafts coal scuttle for bugger all at a sale.' He flicked a few pages on. 'More sales, a walking holiday in Yorkshire, an argument with someone over the price of a piece of Meissen. He won, by the way. Naomi, if there's anything important here we're going to have to go through the lot.'

'What are the more recent entries?' Patrick asked.

'I was about to get to that. OK, last entry was made about ten days before he died. He and Marcus had lunch together and he says: "I told Marcus I would not be in for a few days. I need some time to think things through and get away from it all, though I know, if I'm honest with myself, there is no getting away. I could run away, of course, but that would be cowardly and it would leave those I care for in the firing line. I have no illusions. If they could not find me, they would take their spite out on someone other than me, and that I cannot, in all conscience, allow. So, I have done what I can, made my preparations and it is a comfort to know that all of my affairs are ordered, so far as they can be, and now I must allow events to run their course."'

They sat for a moment in silence, the finality of Rupert's words reaching them, casting a despairing miasma across their little company.

'He knew he was going to die,' Naomi said at last.

Nineteen

Alec left early the following morning. No one had slept for more than a few hours. Reading the journals and examining the laptop had taken the rest of the evening and run on into the early hours. It had been after two when Alec finally gave in and shooed everyone off to bed. He had been up again at six and gone just after seven.

Naomi, sitting in the kitchen and finishing the pot of tea, felt far from happy. She had been in two minds about insisting she go with Alec, but had finally decided that she would be more use at this end. She had woken with a plan of action in mind.

Patrick took her by surprise by padding into the kitchen only a half hour after Alec had gone. Harry wasn't far behind.

'I thought Patrick at least would have slept in,' she said.

'Brain was buzzing,' he told her. 'I thought I may as well buzz down here.'

'And I just can't sleep past seven on a weekday,' Harry added. 'I'm too much a creature of habit.'

'Is it OK with your work? I feel so bad about dragging you all the way up here.'

'Don't. I called them on Friday and told them I'd be gone a few days. I've holiday owing and extra hours built up on flexitime, so it's fine.'

'Thanks. So, what was the brain buzzing about?' she asked Patrick.

'Oh, just the stuff he wrote. I was trying to put it together. I can't get why he hid the earlier journals. I mean, the last one talks about Kinnear and all that stuff...'

'Except it says very little in real terms.'

'True, but reading between the lines, he felt threatened and it was something from way back that he was scared about. Something Kinnear knew about him.'

'It certainly sounded like blackmail,' Naomi agreed. 'But how did Kinnear find out whatever it was? Harry, did the ledger tell you anything?'

Harry filled the kettle and set it to boil before responding. 'It's hard to say. The ledger seemed incomplete. There were references to sales and purchases not actually entered into the ledger, as though he cross-referenced the figures elsewhere. What I suspect is that Rupert was keeping a second set of accounts and that the ledger was part of that. I'd need a lot more information and

I've still not collated all we have here, but I suspect that Rupert was not as honest and straightforward as either Marcus or Alec gave him credit for. Some of the entries concern antiques, so far as I can tell. It's possible that he was either trading for himself behind Marcus's back or he was lying about the price received for certain items.'

'You didn't mention this last night.'

'No. I wanted to be sure. Alec was very fond of this man. I've no wish to sully a reputation unnecessarily or spoil a memory.'

'No, perhaps you're right. We'll have to face up to it sooner or later though. There's the possibility that this house and Alec's inheritance are tied up with this. A serving officer; dodgy inheritance...'

'I can imagine the consequences,' Harry said. 'Some of the more interesting entries referenced the stock market.'

'Oh?'

'Um, do you think Alec would mind if I took another look at Rupert's study? Only if I've read this right there should be records of his portfolio somewhere. Of course, it might be with his solicitor but...'

'No, I wouldn't have thought so. The solicitor gave Alec a pack outlining his inheritance and all the tax side of it and so on. He's had a good look through and he never mentioned anything like that.'

'Right, well, we shall have to see what we can find out. I'd like to think I'd have a handle on this before Alec returns. It would be nice to tell him there's nothing to worry about in that direction, but at the very least it would be good to make him aware of exactly which laws his uncle Rupert had been breaking.'

Naomi nodded slowly. 'There's something else I want to do,' she said as Harry got up to make more tea. 'We've got a list of names and addresses for people Rupert contacted in his research. They may not be remotely relevant, but I'd like to check them out. I thought we could say we were trying to finish his book. A sort of posthumous tribute.'

'Sounds like a reasonable cover story,' Harry said.

'So, when do we start?' Patrick asked.

'Well, I thought this morning, unless Harry wants to get on with the financial stuff?'

'To be truthful I could do with some thinking time. I've stared at those figures so long I can still see them imprinted on my eyelids.'

'Good. So, you and Patrick take half the list and I'll contact Marcus, rope him in for the rest.'

'Marcus.' Patrick was disgusted.

'For what it's worth,' Naomi told him, 'I think you were right. Marcus is holding back. I'm hoping that he'll drop his guard a little if we seem to be involving him. Besides, we can't all turn up on people's doorstep. Two of us is OK, three plus dog is going to look intimidating and, anyway, if we split up we can cover more ground. Unfortunately, I do need a driver. Far as I see it, Marcus is it.'

Alec was exhausted long before he reached the capital. He stopped twice for coffee, lacing the strongest brew he could find with painkillers. He'd heard somewhere that it was OK to take ibuprofen with paracetamol and he hoped it was fact and not something he had made up. He alternated the painkillers every couple of hours, saving the ones the hospital had given to him for the bad night he knew was going to come.

His whole body ached; the bruising on his abdomen was still black, showing a purple hue only at the very edges. The seat belt dug deep just where it hurt the most and his ribs protested vigorously every time he changed gear. He knew he wasn't really fit enough to drive and began to wonder just what the hell he was doing rushing headlong towards a place he hated for its dust and noise and crowds to meet a man who could probably tell him little more face to face than he could have over the phone.

He was aware that he hadn't been entirely straight with Naomi. She was right and he didn't actually have to drive all the way down here and he wondered what it was that had compelled him.

He told himself that he couldn't access the newspaper archive by phone, that he really needed to get to the actual records. He told himself that people opened up in face to face meetings in a way they did not on the end of a telephone. He told himself that he could call on his parents on his way back to Epworth and challenge them about the row with Rupert and whether it had any bearing on present events.

He repeated these reasons and excuses over and over again until he almost believed them. After all, they were all valid and true. But they weren't the genuine motivation, Alec thought as he guided the car through the midday traffic on the Edgware Road. The genuine motivation was that he needed to get away, to escape from the concern and questions and the challenge of it all. He thought he'd known Rupe; his cherished memories of his uncle had misled him into thinking that they were the sum total of the man Rupert had been.

He had never looked further.

Alec had grown up but his thoughts, attitudes, knowledge of his uncle Rupe hadn't grown up with him, they had remained frozen in that infant time and Alec wished fervently that he had been able to maintain that cherished fiction, not been faced with a Rupert who attracted violence. A Rupert who brought danger to those he cared for and who acknowledged that fact in writing in the little leather-bound book.

Naomi had been right, he thought. Rupert had known that he was going to die. The question was, had he gone to meet Kinnear to give him what he wanted – that seemed unlikely seeing as how Kinnear was still looking for it – or did he go to challenge Kinnear in some way, to tell him he wasn't about to give in?

DI Phil Malcolm had arranged to meet on neutral ground. Alec was not, in this case, an investigating officer; there was no profes-sional courtesy to be extended. This was a casual meeting slotted in and arranged as a favour to DS Fine. Alec was grateful for the time.

'You not drinking?' Malcolm asked as Alec came back to their table with a pint and an orange juice.

'Can't. On painkillers,' Alec told him. It seemed the easiest thing to say. Explaining that he'd most likely fall asleep mid-after-noon if he drank at lunchtime seemed in-appropriate and unmanly and there was something about Malcolm – the near shaven

head, perhaps, or the sc⌐
invited Alec to make

'I heard about y⌐
near,' Malcolm

'So I've been tⳳ

He waited until N
his glass, wondered ⳳ
with another before theⳳ
placed the half empty vⳳ
table, centring it with elaboⳳ
cardboard mat.

'Right bastard, Kinnear,' hⳳ
sounded satisfied, Alec thought. 'Yⳳ
faxes?'

'Thanks, yes. Reg Fine gave me copies.
list of known associates you sent. Who woⳳ
your money be on?'

Malcolm wiped the condensation from his
glass with a fat, paw-like hand. Boxer's
hands, Alec thought. Heavyweight.

'If you're asking, then I'd take a guess at
two,' Malcolm said. 'The first choice would
be Colin Berridge, fat man, same age as Kinnear, inside with him for armed robbery on
this last stretch, but the association goes
back to when Kinnear first fetched up here
in the seventies. The two of them worked the
door at some less than salubrious establish-
ments, did the odd job on the side. It went to
Kinnear's head. Listen to him and you'd get
the impression he was enforcer for half the

161

the East End. True, he had
t he was strictly a back-up man.
ded the likes of Kinnear you were
deep shit. My dad had a friend
ex-SAS, reckoned you took the bag
head and pointed him in the right
on, then got out of his way. Only
e was getting the bag back on again.
ear was the same way. Once you'd
ched him on he was like that bunny in
battery advert. Kept on going when
hers had packed up and gone home.'

Alec thought of his own acquaintances in
Special Forces and could not in any way
equate them with this description. True, he
would rather they were on his side if it came
to a fight, but they didn't go looking for one.
Kinnear, Alec thought, would not have got
past the psych test, but he got the point
Malcolm was making and he could not
argue with the reality of his own experiences
with the man.

He dragged his attention back to the matter in hand. 'And your other choice?'

Malcolm drained the rest of his pint and
stood up. Alec gathered that his time was
almost up. 'Derek Reid,' he said. 'Youngish
bloke, early thirties. Bright enough by all
accounts, but could never hold a job down. I
checked up; got out of jail about a month
after Kinnear. They were cell mates for three

months. If I was a betting man I'd be putting my money on him.'

'What was he in for?'

'Like I said, he's a bright boy, just lacking in common sense. Where Kinnear is strictly strong arm, Reid uses what he's got up here.' Malcolm tapped the side of his head. 'Got some scam going selling shares in phoney companies. He'd use legit businesses as a front, usually without the owner's knowledge or consent.'

'How did that work then?'

Malcolm shrugged. 'I'll see what I can get for you, send it via our friend Fine.'

'Thanks.'

Malcolm nodded and left. Alec watched him go as he played with his untouched orange juice.

So, a possible link? The use of legitimate businesses? Alec discounted the first of Malcolm's options. Naomi had been sure that the second man had been of lighter build and, with his record, he felt that Reid was a better fit. So had they tried to involve Rupert? Had they in fact drawn him in to whatever game they were playing?

Alec downed his juice, using it to swill down more painkillers. The combination left a powdery, metallic taste in his throat. He was tempted to call it a day and go back home to Naomi. He felt in his pocket and found his phone, intending to call, but then he put it away again. Hearing her voice would be enough to break down what little resolve he still had, and now he was here there were things to do and he may as well get on and do them.

Retrieving his car from behind a small factory unit backing on to the canal, and thanking the gods of motorists that he had not been clamped, he headed for Colindale.

Twenty

Marcus had responded to Naomi's call with such alacrity that by ten o'clock she was in his car and heading for the first person on their list. He was curious about Alec's absence.

'He never intended to stay more than a few days,' Naomi reminded Marcus, somewhat reluctant to go into details about Alec's trip, particularly as she didn't have a great deal of information herself anyway. 'There were things he had to go back and see to.'

Marcus seemed satisfied for the present. He was, Naomi thought, in good spirits to-day, describing the scenery and speculating as to the relevance of those of Rupert's sources they were going to meet.

'It may have nothing at all to do with this man Kinnear,' Naomi reminded him, 'and remember, Marcus, our story is that we're simply interested in completing Rupert's book for him.'

'Oh yes, quite so. We're here, our first address.'

Mr and Mrs Parry, Naomi recalled from Rupert's notes, had contacted the oral history unit at the local university regarding a story told by Mrs Parry's uncle. Marcus had phoned ahead that morning and recited their cover story and found himself with an immediate invitation.

Naomi's heart sank. She could guess what this was going to be like. They might be getting in easily enough but she wondered how long it would take to escape.

Two hours fifteen minutes was the answer. By this time Naomi knew every last detail of Uncle Wally's treasure rumoured to be buried in the orchard ... or was it the garden...?

Tea, cake, enthusiastic fussing of Napoleon once permission had been granted. Condolences that that nice man had died so suddenly, listened for hours, he did.

Naomi, rather sourly, wondered if he'd had any choice.

'Well, that went well,' Marcus said after they'd finally made their escape.

'You think?'

'Well, yes.' He sounded rather put out.

Naomi sighed. 'Sorry Marcus, I'm thinking like a police officer. Ask the relevant questions and get out on to the next job. I suppose there was never really time for the social niceties.' Thank goodness, she added silently.

'No, I suppose not.' He brightened. 'It's the vicar next. The Reverend Fullerton. Rupert consulted him regarding the parish records.'

Naomi groaned inwardly. She had hoped to have worked through their half of the list by mid-afternoon. At this rate, two hours plus per consultation, it was going to take till the end of the month.

Harry and Patrick were not having much luck. The first three names on their list had been out. The second two insisted that they had told Marcus all they could and they really couldn't be bothered with it all again. Didn't he take notes? The next was an elderly lady called Mrs Thorpe who lived alone if you didn't count the African Grey parrot that harassed them from the second she allowed them to come through the front door.

'Of course I remember Mr Friedman,' she said. 'What a charming man. I had such a nice time with him. He was with me all afternoon one week and then he came back the next. It was so nice; one gets so few visitors, you know.' She turned to look quizzically at Patrick, taking in the baggy jeans, long-sleeved surfing shirt and the canvas record bag he carried slung across his body. She drew in a deep and rather hesitant breath, as though teenage boys were a novelty she wasn't sure she included in the category of pleasant visitors. She turned back to his father. 'He took a lot of notes and even recorded some things I told him. It was very exciting. Please sit down. Do.'

They sat. The parrot came and stood on the back of Patrick's chair. It squawked loudly and dived a beak into his unruly hair.

'Ow!' Patrick protested.

Mrs Thorpe turned and frowned in his direction. She said nothing to the parrot. 'Now how can I help you?'

Harry launched into the story of how they wanted to finish Rupert's book. Mrs Thorpe nodded and smiled. 'Oh, how nice.'

The parrot started on Patrick's ears. He hunched his shoulders and sat forward trying to get out of its way.

Mrs Thorpe looked back in his direction. 'Oh, don't slouch, dear. I do think it's such a shame the way young people slouch, don't you?'

'Um...' said Harry glancing absently at his son.

'It's the parrot,' Patrick protested.

Mrs Thorpe clucked her tongue at him. 'No, dear,' she said firmly. 'My parrot doesn't slouch.' She focussed attention back on Harry. 'Now,' she said, 'where were we?'

The parrot switched tack and hopped down on to the arm of Patrick's chair, out of sight, he noticed, of its owner. Once there it began a concerted attack on his sleeve, pulling viciously at the cuff and sinking its beak through the fabric and right into Patrick's arm.

Patrick yelped again.

'My dear –' Mrs Thorpe stared sternly at him through rimless spectacles – 'perhaps if you are determined to torment my parrot, you ought to go and wait outside.'

Stung by injustice but more than happy to escape, Patrick fled. Outside he examined his torn sleeve and the damaged flesh beneath. The beak had drawn blood. He wondered what nasty diseases you could catch from parrots and whether you might risk going to jail should you wring its neck.

There was a patch of overgrown grass in front of the cottage and Patrick sat down with his back to the wall wishing he'd brought his MP3 player. Instead, from the inside pocket of his record bag he pulled the journal that he had been reading after breakfast and hidden in there when Marcus arrived to collect Naomi.

He wasn't sure why he should be worried about Marcus seeing it – he had made a point of taking the other two journals to his room that morning. Patrick wasn't sure, either, what made him so uncomfortable around Rupert's business partner but something did.

The journal he had brought with him was the second one of the three. The first they had skimmed briefly and the third read in more detail the night before. It contained several references that appeared to relate to Sam Kinnear, but never by name and nothing that added to the sense of what they already knew. The second journal had remained untouched until today.

Patrick had begun to plough through the accounts of cinema visits and restaurants and buying trips detailed in the journal. He flicked back to the page he had been reading that morning. On the face of it there was no reason for Rupert to have concealed these books or, for that matter, the laptop. An initial examination of the laptop last night had revealed the text of his new book, some saved emails and a favourites list of internet sites that were fascinating for the variety of sites he visited if nothing else. Patrick was eager to get back to the task.

He found his place in the journal. Rupert was writing about a film he'd watched the night before and the entry was for June 14th 2004. Rupert liked his films and he wrote short reviews on them. Many of the films seemed to be art house or foreign language films that Patrick had either never heard of or never seen, but this one was familiar: *Memento*, a film Patrick had watched with Naomi. It had been a fascinating story, Patrick remembered. A man who had lost his memory was slowly trying to piece together who he was. The film ended with a twist and Patrick had liked that. He'd enjoyed *The Usual Suspects* for the same reason, that twist in the tail, and had watched it several times over, noting the clues by which he could have worked it out.

Patrick looked up from the book and stared out across the road and into the field beyond. There was something ... something now nagging at the back of his mind. Something about the way the journals were written? He wasn't sure. Patrick shook his head. It would all come together, he thought. It usually did but he had learnt that such flashes of intuition could not be forced.

He read on. Another lunch – Rupert had

been fond of his food – another meeting with a client who collected arts and crafts silver and gave details of what he might be looking for. Patrick read on. His heart skipped. Another reference to a man who was probably Kinnear:

I thought I'd got rid of the man. Last year, when he first barged his way back into my life and started making his demands, I thought I'd done enough to satisfy the man's greed. I should have known better than that. Men like him are never satisfied. I should have cut my losses then, before he got out, cut my losses, signed the business over to Marcus, and gone away. You may not be able to run away from your past, but at least you can try to run from the people you left behind there.

Patrick mulled this over. So, in June 2004 Kinnear was still in prison but already causing problems for Rupert. So, why did Marcus think that the problems were more recent, starting only a month or so before Rupert's death. What had changed?

He read on and found a partial answer a couple of pages on:

It turns out he still doesn't know where I am, a fact for which I give profound thanks.

Elaine returned his letters 'address un-known' and I'm glad she didn't have to lie about that. Glad I never let her know where I was. Elaine was always loyal. God alone knows why. I never did anything to deserve it. But the question remains, how long can I breathe easy in the knowledge that he has lost me. A man like Sam does not give up and go away, especially when he feels he has been wronged and, I suppose, from his per-spective, he has.

But I would do the same all over again. Indeed I would, though to be truthful, the actions I took have done little to assuage the guilt I still feel.

Who on earth was Elaine? Patrick wondered. He flicked through the remaining pages but there was no reference to her again that he could see from that brief check. And what did Rupert feel guilty about? How might he feel he had done wrong by Kinnear?

Patrick frowned, staring down at the neatly written text. Irritated now, he flicked through the book again, then froze. What? Patrick laid the book open flat on the ground and lifted the pages, then flicked slowly. No, not quite right, with those flick books they had to be flicked properly. Fast.

Not quite sure what he'd seen, he did it again. Earlier, when he'd tried to figure out what bothered him about the book, he had intuited that it was something about the way that the words were written – and he'd been right. Every now and again Rupert had changed the spacing of his entries, added a random letter to a line, or what had at first looked like a date, to the foot of a page. Patrick had taken little notice of the odd misspelling or random annotations; his own writing was full of them. He now realized he had assumed Rupert was having the odd dyslexic moment.

Now, he concluded that wasn't so. Rupert's handwriting was elegant and controlled, the letters evenly shaped and fluently written. These tiny additions and alterations, some even in a contrasting pen, some scribbled as though he had just remembered something, *meant* something. They were deliberate.

Patrick flicked the pages again, trying to see some pattern there. Fumbling in his bag he found a stub of a pencil and a moleskin notebook – Patrick was rarely without the means to draw. He stopped at the first page on which he'd noticed something odd and noted down the capital letter A, where it should have been in the lower case. A little later he wrote down the number 2. Patrick held his breath. His heart raced with excitement. He had no real idea what he had found, but he knew that he was on to something here.

Behind him the cottage door opened. Harry emerged, followed by Mrs Thorpe, the parrot on her shoulder. Nervously, Patrick eyed the parrot, expecting to be assaulted yet again. He was thankful to get back into the car.

'That woman could talk for England,' Harry said as they drove away. 'What was it with you and the parrot?'

Patrick showed his torn sleeve and mauled arm.

'Oh my goodness. You'd better get something on that.'

'Did she say anything useful?'

Harry shook his head. 'Not a thing. You know, I think this is just one big wild goose chase. I'm for going back to Fallowfields and getting on with the ledger.'

'Suits me,' Patrick told him. He wondered if he should tell his dad what he'd found out. He hesitated in case Harry should be annoyed that he'd removed the book from the house. After all, it now did seem to be evidence. Besides, he really wanted to find out more first and deliver the revelation in full.

He took the contact list from the glove compartment and skimmed through the addresses, ticking with a pen those they had visited. 'We may as well make one more call though,' he said.

'Oh? Why?'

'The farm that backs on to Fallowfields. It's on the list.'

'Right.' Harry sounded reluctant. He'd had enough. 'All right then,' he agreed. 'We may as well, but I think that'll be the last. I hope Naomi and Marcus have had more luck than we have, that's all.'

The farmyard was reached by a narrow track similar to that at Fallowfields but muddier and even more rutted. The yard itself seemed equally uncared for.

Patrick got out of the car and glanced around, curious as to the arrangement of buildings he had glimpsed through the gap in the hedge. The farmhouse was pebble-dashed and had at some point been white-washed. Now, the covering was crumbling away from the brick and the finish was grimed and weathered. Small windows gave no real glimpse of the inside.

At right angles stood out-buildings including a brick barn. Patrick guessed they were older than the house and looked better built. Bright sunlight angled down, casting deep shadows at the barn's end, almost but not quite concealing the outline of some kind of farm machinery, something with wheels and spikes that Patrick could not begin to identify. Patrick glanced back at the barn admiring its high roof and the way it seemed to sit so solidly in the landscape. By contrast the house seemed to squat uncertainly, as if unconfident of its own foundations. Given the choice, he thought, he'd have chosen to live in the barn.

Harry rapped on the door. Flakes of dark-blue paint dropped on to the flagstones. Absently, Patrick poked at them with the toe of his trainer.

No reply.

'Looks like we're out of luck again,' Harry said. He prepared to knock once more as Patrick wandered back into the yard. A boy, about his own age, stared at him from the shadow cast by the barn. Patrick glanced back at his father and then made his way over to the boy.

'Hi.'

The teenager nodded and glanced warily at Harry, then past him to where there was a narrow path leading to the rear of the house.

He's scared, Patrick thought. He remembered being told about the teenager who'd come to the shop to find Rupert. Marcus's description of him could well fit this boy, though, to be fair, he supposed it could fit maybe half the teenage boys Patrick knew.

'You live here?' Patrick asked. He was aware of his father behind him, watching. Patrick willed him to stay back. He took a few steps closer to the barn.

''Course I live here.' He glanced nervously back towards the house. 'You better go,' he said.

'We came about Rupert Friedman's book,' Harry said. 'We're planning to finish it and—'

'And what's that got to do with us?'

Patrick jumped, so did Harry, only the boy seemed unsurprised. His eyes flicked past Harry and settled for a moment on the man who had emerged from behind the farmhouse, then he moved back further into the shadow of the barn.

'Your name was on a list of people who'd helped him with information,' Harry said to the man. 'We're trying to put his notes in order, so we're checking back through his list of contacts.'

The man snorted. 'Waste of bloody time,' he observed. 'Lucky for 'im he didn't have to work for a living.'

Patrick, now watching Harry, saw his father's shoulders stiffen. Harry could not abide bad manners or slights on people not in a position to defend themselves.

'I'm sure Mr Friedman worked very hard at his business,' he said.

'And he should have learned to *mind* his own, too.'

'I'm not sure what you mean,' Harry challenged. 'Look, I'm quite happy not to talk to you, but your name was on the list of contacts Rupert Friedman made. Perhaps someone else here was Mr Friedman's informant?'

'There is no one else here,' the man growled. 'Now get yourself off my property.'

Patrick held his breath, sure that his father was about to challenge the assertion and draw attention to the boy. He didn't think that would be beneficial. Impulsively, he felt in his bag and managed to tear a scrap of paper from his notebook and grab the stub of the pencil. Hoping the older man would not see, he scribbled his mobile number on the piece of paper.

The boy was watching him and took a further step back as though afraid Patrick might approach. Patrick glanced back to where the two men faced off then looked at the boy. He crushed the paper in his hand and dropped it into a clump of grass in front of the barn. The boy was watching him. His gaze fell for a mere instant, then met Patrick's once more.

'We're going,' Harry was saying. 'And don't worry, we won't be back.'

Stiff backed he marched to the car. Patrick followed swiftly. A glance in the wing mirror confirmed that the boy had slipped away, though the man still watched as if making certain they did not change their minds.

Patrick wondered if the boy would retrieve the number. He worried that the man had seen.

'Thoroughly unpleasant fellow.'

Harry at his most pompous made Patrick smile. 'Back to Fallowfields?' he asked hopefully.

'Oh yes. I'm starved.'

'Did you know,' Patrick asked, 'that round here starved used to mean freezing cold as well as hungry?'

'No, I didn't know that.'

'It was in Rupert's notes.'

'Oh. Well, I'm certainly not cold. It's a wonder you can stand it in those long sleeves.'

Patrick grinned. He hardly ever uncovered his arms. 'I just feel naked with that much flesh exposed,' he said, 'and, yes, I know that's weird.'

'Happy with weird,' Harry told him contentedly. 'Perfectly happy with your kind of weird.'

Naomi and Marcus arrived back at Fallowfields just after Patrick and Harry.

Harry had checked the locks and taken a tour round the gardens. 'No sign of anyone having been here,' he reported.

'No, well I expect they've reached the conclusion there's nothing here,' Marcus complained. 'At least, not that I'm aware of?'

The question was clearly a leading one and for a moment Patrick thought his dad would give a direct answer. Marcus had still not been told about the laptop or the journals. As Harry opened his mouth to respond, Patrick caught his father's eye and shook his head.

'No, nothing useful as yet,' Harry said. 'And I can't say that this morning was very helpful either. Nothing but a wild parrot chase, if you ask me. Come along through, Marcus, we'll all have a bite to eat before you have to rush off back to the shop.'

'Oh, yes.' Marcus sounded faintly put out by the inference that he would have to leave. 'Well, thank you. Lunch would be welcome, yes.'

Harry led the way into the kitchen, Marcus following on behind. Naomi turned her head. 'Patrick?'

'Here.'

'Ah. Parrot chase?'

'A woman called Mrs Thorpe and an African Grey,' Patrick said. 'I'll tell you all about it in a minute.'

'In a minute? Oh,' she said catching on. 'Something neutral to talk about over lunch, you mean.'

'I might do.'

Naomi laughed softly. 'Which means we've

180

got something better to discuss when Marcus is safely gone?'

Patrick squeezed her hand in acknowledgement as Marcus himself stuck his head around the door, clearly wondering what was delaying them.

'Patrick was just telling me about his encounter with a mad woman and a parrot,' Naomi said.

'Mad parrot, too,' Patrick added.

Marcus rolled his eyes. 'Oh, that's going to be nothing,' he said. 'Not compared to our vicar and uncle what's-his-name's treasure buried in the orchard. You know,' he continued, ushering them into the kitchen, 'I really don't understand how Rupert could do all this, listening for hours to other people's boring little stories, I mean.'

'Well,' Naomi said, 'I think he must have had a certain gift, Marcus. Patrick's been reading some of his work to me and I'd guess that by the time the stories made their way into one of his books they'd have been Rupertized.'

'Rupertized!' Marcus laughed. 'I like that,' he said softly and for the first time Patrick looked at him and saw something to like. 'Yes,' Marcus went on, 'I think perhaps Rupe Rupertized his entire little world, and I have to say I think it was a better place for it.'

Twenty-One

Alec had spent a frustrating and tiring afternoon at Colindale, searching the archives for mentions of Kinnear. He had come away with a more complete picture of the man. Kinnear's career had escalated through the early eighties and he had graduated from committing general mayhem at the behest of others to setting up on his own account.

He'd committed three armed robberies in quick succession, all banks, always with a three-man team. It had been impatience that proved his downfall. Three robberies in as many weeks, and in the same geographical area, had put the banks on high alert. One of Kinnear's associates had been killed and another wounded during the arrest. Unfortunately, there had been another death. A member of the security team, a man called Fred Ritchie. The news reports called him a 'have a go hero', but it was far from clear exactly what he had done. Neither could Alec find a definitive account of who had shot him. Some reports blamed Kinnear, others his dead associate, and yet another suggested he had been caught in the crossfire between the police and the bank robbers.

But it was a name mentioned only once that caught Alec's eye and which chilled him to the core. A witness to the shooting: a man called Rupert Friedman.

Alec had searched for records of the court case, but found little of use. The trial was only reported in any depth because of the death of Fred Ritchie and by then, almost two years on in the spring of 1982, interest had waned. War in the Falklands knocked just about everything else out of the news and the trial of a couple of armed robbers counted for very little.

Alec returned to his car and made a few calls. The reports had also mentioned the name of the officer in charge of the investigation. It took a little while, and a few favours, but within the hour he had discovered that the officer in charge of the investigation, DS Billy Pierce, had long since retired.

'I can't give out his number,' Alec's informant, a friend of one of Alec's acquaintances in the Met, told him, 'but I can call Bill, see if he's willing to talk to you.'

Alec agreed and sat back to wait, fighting weariness and wishing he could just drive to a nice hotel and go to sleep.

It was Billy Pierce who called him back. He sounded curious and, Alec thought, slightly wary, but by six fifteen he was knocking on the ex-policeman's door.

Billy Pierce was greying and almost bald, but he moved with the agility and deliberateness of a much younger man. Alec was tall, but Pierce had a couple of inches on him. His handshake was firm and the grey eyes direct and curious as he invited Alec to come inside.

'The wife's away visiting the grandkids,' he said. 'Come on through. I'll make us some tea.' He led Alec into the kitchen at the rear of the house and indicated he should sit down at the table. 'We can go into the living room, if you'd rather.'

'No, I'm fine.' Alec lowered himself cautiously into the wooden chair. His body ached as though he'd run a marathon in lead boots and been trampled by the rest of the field.

'You digging into a cold case, or something?' Pierce asked him.

'Not exactly, no. It's a bit more complicated than that.'

Pierce set the kettle to boil and turned to face Alec, arms crossed, leaning comfortably against the counter. 'Our mutual friend mentioned Sam Kinnear, but didn't say a lot more. Bit of a blast from the past, I have to say. I'd rather thought he'd be dead by now.'

'No, definitely alive and still kicking,' Alec said with feeling. 'Any particular reason you

184

might think otherwise?'

Pierce shrugged. 'I suppose because most of them are from back then,' he said. 'There was Kinnear and the bloke that got shot on his last bank job ... Timkins, I believe the name was. Ivor Holmes who worked door with him, stabbed from what I remember. Clifton something or other, found in the Thames ... I could go on. But you'll get my point.'

'And was Kinnear implicated in any of those deaths?' Alec asked.

Bill Pierce snorted. 'Maybe, maybe not. All unsolved so far as I know. Kinnear was just a member of the same pack.'

'I'm interested,' Alec said, 'in the job you mentioned. The last bank job he did.'

'Any particular reason?'

Alec hesitated, wondering how much he should reveal. He decided on nothing, yet. 'There was a witness. A man called Rupert Friedman. Do you remember him?'

Billy Pierce fixed him with that direct grey gaze. 'You want to tell me why?'

'I'd rather hear what you have to say first. If you don't mind.'

Pierce chuckled. 'All right,' he said. 'I'll tell you what I thought. I thought Friedman was in it up to his neck. It always rankled that I could do nothing to prove it.'

★ ★ ★

185

Back at Fallowfields the afternoon had been spent examining the journals and the ledgers and the buried laptop.

Lunch had been a surprisingly happy affair, laughing at the eccentricities of the people they had met that morning and particularly Patrick's account of the parrot. By tacit agreement neither he nor Harry had spoken of the man and boy at the neighbouring farm and they had all been careful to avoid telling Marcus what they had discovered buried in the meadow. It was as though Patrick's wariness of Marcus was catching and, though Patrick himself could not fully explain from where that uncertainty came, the others were willing to go along with it, for the time being at least.

Harry had been genuinely impressed by what his son had noted in the journals and Patrick returned to the task after lunch, Naomi at his side as he read extracts and together they tried to work out what the numbers and letters meant. It took time, Patrick thought, to get your eye in, but once you had there were more anomalies than he had first thought. The trouble was, none of them seemed connected and on a few occasions he was uncertain as to whether what he saw was a genuine correction, an unintentional mistake or something Rupert had wished to highlight.

By half past five when they adjourned to the dining room and joined Harry with his ledgers, Patrick had collected twenty-three definite anomalies and a half dozen he wasn't certain of.

'Telephone numbers with initials?' Naomi suggested.

'Bank details, maybe,' Harry speculated.

'Have to be more than one then. And what about the letters?'

'Offshore accounts often have much longer codes,' Harry said thoughtfully. 'Sometimes they are alphanumeric, too.'

'Oh, and how would you know that?' Patrick teased.

'Because, my dear boy, I am an accountant. And though that may be a boring job, it's one I'm very good at.'

'Which means,' Naomi guessed, 'that you've made some headway with the ledger?'

'Well, yes and no. The no part is that I don't have all the pieces. There are elements missing which I'd hoped would be in the laptop, and indeed there are a few spreadsheets. What I've not managed to do as yet is tie everything together. Not everything.'

'So, what do you have?'

Harry pulled the ledger towards him and shuffled through the bank statements they had found in Rupert's office. 'Look, these are Rupert's normal statements. He was very organized, did everything he could by direct debit, so every month there'd be utility bills, insurance, that sort of thing going out, plus a weekly amount I'm guessing was for household expenses that he drew in cash and which tallies up with the little account book I found in the kitchen drawer. So much spent in this shop or that supermarket, or whatever. Then there's an amount I can't find a correlation for in any of the normal accounts but which he drew on the fourth of every month and had done for the past six or seven years. Maybe longer but that's as far back as I've been able to check.'

'It's not a big amount,' Patrick commented. 'Fifty-five pounds.'

'No, it's not and it's very precise, which is interesting. It started, incidentally, as forty-five pounds, then increased to fifty and in the past year to fifty-five.'

'That's inflation for you,' Naomi joked.

'Well, quite. I thought at first he might be putting it into a savings account, something like that. He has one with another bank, but that's dealt with by direct transfer every month and the account doesn't show any separate cash payments. But, and this is where it gets interesting, it *is* entered into the ledger he buried.'

'As what?'

'Well, just let me explain a bit about the

ledgers first. All right, you remember I was looking for a stock portfolio. I've searched his study and I'm pretty sure it isn't there, but he's been keeping account of the rise and fall of whatever stocks and shares he invested in in this ledger. Every now and again he records having moved money, sold shares, but I couldn't tell you what because they are referred to only by initials. See, here: shares in F.D., shares in G. Rupert obviously knew what they were and so didn't need to add the details. Neither, annoyingly, did he record who his broker was.'

'Patrick, do any of those initials appear in the journal?' Naomi asked.

Patrick checked. 'Well, there might be an F.D.,' he said. 'But there are numbers in between. Anyway, we don't know if this is the right journal. I've not had a chance to look at the others yet and the date on the ledger entry is for later than the journal. The journal is dated two years ago and the ledger entry is more recent.'

'So we need to look at the rest,' Harry said. 'Naomi, you're sure Alec didn't mention any investments of this kind in the packet the solicitor gave him.'

'No, but I'm sure he wouldn't mind you taking a look when he gets back. He took it with him.'

'Oh?' Patrick was curious.

'He said he was going to call on his parents on his way back. I think he wanted to talk all of this over with them.'

'Well, it will have to wait, then.' Harry tapped the ledger thoughtfully. 'There are large amounts of money mentioned here,' he added.

'How large?'

'Well, if I'm reading this right, upwards of a hundred thousand pounds.'

'Wow,' Patrick said. 'But you said it was linked to the fifty-five he drew every month. How?'

'Well, that's the funny thing,' Harry said. 'It's listed as a related expense and it's broken down into a series of very similar amounts for each month. Twenty-three pounds and four eighty, for example and, well, look for yourself. Anything left from that amount is actually deposited back into his account. Really quite bizarre.'

Patrick was staring at the ledger trying to make some sense out of the rows of figures and initial letters. Maths was not his strong suit, despite his father's skills. He noted the initial written beside the incidental amounts. 'E.,' he said. 'It's got E. written by the side of it.'

'Yes?' Harry questioned.

'Well, I was just wondering if that could be the mysterious Elaine.'

Alec waited for Billy Pierce to elucidate. He seemed, Alec thought, to be almost relieved to have said it out loud, but now was something of a loss to explain.

'What *is* your interest in Kinnear?' Pierce asked him. 'If something else has come to light I do feel that I've a right to know.'

'It isn't so much my interest in Kinnear,' Alec explained, 'as his interest in me. He seems to think I have something belonging to him. I have the bruises to prove how annoyed that makes him.'

Pierce's look was sharp. 'Be thankful it's only bruises. So, what does he think you have?'

'That's my problem. I don't know, but my uncle was Rupert Friedman.'

Billy Pierce nodded and turned his attention to the kettle. 'It was the name that made me agree to see you,' he said. 'I figured there wouldn't be too many Friedman's about. Not interested in Sam Kinnear, anyway. So, what *do* you know?'

Swiftly, Alec brought him up to speed and by the time Pierce had joined him at the table with mugs of tea, he knew just about as much as Alec which, he now reflected, wasn't a whole lot.

Pierce left him and rummaged in the kitchen drawer, pulling out a sheaf of takeaway menus. 'Got a preference?'

'Sorry?'

'I recommend the Chinese. They're about the quickest too. I don't bother to cook for myself, I'm afraid. Lousy at it. Miriam used to leave stuff for me when she went away, but I used to put it in the oven and forget to take it out. Now she just leaves these.' He grinned sheepishly. It transformed the rather dour face and lost him a good ten years in age.

'Chinese, then,' Alec said suddenly realizing how ravenous he was. 'I don't think I managed lunch and breakfast was caffeine based.'

Pierce smiled again. 'Good,' he said. 'You've no idea how I've missed the chance to talk shop. Retirement! Bloody overrated, that's for sure.'

After the food arrived, they settled themselves once again around the table. 'At first,' Pierce told Alec, 'your uncle seemed like a star witness. He was lucid and coherent, which is more than could be said for most of the poor buggers caught up in the shoot out. And that's what it was, I don't care what the official report says. Two men were killed and, frankly, it's a miracle not more were injured. Kinnear was just firing off shots in all directions. Didn't give a damn.'

'What was he armed with? The newspaper reports are a bit vague on that score.'

'Smith and Wesson revolver of all things. Turned out it belonged to his stepdad.'

'Stepdad?'

'His father went off when he was just a kid. She married this other fella when Sam was six or seven. He took his name. From all accounts he didn't make a bad fist of raising the boy, but it was a rootless sort of childhood.'

'I read he was an army kid.'

'Well, so are a lot of kids but they don't turn out like Kinnear. No, it wasn't the moving around, it was the fact Kinnear had such a short fuse no one could get close to him for long enough to build a relationship. Now, they'd no doubt have some fancy label for him. We just knew he was a little scrote. In trouble from the time he was old enough to spell the word.'

'And by the time of the robbery?'

'In so deep he'd need a JCB to dig himself out. Same with the others in his so-called gang. That's what didn't fit, you see. Between them they had the IQ of a chicken, and a very dumb chicken at that, yet they pulled off two very neat little jobs, made themselves a tidy little sum and if they'd waited a bit for the fuss to die down would probably have got clear away with the third.'

'So, you suspect Kinnear didn't do the planning.'

'It was speculated upon, yes.' He took a long draft of beer and then started on his chow mein.

Alec waited, thinking and chewing slowly. He had declined the beer knowing he had to drive and that even if he was still legal he'd be asleep at the wheel within a mile. He felt so bone weary and was having a hard time keeping his head clear enough to focus on what Pierce was saying.

'So, when did you start to suspect Rupert?' continued Alec.

'When it turned out he'd been at the scene of the second robbery.'

'Oh?'

'Took a bit of time to make the connection. He wasn't an official witness, just a name on a list of people questioned because he was in the vicinity. He claimed to have seen nothing and was sent on his way.'

'Miracle, in that case, you even had his name.'

'It was that. Seems they'd put a young recruit on the job who wanted to prove how thorough he was. Rupert Friedman never denied he was there and he had a valid sort of excuse if you believe someone would drive ten miles out of their way because they liked a particular supermarket.'

'Actually,' Alec mused, 'that sounds exactly the kind of thing he would do.'

Pierce laughed. 'Well, you would know.'

'So, how involved did you suspect he was?'

Pierce paused, then rammed his fork back into the foil tray and twisted it round, collecting noodles and chicken. 'Well, it occurred to me he might have been the one that planned it,' Pierce said.

By the time Alec left an hour later his brain was buzzing, as Patrick would have described it. He couldn't see Rupert as any kind of criminal mastermind but, much as he disliked the idea, he could not get away from the thought that this too might be something Rupert could do as an exercise, just because he could. Rupert, Alec thought, had never been much on consequences. Even as a child Alec had recognized that his uncle was an impulsive being. One who gave about as much thought to the responsibilities and outcomes of his actions as did Alec himself.

So, if he had been involved, why hadn't Kinnear fingered him? Unless, Kinnear thought Rupert was looking after their money.

That made a kind of sense.

But, Alec had questioned, why wait until now to try and reclaim what was his? The only logical explanation Alec could come up with was that Kinnear hadn't known where Rupert was.

Alec had analyzed that, put the speculation to Pierce. Friedman was, as he had commented, an uncommon name.

'Your uncle was due to appear as a witness,' Pierce said. 'But he did a runner long before the trial and we didn't have the resources to track him down. Not that anyone was that bothered; there was no doubt Kinnear had been there, was there?'

'Which does not explain why Kinnear didn't look for him.'

Pierce smiled and Alec realized he'd been keeping something back. 'Kinnear thought he was someone else.'

Pierce laughed. 'That's what we figured,' he said. 'Kinnear kept going on about the getaway driver and how he'd been the one that planned it. That fitted with what we knew about Kinnear, but we knew from the start the driver hadn't given him a proper name.'

'Oh? How was that then?'

Sitting in his car and signalling to come off the slip road and back on to the motorway, Alec chuckled at the remembered reply. It was *so* Rupert. Then he sobered, realizing this really clinched Rupert's involvement.

'Because your uncle Rupert had called himself Sam Spade,' Billy Pierce had said.

Twenty-Two

It was very late by the time he reached his parents' home and he worried that they may not be up. He still had a key to their house, tucked away in the inside pocket of his jacket, though that might not count for much if his father had bolted the door.

Only an upstairs light shone out when he pulled across the end of the drive rather than turning into it, remembering almost too late that his father rarely put the car into the garage. He leaned back in his seat and rubbed his eyes, more tired than he could ever remember being.

Feeling in his pocket for the door key he found the locket he had discovered in Rupert's box. It had come to him later that same night why it seemed so familiar, though he had omitted to tell Naomi. Forgotten? No, not forgotten, he'd not wanted to tell her yet, not until he had an explanation. It was one of the things he needed to ask his parents.

His mother opened the door as he inserted the key.

'Alec! Naomi phoned a couple of hours ago, she thought you might be here. Your mobile was off,' she chided. 'And you might have let me know sooner, then I could have made up a bed. I've done it now anyway.'

She stood on tiptoe to kiss his cheek and Alec hugged her back. 'I switched the phone off because the battery was low,' he explained. 'But I should have called. Watch the ribs they're still sore.'

'Yes, Naomi told us about that too. Alec, what were you thinking and why didn't one of you let us know? We'd have been right there, you know that.'

'I know, I know. Is Dad still up?'

'Well yes, we thought we'd give you another half hour and then go to bed. Come on in, come in, do.' Smiling, she reached out to take his hand. 'What on earth do you have there?'

He opened his hand and held out the locket. He noticed the sudden rigidity that took hold of her shoulders. 'Alec...' Then she managed a laugh. 'Good Lord, where on earth did you find that?' She had blanched, her cheeks suddenly pale in the harsh light of the hallway. Then she flushed as though embarrassed or ashamed. Alec did not know what to say.

His father appeared in the living-room doorway. He was dressed in striped pyjamas and a deep red dressing gown. His comfortable dressing gown, Alec remembered. His favourite. Baggy and soft from years of washing and wearing and faded in patches as though the dye had been unevenly exposed to the light.

Alec folded his hand around the gold locket suddenly unwilling to ask questions that his mother's response had already told him the answers to. But it was too late by then. His father, always sharp, always observant, had seen.

'Rupert had it then,' he said.

'In a box upstairs. I didn't remember at first where I'd seen it, then I knew. The photograph of us all at Fallowfields.' He looked at his father's face and invented a lie, one they could all retreat behind. 'I guess Rupert must have found it and forgotten to give it back. Then when you all stopped talking...'

'That must have been it,' his mother said eagerly, then she met her husband's eyes and shook her head. 'Enough,' she said. 'Does it really matter now?'

Alec sat in his parents' front living room, and listened. They were together on the sofa, sitting close, holding hands as though for moral support and suddenly, to Alec's eyes, they looked very vulnerable and oddly young.

'You were seven years old when we lost Sara,' his mother said.

'Sara?'

'She would have been your sister.'

'My sister? I don't even remember you being pregnant.'

'You remember I was ill. In hospital for a time. You went to stay with Aunt Liz and...'

'And missed most of it,' his father continued. 'Sara was stillborn. It was all a mess. Your mother was depressed after and I hid in my work. We just didn't seem to know how to get along for a while.'

'That summer we went to stay with Rupert,' Audrey, Alec's mother picked up the story. 'Rupert was kind and ... well, it never actually came to anything, but it was a close call. I didn't tell your father for quite a while. In fact, it was Rupert that let it slip.'

'I wasn't quite that naïve,' Arthur went on. 'I suspected something. And to tell the truth I deserved for something to happen. I'd just shut myself off there and didn't know how to cope. It wasn't just Sara. My father died around the same time, if you remember, and then Mum was so ill and it all got a bit too much, I suppose.'

'So...' Alec wasn't quite sure how to put this. 'What did happen? Between you and Rupert, I mean.'

Audrey shrugged sadly. 'Not a lot, if you

must know. We kissed then we both came to our senses, or so I thought.'

'But we still visited Rupert, right up to when I was about ten. I remember the visits.'

She nodded. 'We did and if I'd had my way one stupid moment would have been one forgotten stupid moment. I was very careful not to be alone with Rupert and to make clear to him that it was your father I wanted to be with.'

'But Rupert wouldn't let it go. It seems he was quite besotted and one day he said so. I didn't know how to react and we had a big row. I told your mother to pack and we left. I never did get around to making up with him, at first because I felt betrayed and hurt and angry, and then later ... well, later was just too late. You know how these things can be? If it had been anyone else but my brother...'

Alec closed his eyes and sighed deeply. He wanted to sleep, but he had other questions to ask, more relevant to now, and he knew he would want to leave early the next day and be back at Fallowfields as soon as possible.

'I'm sorry, Alec,' his mother said.

'Why did you never tell me about Sara?'

They looked at one another, his father and mother, these adults who had raised him and done a good job by and large. These adults who had twenty-plus years experience ahead of his and he saw only bewilderment on their faces.

'I don't know,' Audrey said at last. 'At first I couldn't bear to talk about it and then it just never seemed to be the right time.'

Alec laid the locket down on the arm of the chair. His father's chair. He let it lie, not quite knowing what to do with it. It was odd, he thought, just how quickly the story had emerged once given the right prompt. They must have talked about it in the days since Rupert's death. Or if not talked, both thought so much about those days that their memories transmitted one to the other by some strange osmosis so that when the right stimulus was applied they both knew exactly what to say and that this was the time to say it.

'I've got to ask you something else,' he said. 'There's no easy way to put this, but did you ever suspect Rupert might have been involved in anything illegal?'

That shared look again. Alec's heart sank. Something else they did not talk about?

'He got fired from a job,' Alec's father said. 'He was working for a firm of accountants. They also handled stock portfolios, insurance, all of that. I suppose they were more financial advisors than accountants in the true sense ... Anyway, he was sacked, accused of what we'd now call insider trading.

Seems a client had given him some kind of tip-off about a takeover. I don't recall the details. I'm not sure I ever knew them, but Rupert was able to sell rather quickly on behalf of several of the firm's clients and, it seems, saved them quite a packet.'

'So they sacked him?'

'It came out that he might have had inside knowledge and they could not be seen to encourage a technical fraud. Rupert was quite bitter about it, I believe.'

'When was this?'

His parents thought about it. 'You must have been about nine or ten. It was around the time we had our falling out, so 1980 or maybe 1981. I can't be sure. Sorry Alec, it was quite some time ago.'

'So, he was already living at Fallowfields.'

'Had been for some years by then. He bought it for little or nothing. I remember telling him, "Rupert, I wouldn't touch that place with a bargepole." It needed a new roof and electrics and all the plumbing ripping out. There was no heating. It was just a shell of a place but he said he liked the location. His job wasn't local to Fallowfields, though. He was just travelling up for weekends then and still had his flat in London. So far as I know he still did. Wasn't it mentioned in the will?'

Alec frowned. 'I'm not sure. The solicitor

gave me a whole folder full of stuff. It's in the car, I wanted to go through it with you but I don't recall anything about a flat in London.'

It all fitted time-wise though, didn't it, Alec thought. The robberies, the annoyance at being sacked. Was that what had triggered Rupert? Some kind of revenge against the financial community at large? His parents clearly knew nothing about that and for the moment at least he thought he would keep it that way. Alec gave up on trying to figure out the motivation. He had another question and this was, on a personal level, the most important.

'How did he buy Fallowfields?' he asked. 'Where did the money come from?'

'From your grandfather,' his father said. 'Alec, there's no mystery about that.'

'I know he left money in his will, but Rupert owned Fallowfields long before that.'

'No, no. You see he set up trust funds for us both and being an old-fashioned soul they were set up so we got them when we married or turned twenty-five. I used mine for the deposit on this place and Rupert used his for Fallowfields. Bought it outright, it was in such a state. Then when our father died, we came into his estate and when Mother became so ill I had power of attorney over her savings as well. We used most of it for nursing care, but what was left when she died was split between us. I invested mine and I'm pretty certain Rupert did the same. You've got to remember, Alec, the stock market actually returned something in those days.'

'I think he used it later to buy the shop,' Audrey said. 'That's what we always understood, anyway.'

Alec nodded, relieved.

'Why the question?' his father wanted to know.

'There's no reason,' he lied. 'In my position though, I need to know.'

His father nodded. 'Of course. Everything must be seen to be legal, I guess. I'm sure his solicitor could verify things if you're worried.'

Alec nodded.

His father yawned and got up. 'I'm sorry, Alec, but I'm off to bed. Way past my usual time and you look all in.'

'I feel it,' he agreed. He made his way up to the guest room but knew, despite his exhaustion, he would find it hard to sleep. Shrewd investments didn't account for all of Rupert's legacy, of that he was certain, but even if it did, Billy Pierce had told him that the money from the first two robberies had never been recovered. So, where was it? That, Alec guessed, was also what Kinnear wanted to know.

Twenty-Three

Patrick rarely slept deeply and the sound of his phone having received a message was enough to wake him. He fumbled about on the bedside table trying to locate his phone, then stared at the screen. One message, unknown number and the time was two fifteen.

Ordinarily, Patrick ignored anything that came up as unknown, but he had a fair idea who this might be from.

Patrick sat up and switched on the bedside light.

The text was brief. *Meet me? Now.*

For a minute or two Patrick stared at it, not sure what to do. Why did he want to meet now and for what? He had hoped the boy would get in touch, sensing something very wrong and also hoping that he was the same person Marcus had reported coming to the shop.

But he'd been unprepared for this to happen in the dead of night.

Patrick texted back, then slipped out of bed and found his clothes. As quietly as he could he made his way past the rooms now occupied by Naomi on one side and his father on the other. Patrick had been given the small bedroom at the rear of the house. The stairs creaked and groaned as he tiptoed down, taking care to keep to the very edge of the tread but flinching at every sound. Had he not been dressed he could have used the excuse of getting a drink if he was found out. He decided if his father woke he'd simply say that he couldn't sleep and remind his dad that he didn't have his dressing gown with him and was far too old to wander about a strange house in just his pyjamas.

But he need not have worried himself with thinking up excuses because no one stirred and he made it through the back door and out into the garden without raising the alarm.

Napoleon, curled up in the kitchen, rolled on to his back and watched him go outside, then trotted after, nuzzling at his hand. Patrick thought about shooing him back, but the presence of the black dog was comforting. He lay his hand on the dog's flat, silky head, stroking his ears.

He should have brought his torch. He had forgotten just how dark it was here, no streetlights, no borrowed illumination from nearby houses.

Patrick stood and waited for his eyes to adjust, pleasantly surprised at the way the world slowly came into grey-blue focus and just how much light there really was from a half fat moon and a scattering of stars. He made his way across the garden, feeling the damp grass soaking through his shoes and wishing he'd worn his boots. There was still some heat in the night air and the scent of jasmine that wafted across the lawn from the terrace wall was almost too intense.

Patrick flinched as the gate creaked open. He cracked it just wide enough to slip through, Napoleon in tow. He had told the boy to meet him in the meadow, checking he knew where Patrick meant. It seemed like a logical place, the boy could get across the field behind his house and was less likely to be seen that way than if he had to come out of the drive and on to the road.

It occurred to Patrick, as he stepped out from the garden and into Rupert's over-grown meadow, that he did not even know the name of this boy he had come here to meet or how long he would have to wait before he managed to get there.

Patrick made his way over to the fence and stared across into the field. The moon cast deep shadows, concealing the bullocks and the nettles and the long grass at the margins. Patrick stared hard and after a moment or two could just make out a figure making its way through the shadow and heading towards him.

'Hi,' Patrick said as he drew near.

The boy glanced back over his shoulder and then cast a searching look past Patrick and into the meadow.

'It's OK. I'm on my own.'

He nodded and then climbed up to perch on his side of the fence. Patrick, taking his lead, wedged himself on the other side with his back against one of the tall ash trees that formed part of the boundary to Rupert's land.

'Didn't know if you'd come,' the boy mumbled.

'Said I would, didn't I?' Patrick told him. 'Who are you anyway?'

His name was Danny Fielding and he was not quite sixteen. He lived with his father, as Patrick had gathered, at what he called White Farm.

Remembering their visit that afternoon Patrick considered that it should have been Off-White Farm or even Grey and Unwashed Farm, but he kept his thoughts to himself.

'Your mum not live there?' Patrick asked. 'Mine lives in Florida. She and Dad got divorced.'

Danny shook his head. 'Me mam's gone,' he said. 'She had a row with me dad and he reckons she left.'

'When did she go?'

'About three week ago. Just before he died. The man what lived here.'

'Was it your mam Rupert came to see?'

'Rupert?'

'Rupert Friedman. The man who lived here.'

Danny nodded. 'Mam grew up round here, she knew all sorts of stories like me granddad used to tell. Dad reckoned they were rubbish but mam liked to talk about them and Mr Friedman was writing a book. He had these meetings at the library, asked anyone what'd got stories to come along and tell them and me mam went. Came back full of it, how he was going to write this book and me mam's stories were going to be in it.'

'Did your dad not like that?'

'Dad don't like anything except stuff to do with the farm. He's been making no money and it's getting to him. Wurriting, me mam says. She wanted him to sell up and move to Epworth, get a job like she did, but he won't have it. Mr Friedman came to our house. He sat there one afternoon talking to me mam when me dad came home and he wasn't best pleased. Thought it were all a big waste of time and said so. She told him he were a big waste of time and they got into a big fight like they always do. Mr Friedman left and after he'd gone the fight got worse.'

'Did you go to the shop to try and talk to him?'

Danny nodded. 'I went to tell him not to come here again. It'd just make it all worse for everyone.'

Patrick nodded his understanding. 'Marcus, the man at the shop, he said you looked scared.'

Danny shrugged. 'I'd rode me bike in, but me dad, he comes into Epworth on market days. I was scared he'd see me. He wouldn't have understood. He'd have thought I was against him too and I'm not. Not agin either of them. I just want them to stop rowing.'

'Why did you go to the shop?' Patrick asked. 'Why not just come here?'

'I did,' Danny told him. 'I did that first thing, but there was no one here and I looked in the garage through the gap between the doors and the car wasn't there. I thought he'd have gone to the shop but the other bloke said not.'

He broke off, cast a resentful look back towards the farm. 'When I got back home she'd gone. Dad said she'd waited till he'd gone out then packed her bags and cleared off. She never left a note or nothing.'

Patrick gnawed on his lower lip not knowing what to say. Danny was so obviously hurting. His dad would never just have gone off like that, Patrick thought, nor, for that matter, would his mum or even his stepdad. He was lucky, he reflected, and not for the first time. His mum and dad had managed an amicable divorce and he got along fine with his stepdad and his stepbrothers. His parents were on good terms too and Harry and his stepdad were perfectly friendly. In fact, the only problem Patrick had with any of it was in being unable to solve the mystery of how his parents had met and married in the first place. Talk about an attraction of opposites.

'Do you know where she went to?' he asked.

Danny shook his head. 'She's not called and I've phoned my auntie and my cousins and they don't know where she is either.'

'What about a friend?'

Danny laughed harshly. 'Me dad made sure she didn't keep no friends,' he said. 'Reckoned they were a waste of time too.'

It sounded as though Danny's dad was the waste of time, Patrick thought, but he bit back the words. He wondered why Danny was telling him all this but he didn't feel able to ask that either. It would sound as if he didn't care and Patrick did care. His heart went out to him.

'Can I do anything?' he asked finally.

Danny shrugged. 'I went to the police station and told them about my mum. They said she was an adult and could do what she liked and if my dad didn't report her missing there was nothing I could do. I'm not old enough to count,' he added bitterly. 'So I don't know what I can do.'

'What's your mum's name?'

'Sharon Fielding. I don't know what else to do. My dad won't talk about her, he just says she's gone and don't care about us so I'd best forget about her.'

Patrick fumbled in his head for something useful to say. 'Look,' he managed finally, 'the man who owns Fallowfields now, Alec, he's a policeman. I might be able to get him to ... well, to tell you what you could do.'

Danny turned his gaze upon Patrick and held it there for so long it began to burn. Then he looked away and shrugged. 'Ask him then,' he said. 'But I keep thinking ... keep thinking how she might be dead.'

It was almost four by the time Patrick got back to his bed and when he did, sleep just would not come. He could understand why Danny felt the way he did. To have a parent suddenly cut off contact like that, with no warning and seemingly no reason, was hard to understand. Danny understood that his mother had been unhappy. He'd understood that it was likely his parents would split up sooner or later. He'd just expected to have a bit more warning and a little less drama, after all, they'd muddled along unhappily for years up until now.

Oddly, it seemed that Danny blamed Rupert. Rupert, Danny sensed, though he did not put it into words, was the straw that broke the proverbial camel. Rupert had, somehow, showed Sharon Fielding just what she was missing out on; clarified and made solid that vague discontent and provided the impetus for action.

Patrick wondered if Rupert'd had any inkling of that.

Had anyone else come asking questions about Rupert? Patrick had asked.

Danny had thought about it and then nodded slowly. A man Danny estimated to be in his thirties, thin and with dark hair, had come asking if they'd seen him. It was a few days before he died, Danny thought, though he wasn't certain. He'd only overheard a part of the conversation between the man and his dad, but it seemed to be something about the man wanting to buy Rupert's car but not being able to get hold of him.

'He wanted to know when he'd be in,' Danny said. 'As if we'd know! Dad told him that. Like we ever see him.'

His dad hadn't always been so angry, Danny had said in his father's defence, but the farm was unprofitable and the bills were mounting and his mam was nagging about chucking it all in. After all, she'd argued, the farm was from her family, not his dad's, so why was it so important to him?

Danny didn't know the answer to that one. He'd have been happy to move closer to his school and what friends he had in town. Patrick got the impression he'd have been glad to have moved anywhere away from his dad.

That was what troubled him the most, Patrick realized. The sense of abandonment. It was almost preferable that his mother might be dead and unable to get in touch than it was to think she might simply have chosen not to.

Unable to sleep, Patrick sat up again and propped his pillows comfortably against the headboard. He had a pad and pen on the bedside table and the first of the three journals. He'd already found four letters and two numbers in this one the night before, but was no closer to figuring out what they might mean. He began work again, picking up from where he'd left off, focussing his mind on something that he might just possibly be able to solve, unlike the Danny problem which, Patrick knew, he probably could not.

Light crept above the horizon and greyed the darkness outside his window. Patrick worked on, finally falling back to sleep with the journal in his hand and the notepad tumbling from his bed as the sun rose up above the garden wall.

Twenty-Four

Alec arrived just before midday. He sounded exhausted and distressed, Naomi thought. Harry had let him in and she hurried through to join them in the hall. His hug of greeting was more like the clasp of someone drowning and, although he tried to sound cheerful and was obviously happy to see her, she could almost feel him pulling her down into the depth of his weariness.

'Coffee,' he pleaded. 'Strong please.'

Naomi laughed uneasily and led him through to the kitchen where Harry was busying himself with the newly acquired coffee maker Naomi had bought when she'd been out with Marcus.

'I hope I've got the hang of this thing,' he said. Satisfied he'd set the process in motion, he told them he was going to rouse his son and left them alone.

'Are you OK?' Naomi asked anxiously.

'No. I need to sleep and I hurt like hell. I'd forgotten how lumpy my parents' spare bed was. It's no wonder they don't have anyone to stay.'

Vaguely, Naomi wondered if the bed or absence of guests came first, rather like the chicken and the egg. She asked, 'Were they able to tell you anything?'

'Not a lot. Only that Rupert once got the sack for alleged insider trading, but that the money used to buy Fallowfields and the share in the shop was probably clean.'

'Probably?'

'Oh, not much doubt really. I'm just in pessimistic mode. Sorry.' He reached across the table and took her hand. 'The locket we found, it belonged to my mother, by the way. She must have left it here when they and Rupert were still talking. Now she's fretting because she'd already claimed for it on the insurance.'

Naomi laughed. 'God, that must have been years ago.'

'True, but you know Mum.'

'And your London trip. Was it worth it?'

'Worth it?' Alec considered. 'Let's just say I discovered a great deal. Worth it ... now, that's another question.'

Harry arrived back and went to tend to the coffee, asked if Alec wanted food as he was about to get breakfast for Patrick.

'Lunch, rather,' he said.

'Not like Patrick to sleep this late,' Alec commented.

'No, but I suspect he was up all night with those blasted journals. I found one of them lying on his bed when I went in.'

'Oh? Did he turn up anything interesting?'

'Well, I'll let him explain that, but yes, I rather think he has.' There was no mistaking the pride in Harry's voice.

Gratefully, Alec took the mug that Harry proffered and sipped the sweet and scalding liquid. He glanced up as Patrick stumbled, bleary eyed and tousle haired, clutching three leather-bound books and a notebook.

'Late night?'

The boy nodded. 'Yeah. You?'

'Better believe it.' He sighed, knowing that he'd better make a start. 'Well, since we're all here...' Slowly and somewhat reluctantly, Alec began to tell them what he knew.

'Kinnear and two others robbed three banks back in 1980. The first two, they got away free and clear, but it looks as though they got greedy. Bank number three was only twelve days after the first and it all went badly wrong. The police arrived. Armed. One of Kinnear's gang was shot dead and the other wounded and a security guard called Fred Ritchie was also shot dead.'

'What was their MO?' Naomi asked.

'Wait for the security van to arrive with the day's delivery. Wait until the guards entered the bank, then grab the nearest person to use as a hostage, threaten to shoot unless the security men handed over their delivery and staff dished out whatever they had in the tills. Double whammy. They'd take the hostage outside with them, car would drive up, hostage released, men were away. They were fast and slick and it was all over in a matter of minutes.'

'So, two or three men inside the bank?' Naomi asked.

'Three. The driver was never caught. Kinnear fingered someone he said was called Sam Spade.'

Harry laughed. 'Someone had a sense of humour,' he said.

'Why?' Patrick asked.

'Sam Spade was a fictional PI,' Alec explained. 'It's exactly the sort of thing that Rupert would do.'

'Rupert!' Naomi was as shocked as he knew she would be.

'Rupert,' he confirmed. 'It was never proved but...'

Slowly, he filled in the gaps, telling them what Billy Pierce had said and the assumptions they had both made.

'But you don't know for certain,' Naomi objected.

'Not for certain, no. But, Nomi, I've got to face facts here and all the facts point to this being so.'

'And to Kinnear wanting his money back,' Harry added.

'Which explains, in part, what he was looking for.'

'Surely,' Harry objected, 'he couldn't possibly think that Rupert would keep the money here. How much would it have been anyway?'

'About £25,000, they reckon.'

'Doesn't sound like a lot,' Patrick said.

'Remember this was back in 1980. That would have bought a substantial detached house round where we live and still left change. It's about a quarter of a million, I'd say, in today's money.'

'Oh,' Patrick said. 'So, if he'd invested it, it would be worth a lot more now.'

'Well, yes, I suppose it would. Kinnear probably assumed he'd taken it and spent the lot,' Alec added. 'I suspect he wanted a share of what Rupert still had. I went through the information the solicitor gave me last night and, from what my father told me about what their father left them and so on, I can more or less account for everything there. I called the solicitor this morning and got the name of his stockbroker, called him and accounted for the figures I couldn't match up last night and the references to the shares Harry found in the study. His broker said he'd talked about online trading but he didn't know if Rupert struck out on his own or not. But, the fact is, without getting in a forensic accountant, I can't see any trace of the money from the raids.'

'Um, I think Patrick might be able to help there,' Harry said.

'Oh? How's that?'

'Patrick found out why he buried the journals,' Harry said.

An hour spent examining the letters and numbers Patrick had written down convinced Alec that they were on the right lines, but he also had no idea exactly what they might mean. He had a feeling that Harry might be right and the numbers may refer to offshore accounts. He agreed they needed an expert to look at this and wondered if one could be suggested by DS Fine.

'Alec, if Rupert was clever enough to set this up, to cover his tracks so far, why didn't he gradually filter this money back into his legitimate business?' Harry asked. 'I mean, the antiques business would lend itself to laundering, I would have thought. There are a lot of overseas sales and a number of trans-actions in cash. Both ways.'

'And how accurately did he keep his books

where they were concerned?' Alec questioned.

'Ah, well now, that's a question,' Harry
replied. He paused, mind working. 'You
know,' he continued, 'I wonder if what I just
suggested is precisely what Rupert was
trying to do. You know the ledger we found
buried with the other things? Well, it's
recent, only been kept over the past six
months or so. From what I've seen so far it's
possible that at long last Rupert decided to
bring that money in line, so to speak.'

'Why now? He didn't need it. His bank
accounts were more than healthy.'

'Because Kinnear came back on the scene,'
Harry said. 'He was trying to pay him off.'

'Obviously not fast enough for Sam Kinnear,' Alec observed.

Alec had gone to bed, exhaustion winning
out over his desire to carry on puzzling this
out. Naomi joined him and Harry went back
to his examination of the ledger.

Patrick took the laptop into the dining
room and set himself up at the table opposite his father. The French doors were open
and the sun streaming in. It was hard to
equate the peace of the summer afternoon
with the violence of men like Kinnear,
though Patrick only had to look at the rein-
forcement and new locks on the doors to be

reminded.

'Dad, why do you think he hasn't tried again?' Patrick asked looking at the door. Kinnear seemed to have gone to ground since his attack on Alec. The routine phone call from Fine that afternoon had once again reported no further sightings. Fine wanted to talk to Alec about getting the media involved; so far his encounter with Kinnear had made it into the local paper only as an attempted mugging. It had made two paragraphs on an inside page, having been deliberately played down at Alec's request.

Fine had gone along with him, preferring to wait until they had more details to go on, but the hunt for Kinnear seemed to have stumbled to a halt.

'I don't know,' Harry replied. 'I can't help but wonder if Kinnear deliberately exposed himself that day. If he made certain that Naomi heard him.'

Patrick nodded. 'The kid from the farm. He texted me last night.'

Harry looked at his son. 'What did he say?'

'He wanted to meet.'

'And?'

Patrick shrugged. 'We met,' he said. 'In the meadow last night.'

Harry took a deep breath and Patrick could see he was biting back words. He could guess what they were. Something along the

223

lines of: Don't you realize how dangerous/ stupid/ irresponsible that was. And just when were you going to tell me about it?

'I'm telling you now,' Patrick defended himself against his father's unspoken question. 'First chance I've had really,' he added as reasonably as he dared. He waited, wondering which way, as regards response, his father would decide to go.

Harry closed his eyes, then opened them again. He'd decided, Patrick realized, to come down on the side of what's done is done. 'Not sensible, Patrick. I'm sure you know that.'

Patrick shrugged, not quite able to concede the point. 'He was upset,' he said, 'but he's definitely the kid Marcus saw at the shop. He said he went to tell Rupert not to go to the farm again. His parents had been rowing about it.'

'His parents? Why?'

Patrick shrugged. Truth to tell he wasn't sure. 'He *said* his dad thought it was a big waste of time and got all resentful of how much attention his mam was giving it.'

'You think he was lying?'

Patrick shook his head. 'I think that's what he thought his dad thought. I think it was just one more thing and if it hadn't been Rupert that made her leave then something else would. I mean, who'd want to live with a man like him?'

'Rupert made her leave? I don't understand.'

'No. Not *made* her. Not like forced. Made her realize she wanted to leave, I suppose. But Danny – that's the boy – he's really cut up about it. She's gone and not been in touch since and he's convinced himself she's dead.'

'Dead? Does he have any reason for thinking that?'

'I don't think so,' Patrick said. 'Just that she didn't say goodbye and she's not been in touch.'

'That's sad,' Harry said. 'Sad and cruel, in my view, but it may be she thought a clean break would...'

He paused, met his son's gaze.

'No, I don't think she was right either, Patrick. But there's one thing I don't understand. Was he worried about coming to talk to Rupert at Fallowfields?'

'No. I asked him that too. He says he came but that Rupert wasn't here and the car was gone too.'

Harry frowned. 'And this was just a couple of weeks before he died, wasn't it? The time Marcus identified when Rupert was behaving oddly, not going into work, that sort of thing.'

'Marcus didn't think he'd even wanted to

leave the house,' Patrick agreed.

'But, obviously, on that occasion he did. Maybe his reluctance to go into work was not so much because he was afraid as because he was elsewhere.'

Patrick shrugged. 'Might have been coincidence,' he said. 'But, Dad, would you want to be on your own here knowing someone like Kinnear knew where you lived?'

'No, but then I wouldn't go and see him on my own either and it looks as though Rupert did just that the day he died.'

'Do you think Kinnear killed him in a way that the post-mortem didn't pick up?'

'I think Kinnear was responsible,' Harry said slowly. 'But as to what he did to cause Rupert to have the heart attack ... It could be that, unless Kinnear tells us, we will never know.'

Twenty-Five

Alec listened to Patrick's account of his meeting with Danny Fielding.

'Do you know the mother's name?'

'Sharon Fielding,' Patrick told him. 'I said I'd ask you what he could do.'

226

'Well, technically, the police officer he spoke to was right. She hasn't actually gone *missing*. She's an adult and her husband hasn't reported her absence.'

'But...'

'But I can have a word with Reg Fine. See if there's any circumstances Danny didn't know about. Did he say that she knew Rupert well?'

Patrick thought about it. 'They were working on some stories she told him but I don't think she knew him before or anything.'

'Right.' Alec was thoughtful. 'Patrick, I think we should assume then that this is a separate issue. I hope her disappearance has nothing to do with Kinnear.'

He felt more alert now, rested after his sleep and his mind was working again.

'What do we have, then? We have a set of dubious accounts. Some kind of code concealed in his journals. Money from two robberies that Kinnear wants back and evidence that Rupert was trying to settle with him. I'm forced to the conclusion that Kinnear didn't want Rupert dead, at least not until he had his money, and it looks as though he may have been willing to give Rupert time to get what he thought he was owed. To legitimize it in some way. The thing in Kinnear's favour is the number of years that have passed since the robberies. Handled carefully, Kinnear may well get away with the money, free and clear, if just a little late.'

'Except that Rupert died before he could finish what he was doing.'

'Well, yes, and that obviously pissed him off big time which is, no doubt, why he came here and started threatening, though quite what he expected Naomi to give him is still something of a moot point.'

'The journals and the ledger,' Patrick said. 'He must have known about them and what Rupert planned to do.'

Alec nodded. 'You're probably right. And his partner, this Reid fellow, he would probably be able to take care of the rest. Financial double-dealing seems to have been his speciality by all accounts.'

'So,' Naomi observed, 'Rupert's usefulness to Kinnear lasted only so long as he was transferring the money. After that ... who knows? I can't think that Kinnear would have had scruples about getting rid of him.'

'How do you think he tracked Rupert down?' Harry asked.

Alec shrugged. 'Probably pure chance. He may have seen the newspaper clipping. Rupert had got greyer, but he hadn't changed that much. Kinnear would have known him.'

'Who do you think Elaine might be?' Patrick asked.

'That, I don't know, but I think you and Harry are right and the E in the ledger is probably her.' He frowned. 'So, we need to think about our next move, I guess.'

'And that is?' Naomi wanted to know.

'Tomorrow, we talk to Reg Fine, see if there's anything we should know about Sharon Fielding. I agree with him that we need to use the media. I was against it before; I thought Kinnear would run and we'd never get to the bottom of things, but now we know what he was after I think there's too much at stake for him to do that. And we need to flush him out, shock him into making a move.'

'Not sure I like the sound of that,' Harry said.

'No more than I, but I don't see as we have a choice. Then, we try and track down the flat in London. My dad gave me what he remembered as the address, but I'll make some calls. Don't worry, Naomi, I think I'm more use here than trekking off south again. I might rope in Billy Pierce seeing as how his retirement is chafing on him.'

'Is that wise? He's not a young man, is he?'

Alec recalled the way Pierce had towered over him, the firm handshake and square shoulders. 'I don't think he's ready for the scrap heap, either. He'll be careful.'

'And what about this Elaine?'

Alec shrugged. 'We keep trawling through Rupe's notes; see if she comes up anywhere else. And we see what else we can find on the laptop. He's got to have buried it for a reason.'

'OK, so that's the morning taken care of?' Naomi joked. 'And after that?'

'Oh, we'll think of something for the afternoon,' Alec told her. 'I might even take another nap.'

Patrick had said little during this later exchange and it was Naomi that noticed. 'Patrick?' she asked. 'Something up?'

'I'm not exactly sure,' he said. 'Dad and I agreed earlier that it was funny Kinnear hadn't done anything since he attacked Alec. It's almost like he thinks he's got another way of getting to what he wants. I mean, I know we've had new locks put on and everything, but he could easily have broken in again if he thought we'd found the books. He must think we're still searching.'

'You're implying someone could tell him otherwise,' Alec said.

Patrick nodded. 'I think if he thought for one minute we'd found the ledger and the books he'd do whatever he had to get them. I think he's got a way of knowing. Or he thinks he does.'

'Well, none of us would tell him,' Harry objected. 'He could threaten us, of course,' he said anxiously. 'Which is why, Patrick, I think you were so unwise last night.'

'First he would have to be convinced we had what he wanted,' Alec soothed. 'No point in trying to extract information from anyone if they don't have it to give. No, I think Patrick has a point. He's holding back, giving us time to unearth what he's looking for, relying on us being thorough and...'

'Us telling Marcus Prescott when we've found it,' Patrick finished.

Twenty-Six

Reg Fine welcomed them into the pokey little office he shared with two other officers. 'Good to see you both. Alec, how are you?'

'Better, thanks. The bruises are now an interesting shade of green.'

Fine laughed. 'So, what can I do you for? Sit yourselves down. Alec, grab a chair from behind that desk. Bristow's in court so he won't be needing it.'

Alec wheeled out a battered office chair from behind another desk, seated Naomi and found a wooden one that looked as if it had come out of an ancient school room for himself.

'So, what do you have to tell me?'

'First,' Alec said, 'I think we should up the publicity here. See if we can flush Kinnear.'

'Oh? And what changed your mind?'

'We now know what he was looking for at Fallowfields. He won't run until he has it and, frankly, we'd rather have control of the situation than let Kinnear get impatient and do something we might not like.'

Fine nodded. 'Seems to be making a habit out of that,' he said. 'So what did you find? What was Kinnear so desperate to get?'

'Money,' Alec told him. 'Or rather, the means of recovering it.'

'And what money would that be?'

'The proceeds of two robberies,' Alec told him. 'From back in the early eighties.'

Fine raised an eyebrow. 'And the connection with your uncle would be?'

'We suspect Rupert might have been driving the getaway vehicle,' Alec said.

Fine raised an eyebrow. 'Well,' he said. 'You've got *my* attention. Tell me more.'

Quickly, but as concisely as possible, Alec filled in the details of the crimes and the part he suspected his uncle might have played.

'You're serious?' Fine said at last. 'You really think this Billy Pierce may have it right and your uncle was involved?'

Alec nodded reluctantly. 'It fits the known facts,' he said. 'Believe me, I'd love to be proved wrong but in the absence of something disproving his involvement ... Rupert was a clever man but he wasn't always a wise one and I suspect ex-DI Pierce was right.'

'Sam Spade,' Fine laughed harshly. 'I like that. But Alec, have you thought this through? Two men died. One an innocent bystander. Do you really think your uncle could have lived with that? Could he have just carried on as normal all these years? I didn't know him, but the impression I've gained from those that did was that he was a good man. An honest one.'

'That's the one thing that causes us to doubt,' Naomi agreed, 'but, as Alec says, we have to work with what we've found out.'

'But you're only hypothesizing about the so-called code you've found in the journals. It might be completely unrelated.'

'Of course it might,' Alec agreed. 'It might even be something Rupert used to throw Kinnear off the trail, but it seems to me that Kinnear believed that Rupe still had the money and from the look of the ledger Harry's been working on, Rupert was drawing money back through the antiques business, effectively laundering it for Kinnear. There are purchases mentioned that he's paid one price for and declared another.

Items sold for a different rate according to which records you examine. Money diverted. Though we don't yet know where. And when we compared this to the stuff his solicitor gave me, details to do with the house and his business and his ordinary accounts, you can't but help see the difference.'

'You're pretty sure that the house and business are clean then. I mean, apart from his recent activities.'

'Pretty sure, yes. It would need a forensic accountant to go back through the books.'

'Well, I hope you've got deep pockets,' Fine said. 'They don't come cheap.'

'I was wondering, 'Alec said. 'If this became an official investigation...'

Fine threw up his hands in a gesture somewhere between horror and denial. 'Alec, you've got to be joshing with me. There's not enough evidence to warrant those kinds of resources. Bring me Kinnear, bring me a direct link to your uncle and something might be done, but as it is, no hope.'

Alec nodded. He hadn't been expecting anything else but he thought he ought to ask. 'But, the publicity,' he said, 'you can handle that?'

'*That* I can do,' Fine agreed. 'We'll get the local media involved and Kinnear's picture out there with a statement to the effect that he's wanted for the attack on you and an attempted break-in at the house of a recently deceased minor celebrity.'

'Minor celebrity?' Alec laughed. 'Rupe would have enjoyed that.'

'Well, he almost was,' Fine said. 'We'll just give it a little spin. It shouldn't be difficult, not with the local writer angle and the circumstances in which he was found. It might take a day or so to build, but I reckon we can get his picture and a brief statement in tomorrow's papers. That would be a start.'

'Good,' Alec told him. 'Then the next move will be up to Kinnear.'

'There's something else,' Naomi said. 'Probably unrelated, but Patrick's befriended a young lad by the name of Danny Fielding.'

'At the farm back of Fallowfields,' Alec elucidated.

'His mother went missing about the time of Rupert's death. Danny is convinced it wasn't as simple as her just leaving home. She's not been in touch and no one seems to have seen her.'

'And you want me to see if there's any previous?'

'Please,' Naomi said. 'It occurred to me there might be a history. I wondered if you could check out the local women's refuges.'

'I could get that done,' Fine said, though

235

he sounded a little wary. 'You realize, though, that I couldn't tell you anything. If she's there it's because she's in need of protection. It'd be up to her if she wanted to make contact with her son.'

Naomi nodded. 'I think it would be something for Danny to know that she was still alive,' she said. 'He's convinced she would have been in touch if she'd been able.'

'So, won't knowing that she hasn't been be harder still on the lad?'

'I don't know,' Naomi told him. 'But we promised to try and find out.'

Fine considered for a moment then pushed his chair out from behind the desk. 'Give me a minute,' he said.

It was in fact almost ten before he came back. He dropped a folder on the table. 'Look,' he said. 'You know I can't go into detail, but you were right. There is history. A half dozen calls in the past three years. Nothing before,' he sighed. 'It's become more common round here of late to be called to domestics. Pressures on farmers have never been greater and tempers boil over. From my reading of the reports though, this was a case of six of one and half a dozen of the other. Sharon Fielding has a temper and so does her old man. She walloped him with a cast iron pan last year. Lucky not to crack his skull. Neither of them have ever pressed charges.'

'I see,' Naomi said. 'So it could be that there was violence this time.'

'You're afraid Danny Fielding could be right?'

She nodded.

'OK, look, I'll do a ring round. I'm assuming they've called the hospitals and the usual stuff?'

'You know, I'm not sure they have,' she said thoughtfully. 'Patrick said that Danny had phoned family and friends, but he's just a kid.'

'Well, we can get on to that,' Alec said.

'They might not let on she's there, you know. Depends if she's told them not to,' Fine reminded him. 'And if she was unconscious and had identification then the family would have been informed. You can give a description, of course, see if they have any bodies they don't have a name for. I'll do the mortuary,' he added. 'Be easier for me.'

'Thanks,' Naomi said though she suddenly felt terribly depressed. What if Sharon Fielding did turn up dead or badly injured?

She sighed. Well, she supposed, at least then Danny would know he hadn't been abandoned. It was, she thought, a toss-up which outcome would be worse for the boy.

Danny Fielding had agreed to come to

Fallowfields that morning. Patrick had thought it might be easier if only he and his dad were there, and Napoleon, of course, Naomi having left him behind. Napoleon was a great ice-breaker and Patrick was relying on him to ease the way.

Patrick met Danny in the meadow.

'Does your dad know you're here?'

Danny shrugged. 'He's out,' he said. 'Don't know when he'll be back.' He had made Napoleon's acquaintance when he talked to Patrick that night he had texted him, and he renewed the friendship now, patting the dog's back and stroking his ears.

Patrick led him through the garden and into the house, entering through the kitchen door. 'You want something to drink?'

'You got coke?'

Patrick got a couple of cans from the fridge. 'Here.'

'Thanks.'

Danny stood just inside the kitchen door as though ready to make his escape. He allowed his gaze to travel around the room and Patrick noted as it fell on the blue bowl filled with eggs, the flowers Naomi had cut in the garden and the various gadgets Rupert had filled his kitchen with.

'Did you make the list?'

Danny nodded and finally left the kitchen door. He took a couple of sheets of lined, crumpled paper from the back pocket of his jeans and sat down at the table. 'This is everyone I could think of. I've ticked the ones I tried already.'

'Did you try the hospitals?' Harry asked. They both jumped, neither having heard him come in from the hall. Danny got to his feet as though ready to run away. 'Don't mind me,' Harry told him, 'I've just brought you these.' He laid on the table a telephone directory and the Yellow Pages and the cordless phone.

'Thanks, Dad.'

Harry nodded. 'I'll just make myself some coffee.'

Danny watched him warily and Patrick found himself observing as though through Danny's eyes. He was so used to his father that he rarely noticed that he looked older than most parents, largely due to the fact that his hair was already grey and a little thin. He wore it cropped short, despising anything resembling a comb-over. Harry's eyes were grey too and his skin a little wrinkled at the corners. Patrick liked his father's eyes. He was, lately, a little fatter round the middle than he really ought to be but, again, Patrick rarely noted that either. Patrick himself, slim and dark haired, olive skinned, resembled his mother, though his eyes, an almost navy blue, were inherited from Mari,

Harry's mother and, so he had been told, were like those of Harry's long-dead sister.

Danny examined Harry and Patrick knew he was comparing him to his own father. From what Patrick had seen so far that would not be an easy thing to do, though for that matter, it wasn't easy to compare Harry to any father he could think of. Harry was, well, Harry. He found himself thinking about his stepfather. A tall, strong, fit outdoorsman with red hair and a beard to match and again wondered what on earth had possessed his parents to get married.

'You can tell my dad anything,' Patrick found himself saying. 'He just wants to help, too.'

For a moment, Danny turned his gaze on Patrick and Patrick got the impression that he had crossed some line, made some incomprehensible statement. He shrugged, muttered something that Patrick didn't catch but which he guessed expressed disbelief.

Patrick pulled the list towards him and began to read.

At Harry's suggestion they worked back through the list from the beginning, starting with those numbers Danny had already tried – his mother's sister, a cousin and a maternal grandfather that he never saw.

There were a few friends listed, some

without numbers. It was clear that Danny had just written down anyone with a connection to his mother, however tenuous.

Harry took over. He sat down at the table and examined the list. 'We should try hospitals,' he said. 'You never know, she might have been in an accident and not had anything with her to say who she was.'

'You mean like, she might have lost her memory?' Danny sounded hopeful.

'I'm not saying that's what happened, Danny,' Harry warned. 'But we should look at all possibilities. Now, you'd better tell me about your mum, her age, what she looked like, what she might have been wearing on the day she left.'

Danny and Patrick watched as Harry found the numbers he needed, asking Danny's advice about local hospitals and which his mother was likely to have been taken to.

Patrick listened with amusement and Danny was in evident awe as Harry began his spiel. 'Oh, good morning. I wonder if you can help me. I certainly hope so, the family is terribly worried...' He paused, listening. 'It's my sister,' he said, his voice shaking slightly. 'You see, she's missing and we're worried she might ... oh, thank you.'

He covered the mouthpiece and said, 'They're redirecting me. This could take a little while.'

'Sister?' Danny asked.

'They won't tell you anything if you're not a relative,' Patrick whispered as Harry resumed his conversation with someone else.

'Yes, my sister. Sharon Fielding. Yes. No, it would have been just over two weeks ago. We did call just after she disappeared but...'

Harry allowed his voice to trail off as though distressed and Patrick could hear the sympathetic tones of the woman on the other end of the line.

Harry repeated the description Danny had given him and then covered the mouthpiece again. 'She's gone to check,' he said. They waited and the woman returned. Harry thanked her and hung up the phone.

'No, no one there,' he said. 'She did tell me though, that if they'd had an unknown patient for this long, they would probably have put out an appeal in the local paper. She gave me a couple of numbers to try, local papers, I think, just in case we missed it. We'll try the other hospitals first and then get on to them.'

Patrick got up and filled the kettle. He was reminded horribly of watching Naomi go through this very process earlier in the year when a close friend had gone missing. She had called the hospitals for him then, asking the questions Harry was asking. Later the friend had turned up dead. Drowned in the canal with a mix of drugs and booze in his stomach and an accusation of murder hanging over his head. Watching Harry do this brought back such painful memories. He could imagine what Danny must be going through.

He made tea and gave Danny another can, watching and listening as Harry worked his way through the hospital list and then the numbers for the local papers. At the end of that he replaced the phone and blew out a frustrated breath. Gratefully he picked up the mug his son had placed on the table beside the directories.

'Nothing?' Patrick asked, though that was self evident.

'No, we can cross those off the list. Now, what else do we have here?' He glanced through the contacts that Danny had written down. 'Let's try the ones you have phone numbers for first,' he said, 'then we'll try to figure out the rest. Do you want to talk to people or shall I?'

'You think you can do it?'

'Sure I can.' Harry smiled at the boy who eyed him speculatively.

'What you doing this for?' Danny asked.

'Why not?' Harry shrugged. 'You need help. And besides,' he added, meeting the boy's eyes and knowing more was required,

'I had a sister once, she went missing. It was twenty years before I found out what happened to her. Twenty years of wondering and never being able to settle properly because there was always that thought that she would come through the door.'

Not the best of analogies, Patrick thought anxiously. Helen had died. Been murdered. But he knew what his dad meant. Patrick had grown up in the shadow of her memory and in the end it had been a relief for everyone that they could finally know what happened to her.

Danny, he noticed, did not ask. He sipped his coke and blinked hard and Patrick knew that he was trying not to cry. He looked away and Harry turned his attention back to the next number on the list.

'Ah, good morning.' The fourth call now and so far nothing gained. 'No, I'm not selling anything. I'm calling about Sharon Fielding ... My son is a friend of Danny's.'

Pause. Harry listened, then, to Patrick's surprise he raised his voice and spoke angrily into the phone. 'Look, I've got the boy here now, sitting at my kitchen table, tearing his heart out because he doesn't know what the hell happened to his mother. If you can't give me a few minutes of your time...'

Pause, Patrick heard a woman shouting down the phone.

'I'm sorry if you feel like that,' Harry said. 'But whatever you might have thought she was still his mother. I'd have thought a little compassion...'

Harry stared angrily at the phone. 'Hung up,' he said.

'What was all that about?'

Harry shrugged. 'Danny, this Ellen March, was she a close friend?'

Danny shrugged. 'I don't know,' he said. 'I just found any numbers I could and writ them down. That was on a bit of paper under the phone book.'

'Right. I see.' Harry leaned back in his chair and stared at the remaining numbers.

'What was her problem?' Patrick asked.

Harry shrugged, but Patrick could tell this was something he didn't want to talk about in front of Danny, so he let it go when his father simply said, 'I think she was just touchy about a stranger asking her questions.'

Danny looked even more depressed than when he had first arrived. 'You think it's worth trying the rest?' he asked.

Harry smiled at him. 'Let's give it a go.' He glanced up at the kitchen clock. It was half past twelve. 'Tell you what, you and Patrick make some lunch and I'll do the rest of these on the other phone. The battery's going on this one. I could hear it beeping on that last call.'

That wasn't the only thing that needed beeping, Patrick thought. He'd caught enough of the woman's language to register that.

Danny shrugged uncomfortably. 'All right,' he said. 'I guess so'

Patrick got up and went to the fridge. 'What do you want?' he said. 'We've got ham and cheese and corned beef. Salad...'

Harry picked up the list and the phone and made his escape. One useful thing he had found out from Ellen March was that she wasn't a friend of Sharon's. From what she'd said to him, Harry would make a bet she was having an affair with Danny's dad.

Twenty-Seven

Danny left just after two and Patrick wandered back upstairs to Rupert's study. He had been flicking through the earlier journals he had noticed on Rupert's shelf, looking for previous references to Kinnear. So far, he had found nothing and the journals did not appear to go back to the time of the robberies, but were obviously a habit Rupert had acquired only in the last ten years of his life.

A car pulling up on the gravel brought him to the window, thinking Alec and Naomi had returned. He was shocked to see Marcus.

'Shit!' Patrick muttered. He had left the journals and laptop downstairs in the dining room in plain view.

Racing downstairs he passed the front door as Marcus rang the bell for a second time. Harry was about to open it as Patrick dashed by, grabbing his record bag from the coat pegs as he ran.

'Patrick?' Harry had the door open now and Marcus was coming inside.

Patrick scooted into the dining room and grabbed the books and the ledger, stuffing them into his bag. Marcus stuck his head around the door to say hello just as Patrick was attempting to do the same with the laptop.

'Hello, Patrick. How are you?' Marcus smiled broadly, then his expression froze. 'You've found Rupert's laptop.'

'No,' Patrick lied. 'It's mine. I've been using it for homework.'

'Homework? I thought you'd finished for the year.'

'I have, but I've got a project to start. Get ready for next term. I'm carrying on with the same subjects, you see, so I can kind of get ahead.'

Marcus eyed him thoughtfully and Patrick knew he did not believe a word of it.

'Coffee, Marcus?' Harry asked. 'Come on through. I was just washing up. Alec and Naomi should be here soon. Patrick, maybe you could give them a ring and find out how long they're going to be?'

Patrick nodded. He waited until Harry had ushered the reluctant Marcus away and then ran upstairs. He put the bag in Rupert's study and locked the door, slipping the key into his pocket. Then he sat down on the top step and called Naomi on his mobile, grateful when she said that they were almost home.

'Marcus saw the laptop,' he said. 'I told him it was mine but he didn't believe me. I've locked it in the study.'

'Good,' Naomi approved. 'Patrick, you and Harry keep him amused, we'll soon be there.'

It was interesting, Patrick thought as he rang off, that they had all come round to his way of thinking as regards Marcus just when, oddly enough, Patrick himself was starting to have some sympathy for the man. He sat for a minute more, analyzing where that feeling had come from and decided it was that he genuinely believed that Marcus cared for Rupert. And if he was scared of Kinnear, Patrick thought, no one could really blame him for that, but what they didn't know for sure was if Marcus and Kinnear were in this together or if Marcus was just acting out of fear.

He thought about it as he went downstairs and joined his father but reached no conclusion. Marcus smiled at him as he came through into the kitchen. 'They're coming back,' Patrick said. 'Should be here in just a few minutes.'

'Oh, good. I was just asking your father if you'd had any luck with the search.'

Patrick shook his head. 'Rupert had some interesting stuff, though,' he said. 'Some great old books and that. He's got maps from the 1640s when they drained the fens and all sorts.'

Marcus smiled again. A genuine smile this time. 'He was working on a second book about the Fen Tigers,' he said. 'I don't know all the details but I know one chapter concerned their descendants who still lived around here. He'd discovered that quite a few of the local families have roots going back to that time, including your neighbour, I believe.'

'Our neighbour?'

'Yes, the Fieldings at White Farm. He was quite enthused by it all.'

'Did you know he wrote poetry?' Patrick asked.

'I knew he tried. I don't recall him showing me any.'

'Well, it's not all that good. He was a much better prose writer,' Patrick said. 'Though I like bits. There's one about the fenland skies that's pretty good.'

'You'll have to show it to me.'

Patrick nodded. He heard Alec's key in the front door and went to meet them. Behind him he heard Marcus ask Harry again about the laptop, saying how odd it was that Patrick had the same model.

'I believe it's a very common one,' Harry said.

Patrick was surprised that Marcus even knew. Laptops tended to look similar, though Rupert's wasn't new and was certainly not as thin or light as many of the more modern ones. Maybe it was this that Marcus had noted. Whatever, Patrick was not easy about it.

After saying hello to Naomi and Alec he took himself back upstairs and into the study, then locked the door and fired up the laptop. In his excitement about the journals he had not taken so much time to look at the computer and, frankly, neither his dad nor Alec were that good.

Methodically, now, he began to open the

250

files in 'my computer' and on the C drive, surveying what was there and comparing the different versions Rupert seemed to have saved. He was still involved when he heard Marcus leave and the car pull away, and then was startled when Alec, unable to access the study, knocked on the door.

'Oh, sorry. Hang on.' He let Alec in.

'You can come out now, he's gone.'

'He knew it was Rupert's computer.'

'Yes, I guess he did. He mentioned it several times. We stuck to our story.' He came round the desk to look at what Patrick had been doing. 'Find anything?'

Patrick shrugged. 'Maybe,' he said. 'It was Marcus that put me on to it actually.'

'Oh?'

'He mentioned Rupert's new book on the Fen Tigers and how some of the families were still living round here. He said the Fieldings were one of them and I thought I remembered seeing something. So I looked and I found this. It's a list of all the people he interviewed for that book. There's like a little file on each of them and this one is on the Fieldings of White Farm.'

He turned the screen so Alec could read it properly.

'It's a rough family tree,' Alec said. 'And some comments on the family. "Husband is a boorish oaf",' Alec read. 'That's a very

251

Rupert turn of phrase. "Wife is a shrew. I pity the boy". Well, that's a little damning, wouldn't you say?'

Patrick shrugged. 'There's more,' he said. 'About the family history and the stories he planned to use.' He sighed and leaned back in Rupert's captain chair. 'I've been looking for financial stuff and there's a couple of files Dad hasn't seen yet. They were nested inside folders he kept his writing in.'

'Hidden?'

Patrick shrugged. 'Burying it in the garden was better,' he said. 'Easy enough to find if you look deeper than the title and no one has so far, which is why we missed it.' He pushed up from his seat. 'You and Naomi get any-where?'

'Well, we've arranged for Kinnear's picture to get into the papers, but Fine can't do a lot more for us. Harry tells me Danny Fielding came over.'

Patrick nodded. 'We didn't find out any-thing.'

'Apart from Ellen March.'

'Ellen March? Oh, angry woman.'

'That would be the one. From what she said to Harry it's likely she and Danny's father were having an affair.'

Marcus was unhappy. Unhappy and now very much afraid. He had been counting on

Naomi and the others playing straight with him. Had convinced himself that they would even though reason told him they had no cause to tell him anything.

The laptop belonged to Rupert, Marcus was sure of it, and Patrick and Harry had both lied. That meant they didn't trust him. Marcus thought about it as he drove home and was bitterly angry and despairing by turns. Angry because if it hadn't been for his insistence they look into Rupert's death, no one would have suspected anything or found anything. No one would have looked further than a heart attack. Alec would have probably sold up and that would have been that. Despairing because he knew Samuel Kinnear would not be understanding of his troubles. Sam Kinnear just wanted results.

He was unsurprised when the phone rang just after he got back to his flat above the shop. Kinnear was watching him, Marcus was sure of that. Kinnear or the quiet one he'd seen once or twice in his company.

'Well?' Sam Kinnear demanded.

'I don't have much to tell. They've found the laptop, that's all I know.'

'And you've got it.' It wasn't a question.

'No, I haven't got it.'

'Why not?'

'I'm supposed to just ask and they hand it over, is that what you think?'

'Works for me.'

'Maybe I don't have, shall we say, your powers of persuasion.'

'I've been telling you that from the start. You reckoned you could get the stuff quietly, no fuss. Seems you can't.'

Marcus sighed. 'Let me have another try,' he said. 'The computer isn't any good to you without the books, or so you said. I don't know yet if they've found the books.'

Kinnear was silent. 'One more day,' he said. 'I'll give you another twenty-four. Get the laptop and find out about the books. You don't, I will. You get the books and you work out what that bastard Rupert was doing with my money, where he hid it and how he planned on getting it back.'

'Rupe had already transferred more than you deserved,' Marcus was suddenly angry.

'I want it with interest,' said Sam Kinnear. 'Way I figure it, he owed me capital and with thirty-year interest on top. Rupert had only just whetted my appetite.'

Back at Fallowfields Alec was on the phone to ex-DI Billy Pierce. He had the approximate address of Rupert's flat from his parents. They had been uncertain of the number and Alec wasn't even convinced it was relevant.

'It's a bit of a wild goose chase,' he told

Billy Pierce. 'My dad is certain he didn't sell the flat, but their contact with Rupert was sketchy at best for the past twenty or so years.'

'Oh, it'll give me something to do,' Pierce told him. 'Keep my hand in. Anything else happening your end?'

Alec told him what had been going on. 'So, it's now wait and see time,' he finished. 'Something tells me we won't be waiting long.'

Twenty-Eight

'We've got trouble.'

Kinnear looked up from the television. He liked to watch the morning news on the BBC. It was very informative, he thought.

'We've always got trouble.'

Reid dropped the first edition of the paper in his lap. It was folded so that Sam Kinnear's picture stared out on the front page. Kinnear picked it up and studied it as though it was unfamiliar. He read the brief paragraphs beneath and then tossed the paper aside.

'And?'

'And they put you on the front page. Every man and his dog is going to be looking for you. Sam, we've got enough, let's get out of here now.'

Kinnear studied him with much the same expression as he'd studied the picture in the paper. Reid swallowed nervously and took an involuntary step back.

'This changes nothing,' Kinnear said. 'Just speeds things up.'

'We've got enough, Sam,' Reid said again. 'Enough to make a start somewhere else. Sam, I want my share. I want out. Now.'

Kinnear got up from his chair and crossed the room in two strides. He grabbed Reid by the shirt front and hoisted him clear of the ground. 'Since when did I give you permission to want anything,' he said, his voice no more than a soft, threatening growl. 'I want the rest of my money. *My* money. You're along for the ride, don't forget that.'

'You need me,' Reid squeaked. 'Need me to do the business. You don't know how...'

'But like as not Marcus does. Don't forget that. Like as not that bloody accountant they've got out at Fallowfields knows. You are not my only option. Don't forget that.'

He dropped Reid letting him fall to the floor. Reid lay there, curled into a ball like a dog expecting a final kick. Risking a look, he saw Kinnear had picked up the phone. He's calling Marcus, Reid guessed. The threat Kinnear had just made gripped his belly, cramped it tight so that Reid thought he might be sick. He'd got himself into this even though he knew what Kinnear was. He'd shared a six by ten space with the man for three straight months. Reid tried to remember just when and how he'd agreed to do this, agreed to help Kinnear, and found he could no longer remember. He recalled getting out of jail, then a few weeks after, remembered the familiar hand heavy on his shoulder and the voice in his ear, 'I've got a job for you, Jimmy boy.'

He couldn't recall ever having agreed. Men like Sam Kinnear didn't ask, they just assumed you'd go along with what they had in mind.

Across the room Kinnear slammed the phone down. 'Bastard's not answering his phone,' he said. 'Get over there and tell him I want to see him. Now.'

'Bring him here?' Reid was anxious. With Marcus, Kinnear would not need him. He'd made that plain.

'Yes here.' He frowned at Reid. 'Thought you were watching him.'

Reid didn't think he could draw attention to the illogic of this statement. I'm here, he thought, getting you your frigging paper and your groceries and your fags. How can I be watching Marcus if you want me here?

Instead, he scrambled to his feet and stumbled back down the stairs and across the yard. He could feel Kinnear's gaze burning into his back as he ran towards his car.

I could run, Reid thought. Get in the car and drive and not stop until he'd put the miles between himself and Sam. He pushed the idea aside almost as soon as it formed in his head. He had witnessed what happened to the last person who had run from Kinnear and she, so far as Reid could see, had only mildly pissed him off. Sam would find him if he ran. As a matter of principle, Sam would hunt him down and Reid, superstitious fear taking place of anything resembling common sense, was sure that there would never be enough places in which to hide.

The sight of Kinnear's face stopped him dead. Marcus stared at the rack, hand hovering over his usual choice of daily paper but his eyes fixed on the local rag he rarely bought. He bought it now though, clutching it in his hand so hard that his sweat leeched print on to his palm even before he was half-way back to the shop.

A thought struck him and he stopped dead in the middle of the pavement.

'Watch it, won't you,' someone said as they

crashed into him with their pushchair.

'Sorry.' The apology so automatic he didn't even think what he might be apologizing for.

He read the text beneath, the words leering at him. 'Vicious attack. Dangerous man. Do not approach.'

'Do not approach,' Marcus said. 'How very funny. Do not approach.' He realized that he had spoken out loud and that a woman turned to look his way. He heard too the hysterical edge to his voice.

'I can't go on like this,' Marcus told no one in particular. 'This just can't go on.'

He slipped into the shop by the back way, relocked the door and let himself into his little office. The shop was open, his part-time girl setting out new stock. Marcus positioned himself so he could see the front shop door and then dialled. Alec answered the phone.

'I've got to talk,' he said. 'Alec, I'm in big trouble and I have to talk to you.'

'Where are you? The shop? I'll—'

'No,' Marcus almost shouted down the phone. 'I think they're watching me, Alec. I'm coming out there. I can't stay here, I...'

He dropped the phone back on to the desk as Alec's voice continued to call his name. Staring out through the glass door of his office he saw that other man come into his shop, the small, dark-haired creature he had spotted with Kinnear.

A second later and the man had seen him too.

Marcus leapt round the desk and turned the key in the office door, then let himself back out through the rear of the shop. He ran to his car and slid the key into the ignition with hands that shook so much they flapped around the hole before managing to slot it in.

'Please start?' His car was temperamental, sometimes taking a second or so to catch. This morning it felt like an eternity.

He turned out of the yard and into the busy street beyond. Where would the man have gone? Did he have a car? Would he guess where Marcus could be going? Marcus glanced sideways at the shop front as he pulled into the main road but saw no one there that resembled the dark-haired man. He sank down in his seat, trying to make himself as small as possible as if that would help. No, the man was not in the shop either. He must have seen Marcus escaping and run back outside.

Marcus turned left at the end of the road and then right, cutting through side roads only a local might use. He reached the junction with the main road and peered out both ways. Clear. Marcus pulled out on to the main road. He put his foot down and accelerated away, relief coursing through his body.

He would drive to Fallowfields, tell them everything. They would call the police, Marcus supposed, but he didn't care about that any more. He just knew he had to get away from Kinnear and from the man who had come to the shop.

Glancing in his rear-view mirror he saw a small red car accelerating fast. His first thought was that kids always drove too fast on these narrow winding roads. He inched across, keeping close to the verge, assuming that they would pass him by if he gave them room and then, as the car pulled closer still Marcus's heart came close to stopping.

It was him. The man who had been with Kinnear.

'Dear God!' Marcus put his foot down and his car surged forward. The small red hatchback behind kept pace and then gained. It was so close now that Marcus could see the man clearly in his rear-view mirror. Foot flat to the floor now, Marcus knew he could not escape.

He felt the bump as the red hatchback hit his rear bumper. It was so gentle, so cautious that at first Marcus wasn't sure it had been deliberate, then he realized that the driver of the red car was just testing out his own skill and nerve. He rammed him then, red car crunching into Marcus, pushing him faster than the accelerator would go. Marcus tried to twist away, wrenching the steering wheel and momentarily freeing himself from his pursuer.

Marcus screamed. A car in the oncoming lane sounded its horn. He glimpsed a pale and terrified face as he wrenched the wheel the other way, could feel the rear tyres stepping out of line before he steered back into the embryonic skid and straightened his line.

How far was Fallowfields. How far?

Marcus realized that it was closer than he'd thought. He could see that wide, sweeping bend coming up and after that would come the sudden left turn into Fallowfields' drive. He had to make it there. He had to make that turn.

Pure willpower seemed to propel his car forward so that it inched away from his pursuer. Marcus found that he was praying. He took the bend wide, pleading that nothing would be coming the other way, then swung across, and dived into the opening in the hedge that spelt safety. Sheer momentum carried the red car forward and Marcus was convinced he would be broadsided. Instead, the unexpectedness of his actions had gained him just enough time. He slithered messily into the gravel drive, the red hatchback clipping his back end and sending him even further out of shape. Dragging on the wheel he straightened out of a second potential skid, the drag of the gravel helping to slow down his sideways slide. Then foot down and spraying small stones skyward he made it to the house, braking just in time.

For what seemed like an eternity he sat quite still, engine still running, front wheel wedged against the ornate porch. He clutched the steering wheel so hard Alec had to prize his fingers free.

Twenty-Nine

The flat that Rupert still owned up until the time he died was on the top floor of an Edwardian house. The area had been on the rise for the past few years and, although this street was still shabby, the neighbouring area had already benefited from the redevelopment grants and the spreading out of people from the more fashionable areas a couple of miles down the road.

Small cafés and restaurants had sprung up and, although the bars had not entirely overtaken the more traditional pubs in popularity, there were signs of gradual encroachment about which Billy Pierce had mixed feelings.

Pierce had spent the morning doing his research. The land registry told him that Rupert Friedman owned the flat. 23c Oban Road. A chat to the neighbours told him that it was rented out and had been for years. To the same woman.

Billy Pierce had examined the mail laid out in open pigeon holes in the ground floor lobby and that confirmed what he already knew.

'Well, well, Rupert Friedman,' he said. 'Weren't you the sly fox?'

There was no one home when he knocked, so he crossed the road again and went into a small café he'd spotted earlier. Sitting in the window, he could watch the length of the road and had the house in view. He had a good idea who he'd be looking for. It was just a case of playing the waiting game.

Pierce sipped his tea and smiled wryly to himself. It felt good to be useful but one thing he had not missed was the mind numbing monotony of surveillance. He had settled in the café just after three and it was almost five when she came home.

Billy Pierce knew it was her. It could, of course, have been one of the other two women – one a wife, one a singleton, who lived in the same house, but he doubted it.

This woman was the right age, right height, *right* from what he remembered, though it was many years since he had last seen her.

He gave her a chance to get inside and then left his seat, aware that the woman who ran the café stared after him as he walked down the street.

At the house, he pressed the buzzer for the top floor.

'Hello?' The woman's voice was light. She sounded happy, friendly, Billy thought.

'Is that Elaine Ritchie?' he asked, though he knew it was. 'I've come to talk about Rupert Friedman.'

Marcus allowed himself to be taken into the house. He was shaking so badly he could hardly stand, and although he could hear the words coming out of his mouth, he knew they were making no sense. They didn't even make sense to him.

Harry handed him brandy and he swallowed in between convulsions, feeling the heat in his throat which warmed him to the core.

'Is brandy really the thing for shock?' Naomi's voice, anxious and uncertain.

Marcus didn't think he cared. The spirit seemed to steady him, at least for the moment, and he extended his glass, hoping for more. Someone obliged and he swallowed again, then leaned back in the armchair and closed his eyes.

He was crying, Marcus realized in horror. Weeping like a child but he couldn't seem to stop. 'I'm sorry,' he whispered. 'I'm so, so sorry.' Not sure if he was apologizing for his tears or for something else.

The driver's side front wing had been wedged tight against the brickwork of the porch by the impact of the crash. Harry inspected it for signs of structural damage but, apart from a few scaled bricks, the porch seemed to have won. The heavy columns on either side were, Harry noted, what was really keeping the porch roof up and the brickwork had only a secondary role.

'It looks all right,' he told Patrick. He glanced anxiously down the drive, expecting at any moment to see Kinnear, or whoever had been chasing Marcus, come charging up. In Harry's imagination, Kinnear would be in a tank or at the very least an armoured car.

'Something red hit the back end,' Patrick said. He stood back from the vehicle, careful not to touch. He'd been around Naomi and Alec long enough to know about preservation of evidence. 'Dad, I think someone rammed him from behind and then hit the rear wing, maybe when he turned into the driveway. Whatever it was hit hard. There's a bloody great dent.'

Harry nodded. Behind him in the hallway he could hear Alec on the phone, calling the police and presumably trying to get hold of DS Fine.

'I suppose we ought to check the end of the drive,' he fretted. 'If the other car hit as hard as you think the driver might have been hurt.'

Patrick cast him a speculative look. 'Do you really want to go down there?'

'No, not really.'

'The police will be here before we know it.'

'We might need an ambulance.'

Patrick sighed. 'OK, we'll take a look. You're not going on your own. Just hold on.'

He slipped back into the house and returned with a heavy iron poker he had taken from the living-room fireplace.

'Isn't that called going equipped?' Alec asked as he came out into the hallway.

'No, I think it's making like a boy scout and being prepared. Dad thinks we should see if anyone's hurt. He's not going on his own and you're not leaving Naomi. Marcus is no use at the moment and Kinnear might try and come here.'

'You're giving the orders now, are you?'

'Not making a habit of it, but...'

Alec nodded. 'OK. But Patrick, you take a quick look and get straight back here. I'd suggest you drive, but both Harry's car and mine seem to be wedged in.' He frowned at Marcus's impromptu parking. If the porch hadn't stopped him he would have ploughed straight into Alec's vehicle. As it was they'd have to shift Marcus's car before either of them could get theirs out.

'We'll be all right.'

Alec watched them go and then shut the door and returned to Naomi and Marcus, glancing into the room to see if Marcus was talking yet. He went through to the kitchen and then the dining room, checking the doors and craning his neck to see the garden.

'Where are they going?' Naomi had heard part of the exchange.

'To see if anyone's hurt. Whoever was following Marcus seems to have collided with him.'

'If it's Kinnear I don't give a damn.'

'Not Kinnear,' Marcus whispered. 'It was the other one. He came to the shop and I ran. I got into my car and drove out here but he must have guessed. He was on the main road. He tried to force me off the road, bumping and barging from behind and then I just managed to make the turn and he hit my back end.'

'Yours is a heavy car,' Alec mused, thinking about the ageing BMW Marcus had been driving. 'Marcus, what was he driving? Who is he? You must have seen him before.'

Marcus stared in bemusement and Alec realized his brain was not capable of processing more than one thing at a time.

'Who is he?' he began again.

'I don't know his name. I saw him with Sam Kinnear once, just by chance. Another time he was waiting in the car when Kinnear came to the shop. He only came that one time and that was just after Rupert died. He was in a dreadful rage. I was just closing up and I suppose he waited until everyone had gone. He said Rupert owned him money and that just because Rupert was dead didn't mean he wasn't still owed.'

'Did he tell you where the money was from?'

Marcus nodded miserably. 'He told me. He said he had proof. He had something Rupert had written, but he didn't show me all of it, just enough to see that it was written in Rupert's hand. He said Rupert had been paying him back, paying him by using the shop and his stock and all sorts of other things. He made Rupert sound like a common thief.'

'Marcus,' Alec said softly, 'Rupert *was* a common thief. He stole.'

'Rupert wasn't a common anything,' Marcus contradicted hotly. 'That man Kinnear, he was blackmailing him. Forcing him to give him money. At first I didn't want to believe him, but it all made sense. All made sense of what Rupert had been doing the past few months. All the things I didn't understand. I thought Rupert was just tired of me, tired of the business. I thought he was getting ready to leave. Somehow, oh I know it sounds foolish, Alec, but this was easier to bear.'

'You cared deeply for him,' Naomi said.

'I cared deeply, yes and Rupert was the best friend I ever could have wanted.'

Naomi bit her lip uncertain if she should push this. 'Were you more than friends?'

Marcus laughed harshly. 'My dear, I was never that lucky. Rupert wasn't interested in me in that way. Rupert should have found a wife, settled down. I thought once there was someone, but he always denied it. I once saw a gold locket in his study. On his desk. I wondered then, but he said it belonged to a relative who'd been visiting and who had left it behind. I thought it was strange. Rupert didn't have visitors here, not for many years.'

Naomi inclined her head quizzically, but she said nothing.

'This man that followed you,' Alec asked, 'what was he driving?'

'A little red hatchback. On the day I saw him waiting for Kinnear he was in something big and black. I don't really know what.'

'Did it never occur to you to go to the police?' Naomi asked.

Marcus shook his head vehemently. 'No,' he said. 'No, never. I didn't want to see Rupert's name dragged through the mud. I thought I could get what Kinnear wanted and then he'd go away. You had the house and the money Rupert left so no harm done there. All I had to do was find the records Rupert had kept. Then Kinnear could get at his money. That was what he said and that's all I know.'

'And you knew what the records were?'

'A ledger Rupert kept, something on his laptop and something he had written in his little leather books. I didn't know which ones, he had so many. Kinnear said they would be recent. He had seen one of them but he thought there might be more. He said to be on the safe side I should get them all, but I failed him, didn't I. I tried to take them away when I helped with the search but the boy was always close by and I'd seen him poking around in the study. I knew he'd notice anything missing from the shelf...' Marcus broke off. 'I didn't even know what to look for, I suppose. Not much use at anything, am I?'

'You were unwise, not useless,' Alec said. 'Rupert hid the things Kinnear wanted. I'm not sure why he didn't destroy them altogether, but maybe he didn't have the time. Marcus, had Rupert been unwell in the weeks before he died?'

Marcus nodded. 'He was always short of breath and complained of pains in his chest and arms. I believe he had a doctor's appointment just days before he died.'

'I think Rupe knew he didn't have long left,' Alec said.

Patrick stared at the overturned car. A motorist had stopped and was pacing around close by. Patrick shoved his poker into the hedge before the motorist should happen to see it. He thought it might take a bit of explaining.

'Did you come from the house back there?'

Harry nodded. 'We've called the police. We, er, heard the crash.'

'Right. Joyriders most likely. We've started to get a few of the buggers round here. I just came round the bend and nearly hit it. Thought I'd better stop back there and get the hazards on. I've called the police too.'

'Joyriders?' Harry questioned. 'Why?'

The motorist shrugged. 'Obvious, isn't it? The driver's done a runner. No, he and his mates'll be long gone across the field. Probably spend the evening boasting about it in some pub or other.'

In the distance Harry could hear sirens.

'Sounds like the police,' he said.

Patrick bent down and peered inside. The car had ended up on its roof, half in and half out of a ditch and wedged beneath the hedge. The window was open, not broken in the crash, so most likely had been open when the vehicle was being driven. The man who had chased Marcus must have climbed out through there. There was blood on the door, Patrick noted. Part of a handprint and crushed grass where he had fallen as he clambered out. The hedge behind was thick and thorny, but he remembered there being a gate just a little further along the road.

'He was hurt,' he told Harry as he went back to rejoin him, the police car had arrived now. 'There's blood on the door.'

Harry nodded. 'Then I don't imagine he's gone far,' he said. 'The police should find him soon.'

Thirty

The hammering on the kitchen door startled Alec. He made his way warily through to the kitchen and then, hearing a young voice, he unlocked the door. 'Danny, I presume? What on earth?'

'He came to the farm. I saw him. I saw him talking to my mum and there was another bloke with him. I saw them. I'd forgot, then I saw the picture and I remembered.'

He was waving a copy of the local paper at Alec. Kinnear's picture stared out from the front page.

'Me dad gets the paper every day. He ain't there right now. I saw this, saw his picture.'

'You're certain? Oh, of course you are.' Alec relocked the door. 'Come on in, it's all getting a bit dramatic. I'm Alec, by the way. Danny, where's your dad now, do you know?'

Danny shrugged and shook his head. 'Always off somewhere,' he said. 'I fed the stock, watered it. I've not seen him this morning.'

Alec thought of Ellen March but said

nothing. He led Danny through to the front living room and directed him to a seat. 'You've met Marcus?'

Danny nodded. 'He runs the antique shop where Rupert ... Mr Friedman worked. Where's Patrick? Why is there a car crashed into your porch?'

'Patrick and Harry are down the road, they'll be back very soon.' The sound of sirens broke into the conversation and Danny leapt up and went to look out of the window.

'Police cars? What's happened, Alec?'

Alec's mobile phone rang. It was Patrick.

Naomi told Danny what had been going on.

'Chased him from the shop?' she could hear the awe in his voice. 'Shit! Sorry.'

'No, I think the bad language is quite appropriate,' Marcus said with dignity. 'That is precisely the way I feel.'

'Patrick says Fine's arrived and is coming up with them. The scene's been secured and SOCO called. There's nothing more he can do until it's released to him so he's going to come and talk to us.'

'What does all that mean?' Danny asked.

'It means they've found the car that hit Marcus?' Naomi asked.

'On its side in the ditch. No sign of the driver.'

'The uniformed officer will have to make sure the scene is secured, that means no one can go into it. They'll lay a single path that everyone has to follow, then the crime scene officers will come in and do their stuff. Then DS Fine will be allowed back and he'll be told what's been found so far,' Naomi explained. 'Alec, any idea what condition the driver might be in?'

'Patrick says there was blood, but he's nowhere close so ... hard to tell. Danny, you say Kinnear came to the farm. Do you remember when?'

The boy shook his head. 'Couple of weeks back.'

'Before or after Rupert died. Do you remember?'

He thought about it. 'Must have been before,' he said finally. 'The other man gave my mum a lift home and she said he was a friend she had met at this meeting with Mr Friedman.'

'She hadn't driven herself.'

'Can't have done if he gave her a lift home,' Danny said reasonably. 'I don't know why. Anyway, they were standing talking and this other man came up. He just drove into the yard like and the dark-haired man took one look and said he'd better go. Mam didn't say anything, but I could tell she didn't like him much. Then a few days after he came to see my dad. I was in the barn and I stayed up there. They were arguing. I could see that, but I don't know what about, except me dad and mam were in a fight later about her having her ... friends come to the farm.'

'Friends?'

Danny shrugged uncomfortably. 'Dad called him her fancy man. But mam would never do anything with someone like him. Never.'

'Danny, this is a difficult question, but the other man, the one your mum said was a friend. Did you get the impression that he was more than that? Or that she'd known him long?'

Danny stared hard at him, his body stiff and unease showing in the set of his shoulders. Finally, he shrugged. 'I dunno,' he said. 'I dunno what she was doing. What's the use in asking me?'

Fine announced that he would walk back up to Fallowfields and left his car parked on the verge at the end of their driveway. He raised an eyebrow as Patrick retrieved his poker from the hedge.

'I thought we should be prepared,' Patrick said. 'But I'd better not leave it there now, someone might think it's part of the crime scene.'

Fine laughed. 'It might muddy the waters,'

he agreed. 'I'm relieved you didn't have cause to use it. I might have been arresting you too.'

Patrick shrugged. 'You think he'd have gone far? You know who he is?'

'Well, the descriptions point to it being Derek Reid,' he said. 'He was always top of our list. Funny though, he has no real history of violence. This seems out of character, at least from what I've seen of his sheet.'

'Fear can make people behave in some very odd ways,' Harry commented.

'True. Is Marcus up to being questioned?'

'Provided Naomi didn't give him any more brandy. By the time we left he was calming down somewhat. I imagine Alec and Naomi will have got his story from him anyway.'

Derek Reid was lost. His one thought had been to get away from the scene. His neck hurt and his head throbbed where he'd cracked it on the steering wheel. The seat belt had dug deep into his ribs when he had been thrown forward and he'd managed to crack his head a second time on something when the car rolled. He'd hit the back end of Marcus's car at an angle, his speed and the angle causing the passenger side to lift and he had flipped, then rolled, ended up on his side confused and shaken and hurting like hell.

He did not recall getting out of the car but did know that he had not had the strength to climb over the gate. Unable to open it, he had slithered beneath on his belly and then stumbled across the cow-churned field as fast as his shaking legs could take him, his one thought that he should get away.

Now, two fields or three fields over and disorientated, he wondered what to do. The day was warm and there were no cows here to snuffle in that curious way they had. Instead he lay at the edge of a field of wheat or barley, he didn't know which but had the vague memory that he had once known the difference. He lay down on the swathe of uncut grass at the field edge and listened to his body complain.

'God, Derek, your dad was right,' he told himself. 'Can't get a bloody thing right. Not ever.'

Except Sharon, he thought. Sharon was right. He'd known that from the start.

Thinking about her gave him the strength to get up and he felt in his trouser pockets for his phone only to realize that it was in his jacket and his jacket was still in the car.

Groaning in despair and disbelief he remembered that it had been cool first thing and he'd slipped his jacket on when he'd gone shopping for Kinnear. A further search of his trouser pockets informed him that all he had in the world was a handful of change and a crumpled five-pound note.

His dad had been right, he thought again. Never could do a damn thing right. It did not seem in the least bit strange that here he was, a man in his early thirties still stung by the words of someone who had disappeared from his life when Derek had still been in his teens.

'Can't do a bloody thing right. Bloody waste of skin.'

Derek sighed and considered the irony that he was in this situation precisely because for once in his life he had tried to do the right thing. Driving away from Kinnear that morning, Sam's words still burning in his ears, he'd finally realized that he was in a no-win situation. Kinnear would use him and then scrape him off like shit on the bottom of his shoe. Kinnear had no intention of giving Derek a share of what he saw as his. Sam Kinnear had waited too long and fomented so much greed in that waiting time that he wasn't about to share any of his spoils now.

He remembered Kinnear talking to him in prison. One long night when Sam had been in a conversational mood, and when Sam wanted to talk you had no choice but to listen. He had talked about this man, this driver, this Sam Spade, and how he knew he had the proceeds from those first two jobs. Derek had laughed. Laughed at Kinnear.

Spitting blood through the split lip Kinnear had awarded him as prize for his humour, Derek had explained that Sam Spade was a fiction. A made-up name. No one would call their kid Sam Spade.

So Derek had decided when he had left Kinnear that morning that he would, for once, try to do the sensible thing. He would talk to Marcus and together they could concoct some story. Blackmail would probably fit the bill, he thought. Go to the police and tell them Kinnear was blackmailing them. It was close enough to the truth to be almost real and, if forced, Derek was now even willing to come clean. Tell the whole truth and nothing but. Do time if he had to. He'd managed before and though his heart sank at the thought of it, he could hack it again if he was forced.

But it seemed that his father's damnation of him had to thwart even his best intentions. Marcus had seen him and taken off like a scared rabbit and Derek knew that his chance was gone.

He wasn't sure why he'd tried to run Marcus off the road but he'd sort of figured it might be the only way to get to talk to him, convince him to go along with his scheme. Failing that he would have dragged Marcus's sorry ass back to Kinnear and looked for another way out, but it was all too late for that now.

Five pounds and a handful of change. Derek started to laugh it was all so bloody stupid. He choked the laughter back; it hurt too much. Would Sharon want him now? Now he wasn't about to inherit part of Rupert Friedman's illicit wealth?

Well, he figured, if he could ever find his way out of this damned field and back to the hotel where she was staying he might ask her. But not just now.

Derek shifted position finding the deepest grass and closed his eyes. He had not felt so bone weary in the longest time. Too bone weary even to despair.

With the sun on his face, Derek Reid slept while just two fields away they searched for signs of where he might have gone.

Back at the crash site, the crime scene officer had managed to open the door. The contents of the glove compartment, Reid's jacket and the assorted debris from the door pockets and floor had settled on the roof.

Pictures had been taken and now he was bagging and tagging everything. No telling what might later be of use. The phone rang and he paused in his methodical search to retrieve it. He straightened up, phone in his gloved hand and waved it at the officer in charge. 'Should I answer it?'

'Is there a name?'

'It says Kinnear.'

'It what? Bloody hell. Yes.'

The SOCO pressed the key to accept the call and listened.

'Where the hell are you? I told you to get back here. You listening to me?'

The SOCO covered the mouthpiece. 'What the hell do I say?' he whispered.

'You listening to me?' Kinnear's voice again. 'Who's there?' Silence.

'He's rung off.'

'Never mind. Bag it and give it here.'

He took the wrapped phone from the SOCO and shook his head in disbelief. 'He put Kinnear's name in his directory,' he said. 'What a wally.'

The SOCO shrugged. 'Lucky break,' he said.

Sam Kinnear stared at his mobile phone and then dropped it on the bed in disgust. He did not know who had answered the phone but it had not been Derek Reid, that was for sure. He was surprised that no one had spoken. Had it been the police, would they not have announced themselves? Whatever, it seemed to Kinnear that this was not good, that it was a warning, that he should clear out while he still could.

A warning too that Derek was out of the reckoning.

Kinnear always travelled light and it took only minutes to shove his clothes back into his pack and select what food did not need cooking. Bread and beans and cheese and ham went into his bag. He had no objection to cold baked beans. Water. Derek had been bringing the bottled stuff.

Finally he reached beneath the bed and took out a fabric bundle. The gun was cleaned and oiled and he had two full clips to go with it. That, he figured, should be enough. He wasn't aiming to have to shoot his way out of anywhere but always best to be prepared.

A last look around to check for anything he'd missed and then Kinnear was gone. Retrieving his car from below in the rundown barn. He knew where he would go. He figured he had one last chance to get what he was owed and, risky as that might be, he had come too far and wasn't about to walk away.

Thirty-One

Elaine Ritchie held the door open halfway and leaned against the frame. She examined Billy Pierce carefully, methodically.

He stood still and waited for her to finish.

She had changed, of course. It had been twenty-five years or more since he had last seen her, sitting in the public gallery as Sam Kinnear was sentenced.

There had been no jubilation that day and that was one of the things he had always remembered about her. Usually the victim's relatives who came to see the sentencing reacted in some way: relief, joy, tears; but with her there had been nothing like that. Elaine Ritchie had listened as the court sentenced her husband's killer and then she had got up and quietly left the gallery. No fuss, no sound, not even a change of expression, and it was that same expression he remembered now. That quiet examination, but beyond that there was nothing he could read.

'I said I'd come to talk to you about Rupert

Friedman,' he said. 'You don't seem surprised.'

She didn't respond to his question. Instead she said, 'You were the copper that nicked Kinnear.'

'One of them, yes.'

'I remember you. You've got old.'

'I'm retired now.'

'So...'

'I'm doing a favour for a friend.' He didn't think Alec would mind the appropriation. It was something he hoped would become fact anyway. He liked Alec Friedman.

'A friend? What kind of favour?'

'Rupert's nephew. There are questions surrounding Rupert's death that need clearing up.'

For the first time concern rather than academic curiosity showed in the woman's eyes. Her eyes were almost green and her hair still quite blonde though he thought that these days it probably had a little help.

'He had a heart attack. His solicitor called me.'

'That's correct, but, well ... May I come in?'

She thought about it and then finally stood aside and let him through. The door opened straight into the living room. It was at the front of the house and the large bay he had seen from outside added unexpected space.

A sofa, overloaded with bright cushions, had been set there, separate from the rest of the room in which the furniture circled around the twin foci of gas fire and television.

A small shelf of books settled in the space between the sofa and the wall on one side and a tiny table – he thought of Victorian plant stands – squeezed into the gap at the other end. He could see a mug had been set down there when he had knocked at her door. Steam rose, carrying the scent of coffee.

She saw him looking. 'Do you want one?'

'Thanks.' He was already sloshing from too much tea drunk in the little café, but making him a drink would help to break the ice and give him a better chance to look around.

The kitchen was small, but very clean, leading off the living room and visible in its entirety from where he stood. Two closed doors he guessed led to bedroom and bathroom.

'Sugar?'

'Two, please. This is a nice flat.'

She handed him the coffee. 'Yes. And now it's mine.'

'Rupert left it to you?'

She nodded. 'There was some weird thing in the will,' she added. 'His nephew wasn't to be told. He was getting the rest but this was a separate thing.' She looked worried. 'Does that mean he's a greedy bastard and might want it back?'

Billy Pierce smiled and shook his head. 'He's already guessed most of this,' he said. 'Alec feels he's already been given more than he could ever have expected.'

She wriggled her shoulders and crossed the room to retrieve her coffee. 'Well, that's all right then. Rupert always said this was my place. Rupert was good to us. All the way through he was good to us.'

'Us?'

She indicted that he should sit down and he chose the chair closest to the television. She took the one opposite.

'I have kids. Two of them. This flat was too cramped, really. I slept out here for years and they had the bedroom. But it was somewhere safe after ... after Fred was killed.'

'You rented from Rupert?'

'Rented,' she laughed. 'I paid a pittance to him but I made sure I always paid.'

'How did you meet?'

Elaine sipped her coffee and considered her response. Billy understood that he was going to get the expurgated version. He figured it would probably be enough.

'After Fred died, Rupert turned up on my doorstep one day. Not here, of course, in the dump of a place we'd had to move to. Fred left us with nothing and the police were all over it. They thought he might have been in on it.'

'Did you think he was?'

She shrugged. 'I was never sure. We were flat broke, two kids, and his job barely covered the rent and heat. I worked behind a bar five nights a week while he minded the kids. It got so we passed in the hall. Anyway, we were broke and Christmas was coming and if he thought he could have got away with it ... I suspected he might have passed on some information. Times they were due to do the pick up, that sort of thing. I was never sure and I never said. I figured he'd more than paid his dues and I wasn't going to let his kids think he was anything but what he'd always been to them. A decent man and a good dad.'

'And Rupert?'

'Turned up on the doorstep. Said he'd been trying to track me down, that Fred had set up a life insurance and we were the beneficiaries. Rupert said he'd sold it to him.'

'You knew he was lying?'

She shrugged. 'Of course I did. Fred didn't have two pennies to rub together, never mind cash to pay monthly for some policy he'd never have thought he might need. And Rupert as an insurance salesman? Pull the other one. But, he had all the paperwork and a big fat cheque and the promise of a monthly amount which would pay the rent and a good bit more and ... so I chose to believe him.'

'Rupert knew you doubted?'

She smiled. 'Rupert knew, but we never broke our cover story. Not ever. Not even when we became friends. He was always the man who'd sold Fred the policy and I was always content to just let it ride.'

'Did you ever wonder where the money came from?'

She was back into study mode now, examining him over the rim of her mug as she sipped her coffee.

'Elaine, this is off the record. I have no authority to ask you now. If anyone asks me, I'll keep your cover story going.'

She nodded slowly. 'I wondered,' she said, 'but I didn't want to know. I had kids to raise and the money helped but it was still hard. Occasionally I wondered if it might be from the robberies. I knew the money had never been recovered but, then again, I figured we were owed.'

'And did you never wonder why Rupert had offered help? Did that not strike you as odd?'

She looked away and he knew that she had wondered many times. Perhaps she even knew. 'He was an insurance salesman,' she said at last. 'I kept all the policy documents he gave me, all the insurance stuff he said I should hang on to. It has my husband's name, his signature, it's dated from six months before he died, that's all I've ever needed to know.'

'Rupert was a clever man. When did you move in here?'

'About two, three years after Fred died. The place we were in was damp and Vicky, our eldest, had asthma. Rupert said he was moving away but didn't want to sell the flat. He thought it might be a good investment in years to come. It was a bit small but, like I said, the girls slept through there and I had a sofa bed in here. It was warm and dry and the rent was so low I don't know why he bothered.' She smiled for the first time. 'He'd taken to visiting us, once a month, the Tuesday closest to the fourth of the month. He carried on after he moved. He'd meet me for coffee somewhere.'

'He didn't come here?'

She shook her head. 'No.'

'And you continued to meet?'

'Right up 'til the month he died. We'd meet in different places. He'd suggest somewhere and we'd both take the train. Have lunch, maybe go to the pictures. No strings, no romance, just two friends.'

'Never any romance?'

She shook her head. 'No, I'd have liked ...

I mean it wasn't that I didn't think about it but, I got the impression there was someone else but that maybe she was married. No woman wants to play second fiddle, you know.'

'I know. Elaine, did Sam Kinnear contact you?'

She scowled, her expression hardening and taking away the residual prettiness. 'That bastard,' she said. 'Turned up one day, asking questions. He didn't come here, he went to my daughter Vicky's place. God knows how he found her.'

'Ritchie isn't a common name. Is she married?'

'No. He started sniffing round, asking about Rupert, demanding she tell him. Her boyfriend came home and they called the police. He cleared off but they'd let slip one or two things.'

'Such as?'

'She wasn't sure, he got her flustered and upset. She thinks she told him Rupert was in the antiques business and it was somewhere up north.'

'How long ago was this?'

'Eighteen months. Sometime around that. I told Rupert when he phoned to arrange our meeting and he said not to worry and he was sorry Vicky had been upset.'

'Vicky didn't tell him where Rupert lived?'

She shook her head. 'She couldn't, she didn't know. Neither did I. You see it was the one thing Rupert was particular about. I paid the rent when I saw him each month and he'd tell me bits and pieces about his business, but he said Kinnear would come looking for him one day and he didn't want me to have to lie. I suppose he realized I wasn't strong enough, not to stand up to someone like Kinnear.'

'He knew Kinnear would come looking?'

She nodded. 'I suppose that's really how I knew,' she said. 'How I really worked it out, but I knew him by then and I knew he'd never have had anything to do with the guns or with Fred dying, so I just forgot I knew.'

'You knew what?'

'That Rupert must have been involved,' she said.

Thirty-Two

By the time he awoke it was late afternoon, the sun had dropped below the level of the hedges and, though it was still warm, Derek Reid shivered.

The headache was worse, a cracking feeling running from his temples through to the back of his neck. His shoulders had stiffened and he recognized the effects of whiplash. This added to his general misery and disorientation.

He did not know which way to go. Back towards the car was out. The police would be waiting for him, wouldn't they? He found it hard to remember why, but he knew that way was danger. So, he plodded on, circling the field, searching for a way out. A gap in the hedge gave access into the next field and he plodded on, grateful that here the massive open, fenland fields had given way to a smaller patchwork.

Twice he stumbled. His ribs hurt now and he found it hard to draw breath and it was getting cold. At first he thought it was just imagination or shock or confusion, but as he glanced upward, attracted by the sudden darkening of the blue sky to charcoal grey, he understood that it was not his imagination. It was rain, collecting in the heavy clouds, rolling in from the coast and getting ready to fall.

On him.

To his relief Derek spied a gate and beyond that a road. A car sped by, its driver no doubt wanting to be home before the promised storm began. He grasped the gate with both hands and tried to climb. It moved beneath his weight and he noticed, much to his relief, that this gate was not locked and chained, merely held closed by a loop of orange twine. Derek pulled it free and staggered through, wincing at the effort it took to close the gate behind him and loop the twine back into place.

He needed a lift. Needed to get somewhere. To Sharon. Yes, that's where he wanted to go.

He heard the car before he saw it and ran out into the middle of the road hoping to wave it down, his feet disobedient to the wishes of his brain and legs. He fell, heard the brakes squeal as the driver slammed them on. Heard footsteps and voices raised in anger and concern.

'Sharon,' he whispered as someone bent

down beside him. 'Need to get to Sharon.'

Back at Fallowfields Billy Pierce had phoned and told Alec about Elaine.

'That fills in so many gaps,' Alec said. 'Billy, tell her we'll keep her out of this if we possibly can.'

'Will do. So, what's happening with you?'

Alec told him about Marcus and Kinnear and Reid and the dramatic chase that had nearly lost him a porch.

'So, we've got a police car parked up on the drive for now, but Fine doesn't have the resources to keep it there for long. I think the best we can do is move back to the hotel tomorrow. We might even head for home.'

'You think Kinnear will have given up and gone away? That doesn't sound like him.'

'Truth? I don't know what to think but I've got people to think about and responsibilities. Kinnear must realize that someone other than Derek Reid now has his phone. I can't believe he listed him by name, that's just too—'

'Human? I don't suppose he even thought about it. Be interesting to know what else he's got in that phone. Hopefully your friend Fine will be able to enlighten you. Right, I think that's all from my end for now. Elaine's got my number in case she remembers anything else. I've told her to give me a call.'

Alec thanked him and went back to fill the others in about what he had said.

'So, we still don't know exactly how Kinnear found Rupert,' Naomi said thoughtfully.

'But once Elaine's daughter had told him north and antiques he was halfway there. Not knowing Rupert's real name must have been the biggest difficulty. Once he had that, he just had to look up north for an antiques dealer called Friedman. It's not a common name and not a particularly common occupation.'

Alec nodded. Harry was right about that. Whatever else Kinnear was, he was persistent and determined and that made Alec feel that Pierce was right.

'He hasn't gone far,' he said thoughtfully. 'I'll bet on it. He'll either dispose of his phone or leave it switched off so he can't be traced, but he won't have gone away.'

Marcus shifted restlessly in his seat. It had been decided that he should stay the night. He felt safer in company than he did about going back to the shop. 'I hope you're wrong, Alec. I truly do. I know it sounds cowardly, but I just want him gone.'

Alec was right when he said Kinnear would not have gone far. He was in fact much closer than they realized.

He had driven his car to within a mile of White Farm, parked in a small copse of trees he had used before when he had gone to the farm, and walked the rest of the way, cutting across the fields on the opposite side of the road to the direction taken by Derek Reid when he had abandoned his crashed car.

Once behind the farm he had watched and waited. He'd seen the boy come round the back of the house and go in through the front door, heard him calling out to his father and get no response.

Satisfied that only Danny was there, Kinnear pushed through the low hedge behind the barn. It was dusk by the time he cracked open the small door set into the larger wooden ones and entered the dark and musty space beyond. He stood for a while, allowing his eyes to adjust to the dimness, the only light fighting its way in through filthy windows set high up on the wall. He had a small torch on his key ring and he risked flashing it once just to get his bearings, decided he'd be best up on the platform he spied that formed a sort of mezzanine floor.

A ladder led him up on to the platform once intended for the storage of hay but now empty but for the junk they had no use for but could not bear to throw away. Empty feed sacks, rope and twine and boxes filled with general household junk. Bags whose logos declared they were destined for charity but which had gone uncollected or un-delivered. A cardboard box filled with empty jars and, when he risked a second brief flash of his tiny light, topped with an abandoned recipe for damson jam.

Kinnear snorted. He couldn't see Sharon Fielding making any sort of jam. She wasn't the homemade jam type. She was the 'grab it while it's offered and the more the better' type and no doubt Derek would find that out for himself now he'd lost the chance of his share of the cash.

Not that Kinnear had ever had the inten-tion of sharing anything. It was his money. No one else was getting a look in. Agreed, Derek had been useful doing the research that had led him to Friedman's real name. Derek's search through the news reports had turned up a picture of a so-called witness, and guess who it had been? Kinnear had to admit that brain occasionally had its uses over brawn.

A small window at the end of the gable gave him a view on to a section of the yard and out on to the field beyond. Not quite what he wanted but a quick flash of the torch reinforced his guess that this was the best he could do.

Kinnear dumped his pack and his water. The gun weighed down his pocket and the spare clip offered some kind of balance on the other. He took out the clothing and bits of bedding packed up for the charities that never got them and he made himself a rough bed beneath the window, then settled down, knowing that no more could be achieved that night. The police would be all over Fallowfields. Kinnear was good at playing the waiting game. He was aware he had a reputation for impatience, for having a short fuse, but he could think of no one else he knew who would have kept it up as long as he had, this search for the bastard who'd done him out of his money and worse, who'd tried to make a fool out of him.

He had waited this long. He could afford to wait another day.

Thirty-Three

Kinnear's phone was off and likely to remain so but DS Fine had been working his way through the list of numbers in Reid's mobile. By rights he should have got on to this a while ago, he thought, but it had gone off to be printed and the SIM card backed up – a precaution against ham-fisted DSs like himself accidentally deleting the very information he needed to recover.

Now he had it back, and the prints had confirmed the identity of the owner as one Derek Reid, Fine was happy to be getting on with the task in hand, particularly as he had now been told that Mr Reid had just been picked up and taken into hospital, apparently in a pretty bad way. Fine wasn't going to be able to talk to him until the medics said so and from the sound of things that wasn't going to be soon. Fine was preparing for a very late night.

In fact Derek Reid's phone was a little disappointing. Either Reid had very few friends or he had bought the mobile recently. I mean, Fine thought, who has the local takeaway on speed dial.

Wan's Kitchen was one of only five entries. Kinnear of course, someone called Bee who was unavailable, a taxi company and Sharon.

That one caused Fine to pause. Danny had said Reid and Kinnear had been to the farm. It was too much to be a coincidence.

Fine pressed the button and called. Sharon Fielding picked up on the second ring. 'Derek? Where the hell have you been. I've been waiting to hear from you since last night.'

'Mrs Fielding. No, please don't hang up,

301

this is DS Fine. Derek's been hurt.'

'Hurt? Oh my God, what did that effing animal do to him?'

He guessed she must mean Kinnear. No one, Fine reflected, had much of an opinion of Sam Kinnear.

'He was involved in a car accident, Mrs Fielding.'

'A car accident?'

'Yes. Now, Mrs Fielding, I'd like you to tell me where you are.'

'Why?'

'Two reasons. One, I'd like to take you to see Mr Reid. The other is that there's reason to believe Sam Kinnear is on the move. He thinks Derek's let him down. I suspect he may think you had something to do with it.'

Well, he reflected, what was a white lie between friends. It was the kind of lie that might reveal how much she knew about Kinnear, if nothing else.

It appeared she might know quite a lot because he had the address of the hotel within the next breath. That and an appeal for someone to come and get her. Now.

Fine told her he was on his way. At least, he thought, he'd be able to tell Danny that his mother wasn't dead. Not totally dead, he amended, just dead from the neck up.

Sharon Fielding was in the lobby with her

bag on the floor at her feet when he arrived. She looked scared, Fine thought. Scared and tired as though she'd not been sleeping. He found himself hoping this was the case. She had cost her young son too many sleepless nights and in Fine's book that was stepping way beyond the line.

A female officer was waiting for them in the car. Fine asked her to drive and then seated Sharon in the back.

'You've got your mobile on you?'

'Yes.'

'Then phone Danny. Do it now. Do you have any idea what you've put that boy through?'

'Danny?' she sounded puzzled.

'Danny. Your son.'

'I know who he is.'

'Really? He's not so sure.'

'I left him a letter. I left it on the kitchen table, a letter explaining where I'd gone and why. It's Danny hasn't tried to contact me.'

'I don't think he got your letter,' Fine told her.

'That bastard. His dad must have got to it first. But he could have called my mobile?'

'Could he? Does he have the number?'

''Course he does, he ... God, no, he doesn't. The phone. I left mine so *he* couldn't call me.'

'Your husband?'

'Yes. Him. This is new, Derek got me it. He had one the same.' She took her mobile from her bag and weighed it in her hand as though really thinking about it for the first time. 'God, I'm stupid. I should have guessed he'd hide the letter.'

'Call him now.'

Fine watched as she dialled White Farm. 'If *he* picks up I'm hanging up.'

'Don't you have the number to Danny's phone?'

'Not in this one. I don't have jinx.' She listened. Fine could almost hear her holding her breath. Someone picked up.

'Danny? Oh Danny love, are you OK?'

'Mum? Mum, where are you? I thought you were dead. Are you coming home?'

'Dead? Why on earth? Oh Danny...'

Danny Fielding cradled the phone close to his ear. He could hardly believe it. She was OK, she was talking to him. It was going to be all right. He saw his dad come through and stand in the kitchen doorway. He was scowling, glowering at the phone. Danny held it closer, afraid he might snatch it away.

'Why didn't you call me? Why didn't you ... what letter? No, I never got it. Oh, mam, when are you coming home?'

'I don't know yet love, I've got to talk to the police before I do anything else.'

'The police? Why?' He could hear it in her voice. That was just a delaying tactic. The truth was she wasn't coming back. He had known it all along but...

'This is because of that man, isn't it? Isn't it?'

'Danny, it isn't like that. Danny, you've got to let me explain.'

But for Danny there was nothing to explain. He could not put into words how deep the sense of betrayal or by whom he felt the most betrayed. His mother who was leaving him or his dad who had lied about knowing, who had told him she had left no goodbyes.

Unable to bear any more, he lowered the phone and turned to face his father.

'She said she left a note.'

His father glared at him, then turned away and picked up his jacket from the back of the kitchen chair. He strode past Danny, down the hall, out to the car, and drove away.

Danny was once again alone.

From his window in the barn, Kinnear watched Danny's father go.

'He hung up on me.' Sharon was shocked. Horrified.

'Can you blame him?'

She shook her head.

'You've made a right pig's ear of things, lass. It'll take more sorting out than a single phone call.'

305

Thirty-Four

Sharon stared through the glass panel in the door. 'Oh my god, what happened to him?'

'The car rolled. He walked away but by rights he should have stayed put and had himself hauled off to the hospital like a sensible boy.'

'But how, was he driving too fast? Derek didn't drive fast. He was careful, cautious even.'

'We don't know everything. The doc hasn't let me talk to him yet, but we know he was chasing after Marcus Prescott. We know he rammed Prescott's car and we think he flipped when he crashed into his back end. The details we'll have to discuss with Derek here when he wakes up.'

'Chasing Marcus Prescott? I don't understand.'

'Kinnear,' Fine said. 'We assume he was following orders from Kinnear.'

'Him. I told Derek he should just walk away but no, he said. He was going to come into money if he stuck with Kinnear. We could go off somewhere, start again.'

'And you believed him?'

She looked sharply at Fine. 'Yeah,' she said softly. 'I believed him, but you know what, after a little while it didn't matter any more.'

'And you two met, where?'

'Oh, one of Rupert's little get-togethers. He liked his storytellers to get to know one another. Thought if we exchanged information we might remember more. Oral history, he called it.' She shrugged. 'Actually, I liked old Rupert. He was one of the good guys. Kind, considerate, good listener.'

'And Derek came along to one of these meetings?'

'At the library, yes. We called ourselves a study group but ... well, we'd have a good gossip, talk about Rupert's latest bit of writing and then all go off to the pub. Mostly it was the same crowd but Derek turned up one night out of the blue and I fell. Big time. He was charming, curious, talkative and shy, all at the same time.'

'Sounds like a contradiction.'

'Yeah, well. Will he be OK?'

'We hope so, yes. Your son tells me Kinnear came to the farm.'

She nodded. 'Yeah.'

'And did you have much to do with him?'

'Too much. Look, it was obvious from the

start Derek didn't know anything about local history. He claimed his family came from round here and he wanted to find out more about his past. Their past. Rupert didn't care and like I said it was more a social club anyway. But after a while, when we got more involved and I'd seen him hanging round with Sam Kinnear, he told me Kinnear was after something Rupert had. Something Kinnear thought that he was owed. He was scared of the man, too scared to tell me any more but one day when he was with me Kinnear phoned him. He wasn't supposed to be with me but if he'd taken me home I guess he'd have been late answering his master's call so he took me along. Not inside though, made me wait in the car and lie down on the back seat so Kinnear didn't see but I knew where I was.'

'You can take me there?'

She nodded. 'I think so. It's an old farm, deserted. There's a few places round here just left to go to rack and ruin. The big companies take them over, use the land, leave perfectly good homes to fall down when there's local kids crying out for cheap housing.'

Fine nodded. He knew. 'But you can take me there?'

'Yeah. Look, I need to talk to Danny, when can I go home?'

'Tomorrow. Not tonight. The last thing your boy needs is his mum and dad rowing over him again tonight. Tomorrow I'll arrange a meet, maybe at Fallowfields. He's got friends there.'

'You can't stop me going home.'

'No, I can't but just now you're going to take me to where Kinnear was holed up. You've not seen him for this long, best make a fresh start tomorrow, eh?'

She nodded slowly. 'Friends at Fallowfields?'

'The new owner, Alec Friedman, he's got some friends staying. Patrick is just a bit older than Danny. They've hit it off.'

'I'm glad,' she said. 'He never seems to have that many friends.'

She was fairly sure where the farm was but in the dark they made a couple of false turns which meant Fine's car and the patrol cars that followed had to carry out some awkward manoeuvres on the narrow roads.

The farm had once been called The Ash Trees, or so the sign on the sagging gate claimed. Fine thought it was one of those owned by a big frozen food corporation but he couldn't be sure. The dark and the twists and turns had lost him too and he was glad of his GPS which would at least be able to guide him home when he told it to.

The farm buildings were not in bad shape, he thought, or as far as he could tell in the light of his torch. The door was open, though not wide. He looked around, noting the outbuildings and rusting machinery, the muddied yard with the remnants of cobbles in front of the farmhouse door. They kept well back, vehicles pulling up on the road at the end of the drive. Once out of their cars, they all crouched in the shadows behind the engine block, although that still felt too exposed. Fine worried that he was still in there – for all that seemed unlikely. That he might be armed.

He signalled for the armed support unit to move in, content to let them do their own thing. They would search, make everything secure. He heard their commander calling out 'armed police' and instructing anyone inside to come out with their hands raised.

Nothing moved. Kinnear was gone, Fine was sure. All around them country silence reigned. Even the birds had shut up for the night and the faint rustlings in the undergrowth that Fine had been aware of when they first got out of the car had ceased as well.

'Where was Kinnear holed up?'

Sharon pointed to one of the outbuildings. 'In there. Derek said the owners started a conversion, ran out of money, then they sold up and moved on.'

'So he knew something about this place. Did he know the owners?'

She shrugged. 'Maybe Rupert did. Rupert knew everyone. He might have mentioned it. They talked a lot about lost villages, the death of communities, that sort of political stuff. Round here Rupert was all het up about drainage or something.'

'You mean way back when?'

She shook her head. 'No, something about the water table. There was a report or some such a couple of years ago. I didn't take much notice. Sorry.'

Fine nodded, he vaguely recalled it. There was some big debate about the extensions of the Peatlands trails and draining of what was left of the fenland. Worries too that peat ex-traction would lead to the flooding of farm-land. Fine was familiar with the anxieties.

He watched as the armed commander pushed the door, then gestured the other officers forward. 'Armed police,' he shouted. 'We're coming in.'

Minutes later and he emerged again, ges-tured that Fine could come inside.

'Long gone,' he said. 'We'll secure the scene and get SOCO in first thing.'

'Not tonight?' Sharon asked

He grimaced. 'SOCO are civilians. Hard to get them out after hours unless it's an emergency. I don't think this qualifies.'

'Not like CSI then.'

'No, not like CSI. Get back in the car. I've arranged a stay at a safe house for you tonight. Tomorrow I'll take you to see Danny.'

It was late by the time Fine got to Fallowfields but everyone was still up.

'We'll be leaving in the morning,' Alec told him. 'Going home, I think. You've enough to do without protecting us.'

Fine nodded. The chair in which he sat was comfortable and he could easily drop off to sleep. 'At least Danny's mum's OK. That's one small blessing, though I think it's going to be a long haul making up for all this.'

'When will Reid be fit to talk?'

'Morning, we hope. I've got someone with him all night. Not much more we can do. I just thought I'd bring you up to speed.'

'Appreciate it,' Alec said.

'Oh, and there's one more thing. The laptop and the books. I think we can safely consider them evidence now. I should take them away.'

'Welcome,' Alec said. 'Patrick, will you do the honours?'

Fine bagged the books and laptop. 'I'll get these checked in tonight, then I'm off to my bed.'

'Sounds good to me,' Alec agreed. 'Reid should be able to give you the info on Kinnear and hopefully the worst is over now.'

'I hope you're right,' Fine said. 'I really do.'

Thirty-Five

Danny had risen early and come downstairs looking for something to eat. No bread, no cereal, no milk to speak of and his father was still absent.

He missed his mother.

He didn't regret hanging up on her the night before. She deserved his punishment, Danny felt, but at the same time he would have welcomed a call from her now, if only so he could hang up again.

He wanted her home, or wanted them both to be somewhere else or ... something. Danny really wasn't sure.

He made some tea, taking the last of the milk and ate dry cereal, wondered if there was any money in the house. If so, he could at least get some shopping done. His dad didn't seem to have thought about that in a while and had been impatient when Danny

313

pointed it out to him.

He found a five-pound note and some pound coins in the biscuit jar, a place his mother regularly kept a spare bit of cash for emergencies, and another ten in his dad's best jacket. Danny felt no qualms going through his parents' things like this. He felt they'd both let him down so far and now it was up to him to manage any way he could.

He didn't want to stay here any more.

Danny went back into the kitchen and stared hard at the phone, willing it to ring. It was only just after eight and he'd already been up since six. He wasn't sure what time they'd all wake up at Fallowfields. He thought about calling his aunt. She had invited him to stay when his mum had left. He liked his auntie Paula but wasn't sure if he could face the questions and the pity and the sharing a room with his cousin.

He wanted his dad to come back or his mum to call.

'Fat chance,' he muttered and turned his back on the offending telephone.

His mobile did ring though a few moments later. He grabbed it, read the name on the display. Patrick.

'Yeah?' He sounded too eager, Danny thought. He tried to modify his tone. 'I mean, hi.'

Fine had called, Patrick told him. He'd

asked if Danny's mum could come over to Fallowfields so they could meet on neutral ground. She'd be there about noon but if Danny wanted to come for breakfast to come now, Harry was cooking.

'I'll be there,' Danny told him. He wasn't sure about the meeting with his mother but breakfast sounded good.

He pulled on his shoes and slammed the farmhouse door, only wondering later, as he set off across the field at a steady run, if his father had his keys.

Kinnear heard the door slam and looked down. He saw Danny crossing the yard. Earlier, the boy had gone out to check the feed bins for the cattle. The father had still not returned.

Kinnear had been thinking hard about what his next move might be. He needed to scout the police presence at Fallowfields. They'd be out looking for him, of that he was certain. He wondered what had happened to Derek Reid, not because he felt concern, but because whatever Reid had told the police might direct their next moves and so affect Kinnear's. Puzzled, he saw the boy was heading across the field, not towards the road. He fished in his pack for the binoculars he'd brought with him. Trained them on the running figure of Danny Fielding.

Danny was running towards a gap in the hedge. Looking closer, he glimpsed a second figure waiting by the bit of a fence that blocked the way.

There was only one place the second figure could have come from, wasn't there? It all clicked into place. Danny was headed for Fallowfields, coming in by a back way.

Kinnear restrained his urge to chase after the boy right then and there. No, give them time to get inside. He didn't know if he could be seen from the house should he choose to follow. Take it slow, take it steady.

He packed his belongings back into his pack, undecided if to take it or to leave it in the barn. In the end he hoisted it on to his shoulder and started down the ladder back into the body of the barn. His gun felt heavy in the pocket of his coat and he felt hot, the day already warm, but it was a reassuring weight and the easiest way to carry it. Kinnear was not one to risk shoving a loaded gun into the waistband of his trousers.

Checking for signs that the father might have returned, but finding none, Kinnear strode straight across the yard and behind the house. Once in the field he breathed a little easier. He took his time, following the perimeter of the field, doing his best to ignore the bullocks and avoid their dung. The fence was an easy climb and the overgrown meadow no real obstacle. But then there was the wall.

Kinnear swore. Seven feet tall, he estimated, little in the way of handholds, still fewer places for his booted feet. The gate, when he tried it, was locked. He could kick it down but that would be noisy and he had no way of knowing how far he was from the house. A fair way back, he guessed, seeing as how he had to stand well back, close beside the fence, even to glimpse the roof ... If he could do it without noise then he better had.

Kinnear followed the wall right round, found a possible place to climb where the field curved and a tree branched further into the grassy area in which he stood. He dropped his pack and climbed the tree, edging along the branch. He could now just see over, well enough to get his bearings as regards the garden beyond and the house beyond that.

He sensed movement in what looked like the kitchen and an open door. Kinnear grimaced. He could see, but still needed to get over the wall. He was a heavy man and not the most agile; the branch he sat astride was some five feet off the ground, but it was a lone limb, reaching out with nothing above to grip. Vainly, Kinnear tried to get to his feet, balance on a moving branch that shook beneath his efforts to balance.

Kinnear fell, heavily. He lay, winded, sure he must have been heard.

In the kitchen at Fallowfields, Danny wolfed down his breakfast. Bacon, eggs, sausage. Toast to follow. He hadn't eaten this well in ages. lunch with Patrick and Harry a couple of days before being the last decent thing he'd had.

'You're leaving then?' he asked. Suitcases stood in the hall and Naomi had excused herself to finish off her packing. Napoleon had followed, disliking the upset of people moving around him with big bags. He liked a settled life. She had asked Patrick and Danny to come up when they were done, help her down with her things.

Patrick nodded. 'Sergeant Fine can't promise police cover, Alec's handed over all the evidence we've got on Kinnear and Rupert, but until things are sorted he does not feel he can have anything much to do with Fallowfields. So, we're off home.'

'If your mother agrees, you could come and stay for a while,' Harry offered. 'It is the holidays after all. No school to worry about.'

Danny looked eagerly at Harry, wondering if he meant it.

'I could use the company,' Patrick said. 'If your mum and dad say its OK.'

Danny didn't think they'd have any right to

object, not really. 'Thanks,' he said. 'I'd like that.'

He finished off his tea and stood up. 'Better go and help Naomi,' he said. 'Thanks a lot for breakfast and, you know, everything else.'

Harry nodded. 'You're welcome,' he said.

'I like this place,' Danny said as he and Patrick wandered into the hall.

'Yeah. I could live here, I think.'

'It's a bit out of the way for a townee.'

'I'm not much of a townee,' Patrick said. 'We're right on the edge of town anyway. Where I live you can get down on to the canal and walk right out into the country and the sea's only five minutes the other way. That's the only thing living here. I'd miss the sea. My mum lives near the sea too. In Florida. When I visit my room looks right out on to the ocean.'

'You get on OK with your mum?'

Patrick nodded. 'When mum and dad got divorced I went to live with her. She met my stepdad when she was out there on business. He's OK, got two sons of his own, but I didn't fit in there and I missed my dad and, I don't know, I came home for a trial, just to see how it worked out and I decided to stay. Florida's nice and my mum's family are nice, but it never felt like home.'

Danny shrugged. 'Don't know where I'll

end up,' he said. 'Mum won't come home. Dad is acting strange, like he doesn't belong at the farm any more. You know what I wish? I wish they'd just sell the lot, set up somewhere else and just ... I don't know, make their minds up. It's crap this idea of staying together for the kids. Mam said a couple of years ago that they wouldn't split up 'cos of me. I mean, like that makes me feel better or something.'

Patrick nodded. 'Maybe you need to tell them that,' he said.

Kinnear had found his entry point. It was off towards the road end of the meadow and far too distant from the house for his liking, but there was a place where a stretch of dilapidated-looking fence met the wall. He tested the fence nervously. He was no lightweight. It creaked ominously, but held. Panting with the effort, Kinnear hauled himself up on to the wall and rolled, keeping his body low, then dropped, lowering himself the length of his arms, down on the other side.

Pausing only to check his weapon, Kinnear raced across the lawn and towards the house. He entered through the kitchen door.

Harry and Marcus were clearing away the breakfast things. Marcus was still nervous, still jumpy. He planned, he told Harry, to close the shop for a while and go away. Far away. He had friends in Scotland, surely that was distance enough.

'Depends what you're running from.'

Marcus froze. Harry, turning from the sink found himself facing Sam Kinnear, gun in hand.

Dimly, Harry recognized it as an automatic and some odd bit of his mind suggested that Patrick would know the make and model. It was the sort of oddity that Patrick always knew when they watched films together. But this was not a film.

Marcus had begun to panic. Gibbering wordlessly. Harry shushed him impatiently. 'What do you want?' he asked Kinnear.

'What do you think I want?'

'I wouldn't know.'

'Don't try to be smart,' Kinnear told him. 'Give me what I came for and I'll be out of here. I want the numbers, the accounts. I want the lot, everything he owed me.'

'I don't have them,' Harry said, oddly relieved that he could tell the truth. Harry was never very good with lies. 'The police have everything we found.'

Kinnear laughed out loud. 'Like I believe you.'

'Harry, give him what he wants.'

Harry glanced sideways at Marcus. 'You know I can't do that. Sergeant Fine took the books away last night. You were here, you saw it.'

'But your notes, you must have kept notes. I know you kept notes.' Marcus started to run, he leapt for the kitchen door. Kinnear fired and Marcus went down. Blood poured from his torn calf.

Harry grabbed a towel and made to move towards the fallen man. He could hear footsteps, running down the uncarpeted hall. 'Alec, stay back.'

'And you bloody well stay there.' Kinnear had crossed the space between them and the muzzle of his gun pressed hard against Harry's side.

Alec appeared in the doorway and Kinnear motioned him through. Harry could see Alec cursing himself for running in like a green fool.

The boys and Naomi were still upstairs, Harry thought. He prayed they had heard the shot but would have the sense to stay put.

'You. Who else is here. I know about Danny and there's another one, I saw him. Anyone else?'

'No,' Harry said firmly.

Alec shot him a look, nodded almost imperceptibly.

He hoped fervently that Marcus would not contradict but the man was lying on the floor clutching at his injured leg and seemed not to have even heard.

'You.' Kinnear prodded Harry in the side. 'Tie them up.'

'Marcus is hurt, at least let me help him first.'

'Just do as you're told.'

Having nothing else to hand, Harry tore the tea towels into strips and used them to bind Alec and Marcus's hands and feet to the kitchen chairs. He dare not tie them too loosely, knowing Kinnear would check. He tied another strip around Marcus's bleeding calf, padding it with a towel and hoping that the bleeding would stop. It looked very red, Harry thought. Very red and very painful. He tried to think if there were any major arteries Kinnear might have hit, but he really didn't know. He found himself thinking that Patrick would know that too. Patrick or Naomi.

Harry took a deep breath. He was oddly calm in the face of the gun; less so having witnessed the sheer unpredictability of Kinnear. Last year he and Patrick and Naomi had found themselves caught up in a hostage situation, Harry's first encounter with weapons. He had seen then just what a gun in the hands of a madman could do, but he had faced his fear back then and somehow that fear had diminished.

He was wary, certainly, but as he set about

323

the practical task of binding Marcus's wound and tying his friend's hands and feet he found that his mind was oddly calm. Out of sight of Kinnear, he slid his hand into his trouser pocket and withdrew a small pen-knife, the twin to the one Patrick had given Alec last Christmas. He managed to open the knife, slid it into Alec's hand.

So far no sound of running feet on the stairs, no indication that Naomi and the boys were coming down. Harry held his breath, released it slowly. He straightened.

'What now?'

'You come with me.'

Harry went.

'That was a shot.'

'A what?' Danny stared at her. 'Didn't sound like no shotgun.'

'That's because it wasn't,' she told him. Of course, Danny would be familiar with the sound of shotguns and maybe even rifles. 'That was a pistol, Danny.'

'Kinnear,' Patrick said. Then: 'Dad.'

He was making for the door. Naomi threw herself in the direction of the sound and grabbed at him. 'No, stay up here. In the study. Danny, do you have your phone?'

'Yes, but there's not much credit on it.'

'You don't need it for the nines. Quick now. We've got to contact Fine.'

Patrick led the way and they piled into the study. Naomi locked the door.

'What if he shoots the lock?' Patrick said.

'The desk. Do you think you could move it between you? I can help if you tell me where I'm going.'

'Give it a try.'

The desk was heavy, antique oak. They struggled between them to drag it across the rugs and bare floorboards, hating the noise it made, though Naomi guessed that Kinnear would know where they were anyway. They shoved it hard against the door and then Naomi called the police, telling the controller where she was and what was wrong and to patch her through to Sergeant Fine.

It wasn't easy persuading the woman but Naomi persevered. To her profound relief, Fine's voice was soon on the phone.

'He's here. Downstairs and he's armed. One shot fired. I'm in the study with Patrick and Danny. I don't know what's happening with the others.'

'Hang tight,' Fine said. 'The cavalry's on its way.'

Kinnear forced Harry upstairs. 'Where are they?'

'In the study, I think,' Harry said. 'The door locks, none of the others do.'

'Come on out,' Kinnear yelled through the

door.

'Danny, Patrick? Are the two of you all right in there?'

'Two of us,' Danny whispered. Patrick shrugged.

'Don't know what he has in mind but ... Yes, dad, we're both fine. What's going on?'

'Marcus is hurt.'

'Enough. Your notes, Marcus said you kept notes.'

'And Marcus was wrong,' Harry said patiently. 'The police took everything away with them last night.'

'He's telling you the truth,' Patrick shouted through the door. 'The police said it was evidence and they had to have everything. Sergeant Fine has it all.'

'Then we'd better talk to bloody Sergeant Fine,' Kinnear snapped. 'Downstairs. You know his number?'

'I know his number,' Harry agreed.

From inside the room they heard two sets of footsteps retreating down the stairs.

'So,' Naomi said, 'the gunshot was probably Marcus. Alec must be out of action in some way and Harry's lied about how many of us there are.' She relayed this to Fine. Below, they could hear the murmur of voices as Harry spoke on the phone.

'He's coming in on the other line,' Fine said. 'Hold on.'

Moments later he was back. 'Naomi, we're only minutes away, hang tight. Armed officers will be maybe ten minutes after us. Kinnear's on his own.'

'True, but he's already proved himself ready and willing to use his gun. Reg, I think he's lost what little balance he had.'

'You're there on scene, Naomi. I'll take your point. I've told him I've arranged for the paperwork to be brought to Fallowfields. I don't think he believes me but it might buy us a breathing space. What's happening now?'

'I think they're coming back up the stairs.'

She fell silent, listening. Kinnear was now banging on the door. 'Open up. I'll shoot.'

The sound of sirens distracted him. Fine was coming in mob-handed, Naomi thought.

They heard Kinnear move from the door, presumably taking Harry with him.

'He'll either force us out or force his way in,' Naomi said. 'Patrick, ordinarily I would not advise trying to fight back, but I think this man's beyond reasoning with. We may have to do just that.'

'Right. Look, there's some stuff hanging on the walls. A snooker cue, some kind of Indian club thing. Danny, give me a hand.'

Naomi heard them climbing on chairs, pulling objects down from the walls, felt something placed in her hand. 'What's this?'

'Rusty. Hope your tetanus is up to date. It's a fancy knife.'

'Patrick, I'm more likely to stab one of you. Danny, you hang on to it, but remember. Emergency only.'

They could hear Kinnear shouting at the police, presumably from one of the bedroom windows.

'We need a plan,' she said. 'If he gets in, we need to think what we're going to do.'

Down in the kitchen Alec was sawing through the tea towel ties that bound him to the chair. While he gave Harry ten out of ten for nerve and on the spot thinking, it was proving very hard to manipulate the knife enough to have any real effect on the tough cloth. He wasn't getting very far.

Beside him, Marcus was whimpering in pain. 'Hold on, you heard the sirens, the police are here. Naomi must have called them.'

'What can they do? He has a gun.'

'So do they, Marcus. So do the police. Lots of guns.'

He knew he sounded impatient, but could not help himself. Marcus's wailing was getting on his nerves. He tried to remind himself that the man was in pain, but it was still getting on his nerves. Painfully, he sawed the knife against the cloth. Painful because he kept missing the linen and jabbing himself in the wrist. He felt a bunch of fibres give. It gave him just a little more room. He twisted the knife in cramping fingers and tried again. One by one the fibres parted but it was so terribly slow. So awfully, numbingly slow.

Kinnear had lost patience. He stormed back across the landing, Harry dragged along with him. He wasted two shots shooting the lock of the study door.

Danny squealed, Patrick shouted something she could not make out. Naomi dived for cover, hoping the others would have done the same. She held the mobile in her hand and Fine was demanding to know what was going on. She didn't speak, just held up the phone so he could hear as Kinnear raged and swore, threatening to shoot Harry if they did not move whatever was blocking the door.

'Help me,' Patrick said to Danny. Naomi scrambled to her feet, leaving the mobile where it lay on the floor. Danny grabbed her hand and shoved her into the position they'd agreed, and then he and Patrick dragged the barricade away from the door. They've got to get it far enough back, Naomi thought. Far enough but not too far.

Kinnear pushed Harry through.

'Now,' Danny yelled. Patrick threw himself at his dad and pushed him to the ground. Naomi was behind the door, she slammed it hard against Kinnear, Danny piling in with her. She heard the man shout and knew Danny had pierced his hand with the knife he had found. She heard the gun fall to the floor, heard Danny kick it aside. It hit her foot and she dropped to pick it up.

Then she heard Kinnear roar, rage giving him even greater strength as he tossed them aside like so much flotsam. Danny yelped as he fell back and then she knew Kinnear had turned the focus of attack on her. She heard Harry shout, Patrick yelling a warning, and then she fired. No thought to it, no logic and no reason. Her hand was positioned awkwardly on the grip and she felt the slide bite a sliver from the web between her finger and her thumb as it reset. She fired again, compulsively this time and only then did she allow herself to think, to remember, as if it wasn't obvious, that she couldn't see and she had no way of knowing if she'd brought him down or killed one of her friends.

She knew only that she had heard someone fall.

'Naomi!'

'Harry, is everyone...?'

'We're all OK. You'd better give me that though.' Gently, he took the gun from her hand. 'Um, Patrick, make it safe will you?'

'Kinnear?'

'On the floor bleeding,' Danny said. He sounded pleased. 'Like, wow.'

Thirty-Six

A very subdued group left for home late that afternoon. Statements had taken forever, Naomi thought and the 'neutral ground' set for the meeting between Danny and his mother turned out to be a spare interview room at the police station. She had not been there, didn't really know how it had gone, but Sharon Fielding had spoken to her afterward and said thanks and nice to meet you and she'd make sure Danny stayed in touch and all the usual stuff.

Patrick seemed more satisfied. He told Naomi that Danny's mum had agreed to his coming to stay for a while. So, she supposed, that was all right then.

'Do you think he'll make it?' She meant Kinnear. She didn't have to say who.

Alec shrugged, then remembered that wasn't enough and said. 'Don't know. Not sure if I care.'

'I care.'

'Why? He would have killed you without a thought.'

'I know, but I'm not like him.'

'We've been through this before,' he said softly, remembering the events of the previous year.

'I know.'

They drove in silence for a little while, Naomi thinking of all the things that would have to be sorted out. The money, whether or not it jeopardized Alec's legacy, the trial that would come if Kinnear survived. She had shot him in the chest, it seemed, punctured a lung but missed the heart. Then shot him in the shoulder as he fell.

Everyone else seemed impressed but Naomi didn't see how she could have missed anyway from just a few feet away and it wasn't as if she'd thought about it. One thing they did know – but she wasn't sure that knowing was an improvement – was the way Rupert had died.

It was a heart attack, brought on by the threat and stress and the anxiety of what Kinnear had put him through. Derek Reid had described it, told how Rupert had fallen down, clutching at his chest and gasped for breath.

'He didn't ask for pills,' Reid said. He was adamant about that. 'He never asked for any pills.'

'I think I might sell the house,' Alec said. 'That's if I get to keep it, if you see what I mean.'

She nodded. 'We could buy somewhere closer to home.'

'We?'

'Unless you've gone off the idea, but I want a nice wedding, Alec. All the fuss.'

He laughed. 'I've only been asking you for the past ... how many years? What made you say yes now?'

'What's wrong? Have you got cold feet?'

'Couldn't be warmer.'

She reached out and he took her hand. 'You'll like being Mrs Friedman,' Alec said.